THE WONDER LANDS WAR

Also by Peter Darbyshire

Has the World Ended Yet?: Stories
Please
The Warhol Gang

The Book of Cross
1 *The Mona Lisa Sacrifice*
2 *The Dead Hamlets*
3 *The Apocalypse Ark*
4 *The Wonder Lands War*

THE WONDER LANDS WAR

PETER DARBYSHIRE

The Book of Cross 4

Published by Poplar Press
an imprint of Wolsak and Wynn Publishers
280 James Street North
Hamilton, ON L8R2L3
www.wolsakandwynn.ca

Acquiring editors: Ashley Hisson, Jennifer Rawlinson, A.G.A. Wilmot | Editor: A.G.A. Wilmot | Copy editor: Ashley Hisson
Cover design: Michel Vrana
Cover image: iStock.com/ilbusca.
Interior design: Jennifer Rawlinson
Author photograph: Pacific Newspaper Group
Typeset in Caslon Pro and Gibson
Printed by Rapido Books, Montreal, Canada

The publisher gratefully acknowledges the support of the Canada Council for the Arts and the Ontario Arts Council. We also acknowledge the financial support of the Government of Canada through the Canada Book Fund and the Government of Ontario through the Ontario Book Publishing Tax Credit and Ontario Creates.

Library and Archives Canada Cataloguing in Publication

Title: The Wonder Lands war / Peter Darbyshire.
Names: Darbyshire, Peter, 1967- author
Description: Series statement: The book of Cross ; 4
Identifiers: Canadiana (print) 20250273691 | Canadiana (ebook) 20250273985 | ISBN 9781998408290 (softcover) | ISBN 9781998408368 (EPUB)
Subjects: LCGFT: Paranormal fiction. | LCGFT: Thrillers (Fiction) | LCGFT: Novels.
Classification: LCC PS8557.A59346 W66 2025 | DDC C813/.6—dc23

A STRANGE ANGEL

I found Alice again by getting killed in a Paris library by a strange angel.

I wasn't looking for the angel, but they have a way of showing up when they're least expected. I hadn't even intended to be in Paris that day, and I wasn't certain how I'd wound up there. I'd passed out drunk the night before under a bridge in Prague, while resting my head on a discarded jacket and listening to someone sing Édith Piaf's "Mon Dieu" from somewhere deeper in the city. Yet I woke under a different bridge in Paris. I knew it was Paris because I sat up to see tourist boats making their way down the Seine, the people on board staring at me as if puzzled by my presence. I was more than a little puzzled myself.

I had no memory of how I'd come to be there on the wet stones of the riverside walk, so I searched through my pockets for some clue. They were empty of anything but a few coins and crumpled receipts from hotels and bars I'd visited around the world while searching for Alice after she disappeared.

No, there was one thing. A simple note scrawled on a folded piece of stationery. It was from a hotel that had been destroyed in London during the Blitz some number of decades past. Even stranger, the note was in Latin: *Tu es in debitum.* Someone was telling me I was in their debt.

Maybe one day I would find out who had brought me to Paris and why. There's a story to everything. Then again, maybe I wouldn't. Often the best stories are those that never get told.

And some stories are better off forgotten. I wanted to get drunk again and forget about everything that had brought me here. I wanted to forget about how the world had nearly ended at the Sunken City, when Noah had tried to use God's bible to wake the Sleeper there. How it would have ended if I hadn't fought a mad battle alongside the Atlanteans, Ahab and the white whale, and countless scores of the damned from Hades to defeat Noah and destroy his apocalyptic ark. How even then the world would have ended if not for Alice.

Most of all I wanted to forget how Alice had thrown herself into the path of a spectral cannonball to save us and had been lost to the whirlpool it created. God's bible had been lost along with her, but I cared less about that than I did her. The bible had done more harm than good in its time. That's the way of most bibles. But Alice? She was my oldest and dearest friend, ever since she'd ventured out from the pages of that Wonderland book. And the Sunken City hadn't been the first time she'd saved me.

Only I didn't have enough money in my pockets to buy myself a single drink, let alone enough to forget such memories. Nor did I have even a breath of grace left within me that I could use to turn water into wine. I had been searching for Alice so long I had neglected everything else. I had nothing. Same as it ever was.

I breathed deep, letting the air clear my head as I scanned my surroundings. My gaze immediately caught on the dome of the building across the water. I knew it all too well. The Institut de France, which housed the Bibliothèque Mazarine, one of Paris's most noted libraries and a place with a history nearly as troubled as mine.

Alice and I had our own history with the library. I'd found Alice there once many years ago, and she had led me to a forgotten book hidden in the library's shelves. That book had helped me stop a plague of ghosts haunting the city during the Revolution, after the angel Gabriel had raised them from the dead in an effort to drive everyone away. He'd had some mad scheme about turning Paris into a refuge for the angels until they could find their way back to Heaven, but that's a different tale.

It seemed I had been left in Paris for a reason. It was time to find out why.

I picked myself up off the ground and waved at the tourists, who all found something else more interesting to look at. I walked along the bank of the Seine until I reached some stone stairs and climbed them, making my way to the bridge, which turned out to be the Pont des Arts. The railings of the bridge had once been covered in locks that lovers had left behind to symbolize their enduring love – so many locks that the bridge had threatened to collapse under their weight. Paris's rulers had to remove them and replace the railings with glass panels. So much for things lasting forever.

At least the new glass panels offered a view. I paused for a moment and took it in. The Louvre was behind me, and most of the people on the bridge were heading toward it. Many of them would want to see the *Mona Lisa* once inside. If they only knew the truth about her. Farther down the Seine was Île de la Cité, a small island with the spire of Sainte-Chapelle rising above the forested park near its end. A man and woman in matching jackets had paused to take photos of it. I wondered if they knew the history of the island and all the executions that had taken place there during the Revolution. Then again, there wasn't a street in Paris that hadn't run red with blood at one time or another.

I continued on, across the bridge and to the institut. The Mazarine extended from the front of it here, directly across from the Pont des Arts. I lingered in the square outside, until a group of men and women who looked like researchers climbed the steps of the facade and queued up in one of the arched entranceways. I fell in behind them and hoped no one would take note of my dishevelled clothes. It must have worked because no one glanced twice at me.

The man in front of me was drinking coffee from a disposable cup and wearing clothes nearly as worn and dirty as mine. Likely a professor. I pointed out to him that his shoe was untied, and he bent down to retie the laces. He absently handed me his coffee to free his hands, and I drank most of it down. He didn't seem to notice when I handed the cup back.

"Built in the seventeenth century by the Cardinal Mazarin," he said, gazing around with the sort of wonder you typically see on the face of a child, not a grown man. "They don't make them like this anymore."

I'd heard people say that since the days of the Colosseum, but I just nodded politely. "It was a different age."

"Did you know that many of the royal libraries across Europe are modelled on this one?" he said. "Visitors came from across the continent to see it."

"I'd heard rumours along those lines." I didn't bother mentioning I'd been one of those visitors once upon a time.

"It was the largest library of its time," he went on, slipping into lecture mode. Professors often can't help themselves. "Until the civil war, of course, when the nobles rose up against Mazarin and looted his collection. Who knows what was lost in that time?"

"It's just as well," I said. "Mazarin's librarian had acquired a collection of demonology books from an abandoned monastery in Germany that was better left forgotten. That's what the nobles were actually after, and they divided the collection among themselves. Not that it did them any good in the end." I figured I owed him for the coffee – maybe he'd find an interesting new area of research.

The professor frowned at me. "I'm not aware of any such scholarship. What are your sources for this?"

"Cardinal Mazarin," I said as we made our way inside.

The professor's eyes widened. "Have you discovered some secret correspondence or journal?"

"Something like that." I pointed at the others, who were lining up to sign in. "Registration is that way."

The professor shuffled after them, muttering about citations and peer review. He didn't notice me slip away in the other direction, where I could lose myself in the stacks.

It was true the nobles had looted the library and burned many of its books back in the seventeenth century, but the collection had been built up again during the Revolution. Most of the books and artwork the revolutionaries confiscated from those they executed or imprisoned wound up here. Thankfully, the bulk of them were of a less dangerous nature than the demonology texts.

I went through the library slowly, searching for a book, any book, that was out of place. When I found one, I pulled it from the shelf and looked around. This was how I'd always found Alice before. Pull the right misshelved book out, and she will show herself like she's been there all along. Sometimes she comes down the row like another patron searching for a book, sometimes she climbs out from amid the books themselves and yet other times she'll make her presence known in another part of the library. The last time I'd found her in the Mazarine, she'd been wearing the bloody dress that Marie Antoinette had on at the time of her execution, and she'd been carrying a basketful of talking books. That had drawn some attention given it was the 1980s and there had been a different tour of visiting scholars from some academic conference or another going through the place.

Alice didn't show herself this time, though, no matter how many books I pulled from the shelves. I tried to remember if I had already gone through the Mazarine looking for her, but I couldn't be sure; it felt as if I had searched every library in the world since she'd gone missing. I was beginning to lose hope.

And then my eyes caught on a book on one of the top shelves of the row I currently wandered.

Through the Looking-Glass.

"Well, that has to be some sort of sign," I muttered to myself and took the book down from the shelf. The cover was red morocco, with the title and motifs in gilt on the spine, and gilt edges. An illustration of a queen in profile holding a sceptre over her shoulder was on the front. It was a first edition, if I wasn't mistaken, which meant it was worth a small fortune. It also meant it wasn't the sort of book that should have been left in the stacks. I glanced up and down the row once more, but still there was no sign of Alice. I opened the book, hoping to find some clue inside.

That was when the angel erupted from its pages and buried a sword in my chest.

THE WHITE KNIGHT

The sword that the angel rammed through me was ablaze with white flame, which made it hurt even more. Not for the first time, I really wished angels didn't love flaming swords so much.

The angel had taken the form of an old man with long hair and a wild beard. The plate armour that covered every part of his body except for his head and wings was as white as the flames. I wasn't sure why he was wearing it, as I hadn't seen an angel in such armour since it had gone out of style a few centuries ago. Then again, I couldn't recall the last time an angel had come out of a book to attack me either. And I knew he was an angel, because this close I could sense the heavenly grace inside of him.

"You will observe the Rules of Battle, of course?" he asked, in what seemed an overly friendly manner considering the circumstances.

I dropped the book and slumped against him, making a few sounds of the sort one does when impaled by a burning sword. The angel raised his bushy brows at me.

"You didn't cry so much as I thought you would," he said.

There was something familiar about the words he spoke, but I couldn't place it right away. It was hard to think on account of the sword in my chest. For that matter, it was also hard to keep standing and even draw breath.

He shoved me back and planted his left foot against my stomach to push me off the sword so he could free it for another strike but I managed to find some strength and kicked his other foot out from underneath him.

He fell into the shelves, and I stumbled away, ripping the sword free of his grip. I took hold of it and pulled it from my chest, and the world turned nearly as white as the angel. But I managed to stay upright for a moment longer. This wasn't the first time an angel had stabbed me with a burning sword. I'd had far too much practice with this sort of thing.

He came at me in a rush that was careless given I was a few seconds away from dropping. It was almost like he wanted me to stab him. So I obliged and lifted the sword to his throat. The point sank into his flesh. Blood welled out. He tried to stop himself, but his momentum carried him forward until the sword came out the back of his neck.

"A glorious victory," the angel said, although the tone of his voice made it seem more like a question. It was another odd thing to say, but I was in no condition to make sense of things.

I managed to wrench the sword free; I'm not the type to leave a good weapon stuck in someone else. You never know what they may do with it. I didn't have anything left after that, though, and I fell against him as the life drained out of me. The world went black as I died.

And then everything flared to light again as his blood poured over me, and the heavenly grace that was his essence sank into my body. I was bathed in that grace, enough of it that it filled the emptiness within me and I resurrected even as I was dying.

The angel was pushing me off him with one hand while lifting the other to his throat, trying in vain to stop the blood and grace from escaping. He made a surprised sound when I stood, and his gaze flicked to the hole in my chest. It was shrinking as I used his grace to heal myself. It was like he didn't know who I was.

He sprang into the air, and I hacked at his closest wing with the sword. I put some strength into it and was able to sever the wing, which burst into flames from the sword as it fell. So did the one still attached. The angel veered away wildly, his flight thrown off by the loss of his wing, and crashed into the bookshelves farther down the row. I muttered a curse, for I knew what would happen next.

His burning wing raked across a row of books older than most of the bones in the catacombs under Paris, and the flames quickly spread to the shelves. The wing I had severed landed on the fallen copy of *Through the*

Looking-Glass and did the same to it, as well as the nearest bottom shelf of books.

The angel stumbled farther along the row, keeping his gauntleted hand to his throat. As if that was going to make a difference. His armour was crimson with blood now, and the air was thick with his grace. I stomped out the flames on the book at my feet and then followed him. I grew stronger with each step I took thanks to all that grace.

"Where is Alice?" I asked. Given that the angel had come from the book, I figured he must know something. This couldn't just be a coincidence.

"I'll tell thee everything I can," the angel said, but then he choked on his own blood.

The fire was racing up and down the aisle, smoke reaching to the ceiling. Alarms began to sound, and then the fire suppression system turned on and water sprayed from hidden nozzles overhead.

Only the water was not water at all but ink. It rained down on the entire library, turning everything black – the books and shelves, the tables and chairs, the people who ran screaming for the exits. Even the angel and myself. The air filled with the smell of it, only it wasn't the typical chemicals of ink. For some reason it smelled like the sea.

The ink did more than turn the angel black. It doused the flames that had been burning him, washing them away. Then the ink began to wash the angel away, too, melting him as if he were insubstantial.

I rushed toward him, intending to shield him with my body. I didn't understand what was happening, but I was willing to risk him killing me again if it helped find Alice. I slipped and slid on the ink underfoot, and by the time I reached the angel he was already gone. I stared at the river of ink at my feet as it flowed down the row and into the flooded reading room. I wasn't sure if this was some angel trick or not.

I turned to make my way back to the book before it was washed away as well. But ink ran down my face and into my eyes, which began to sting as fiercely as that time Rasputin had thrown acid into them after a disagreement over cards. I tried to wipe the ink away, but it was so thick I ended up just smearing it and blurring my vision even more. Luckily the river underfoot carried the book down the row to me, and it bumped into my leg. I managed to scoop it up and snuff out the lingering flame that burned on part of its cover. I hesitated then, looking around once more and trying to make out any familiar shapes around me.

Alice was still nowhere to be found.

I took a minute to catch my breath and savour the grace, for I had been too long without it. Normally grace is the best high in the world – it's like mainlining Heaven itself. It usually puts me into a stupor where I forget this world and all my problems, forget myself even. It's pure bliss, an addiction I just can't quit. Which helped me understand why the angels were so upset about being abandoned here on Earth and cut off from their home. If Heaven was anything like their grace, well, even I couldn't imagine their loss.

This time, though, the grace had a totally different effect on me.

Laughter erupted from inside me as I gazed upon the chaos of the library. I suddenly swept an armful of books from a shelf into the ink flowing around my feet without thinking. I used some of the grace to turn another shelf of books into parrots for no reason I understood, each one a different colour of the rainbow. They flew off in every direction, shrieking in an infernal tongue. They were speaking the words to some sort of spell, but I wasn't paying attention. I stumbled out into the reading room. It was mostly empty now on account of the ink surging through it, but there were still a few people struggling to get out – a librarian helping a man with a walker and a woman with a prosthetic leg who was hanging on to tables to remain standing. Then a wave of ink rose up and washed them away, toward the exit. I wasn't sure if I had caused it or if it had happened on its own. The entire scene was madness, but the madness was also somehow within me.

I closed my eyes and took a deep breath to steady myself, but my vision flashed with wild colours, some of which I had never seen before. When I opened my eyes again, I was standing outside the library with the copy of *Looking-Glass* in my hands. People stood around me covered in ink, yelling into phones and staring at each other in disbelief. Sirens sounded in the distance, coming closer. The parrots I had created flew away from the library, and the air rippled behind them as if it were heated.

I wiped my hand over my eyes again, this time sending some grace through my fingers to clear the ink from my vision. I looked back down at the book and flipped through its charred and stained pages until I found the scene I was looking for. Alice's encounter with the bumbling White Knight, after he rescues her from the Red Knight. Everything the angel had said to me during our fight were lines the White Knight spoke in the book.

The angels I'd encountered over the ages each had their own quirks, but I had no idea why one would pretend to be a character from a children's tale. I wondered if perhaps he had been possessed by some mischievous spirit, like the *Hamlet* ghost I had once encountered. The grace that I'd taken from him had been corrupted in some way, after all, to cause that temporary madness in me.

I saw the professor making his way through the crowd, trying to get to my side. He had his mouth open as if he had some question to ask me. Whatever he wanted to ask, I was pretty sure I didn't want to answer.

The sirens were getting closer now. I definitely didn't want to be here when they arrived. I wasn't sure who was actually in charge of Paris behind the scenes these days, but I figured whoever it was wouldn't take kindly to me wrecking yet another of the city's cultural establishments. There were still those who wanted to chop off my head after the Paris Flood incident in the early 1900s.

I joined the exodus of people walking the Pont des Arts across the Seine. Hopefully I could lose myself in the city long enough to make sense of everything that had happened since I'd laid down under that bridge in Prague.

I kept looking at the book as I went, trying to understand what it meant, right up until the moment someone stepped out of the crowd and ripped it from my hands.

THE FAERIE COURT OF THE DEAD

A teen with dyed red hair and a large nose ring had taken the battered copy of *Through the Looking-Glass* from me. He was juggling three wine bottles despite the crowd around us, and he added the book to the mix as if it were part of his act.

"What sort of mischief have you gotten yourself into this time?" he asked. I knew his voice instantly.

Puck.

I'd not seen him in this body before, but that was nothing new. The faerie were always finding new bodies to possess given their own had crumbled to dust long ago. There was a reason for all those tales of them stealing babies.

"I should have known the faerie were behind this." I reached for the book but instead came away with a bottle. Even worse, it was empty. "Where's the rest of the court?"

"Oh, whatever trouble you're in isn't our doing," Puck said as he continued to juggle the remaining bottles and the book. He managed to turn the pages of the book as he did so, flipping through it with a bemused expression. "We just sensed some chaos and came to witness it. And look who I found. The ultimate trickster himself."

"You're thinking of Judas, not me." After all, Judas had caused way more problems for the world over the ages than I had. Probably.

"I have trouble telling you apart. Remind me, was it you or Judas that killed your love and your unborn daughter along with her?"

I threw the empty bottle at him. He caught it and added it once more into the rotation, although he took a few steps back when he did so. He was getting dangerously close to the side of the bridge. I didn't follow, for I had a sudden vision of him dropping the book into the Seine, perhaps on accident, perhaps not.

"Wait, I remember," Puck said, fixated on the book now. "Judas is the one who *isn't* a corrupted soul that's taken over the body of God's only son."

I glanced at those around us to see if anyone was listening – I don't usually like to advertise my particular nature in public. People tend to treat me differently when they learn I'm an immortal, angel-killing drunk and thief who was born in the body Christ left behind when he went wherever it was he went. But no one was paying any attention to us. Maybe Puck had enchanted them. Or maybe they were just used to seeing odd characters like Puck and myself. This was Paris, after all.

"You redeem these other mortals for me, you know," Puck said. "I sometimes think that maybe there's hope they can cause as much madness in the world as you have." He tossed one of the bottles back in the direction of the library and it shattered on the bridge.

"Whatever happened in the Mazarine wasn't my fault," I said, although that was perhaps stretching things a bit. I turned away, scanning the crowd once more. "Why am I even having this conversation with you? Where is Morgana?"

"My queen is nearby with the others." Puck giggled. "Would you like to see them? Would you like to see your daughter again?"

I couldn't draw breath for a moment and the crowd seemed to fade away, as if they were no more than background extras. When I was finally able to speak again, I could do little more than whisper.

"Amelia is with you?"

Puck grinned and strode away, letting the remaining bottles smash to the ground. I managed to at least pluck the book out of the air this time, though, which drew a disappointed sigh from him.

"I was looking forward to reading more of that," he said. "It's most intriguing."

"When did you learn to read?" I asked, following him. I inspected the book as we walked, to make sure he hadn't switched it with another. He was a faerie, after all, and we had a history.

"I just make the words in books mean what I want," Puck said. "Isn't that what everyone does?"

He took us down Boulevard Henri IV and to the Place de la Bastille, the square where the infamous prison had once been and where I'd killed a man for a chunk of mouldy bread. I was a different person back then. Mostly. We continued on until we reached the 20th arrondissement and the Père Lachaise Cemetery, where I'd drank several bottles of wine with Leonardo da Vinci many years after he was supposed to have died. We had left the crowd of people from the library behind and my stained clothes were starting to draw a few looks. Puck wasn't helping the situation, because he was gnawing on a large piece of cheese he had acquired from somewhere when I wasn't looking. Luckily the cemetery was mostly empty at this time of the day.

Like the Mazarine library, the Père Lachaise Cemetery is one of those places you should visit when you find yourself in Paris – and everyone finds themselves in Paris at some point or another. It's the largest cemetery in the city, with wandering paths and crowded graves. I've heard there are somewhere around a million dead interred there, including my old friends Édith Piaf and Oscar Wilde. Jim Morrison is there, too, but I could hardly call him a friend after that peyote incident out in the desert.

Puck led me to the rest of the faerie, who were having a picnic at the ossuary within the cemetery. They were spread out around the Monument aux Morts in front of the ossuary, which depicted a crowd of grieving people carved from stone, with two of their number entering a tomb that led to the ossuary. There were a couple dozen fey, the servants of the faerie, scattered about. I recognized them by the typical dazed look of those who had been tricked into service by the faerie. I tried not to pay attention to them – I'd learned long ago there was nothing I could do to help their kind.

There were only a few faerie. Like Puck, they wore different bodies since I'd last seen them, after the *Hamlet* ghost madness. But I recognized them all the same.

Mustardseed sat on a pile of grave markers stacked to form a bench of sorts, dressed in the body of an old man in a housecoat, drinking wine straight from the bottle. He paused long enough to blow a hazy circle of wine into the air, like a smoke ring, then returned to drinking as the ring drifted away and disappeared.

Cobweb stood before the monument wearing the body of a young woman in a summer dress. She stared at the sculptures like an art student in rapture. Dead insects carpeted the ground at her feet, which is how I knew it was her.

I would have recognized Morgana even if she didn't step out of the entrance to the tomb in the body of a dead woman in a mouldy black dress and even blacker hair. Her appearance didn't matter to me; I always yearned for her as soon as I saw her, no matter what her form. It was the lingering effects of when she had once claimed my soul. That's what I told myself anyway.

And then there was Amelia, standing off to the side of the monument and regarding the scene as if she didn't know any of them. Amelia, my daughter. Killed in the womb in Hiroshima along with her mother and my love, Penelope. But here now because she had been birthed by Morgana and raised in the faerie court as one of their own. Perhaps as an act of mischief. Perhaps as a favour to me. I was still undecided on that one.

Amelia had aged again since the last time I'd seen her, when she'd been no more than a teen. She looked to be in her mid-twenties now, although that didn't mean much for someone of her peculiar nature. Her hair was all white, as if she'd been exposed to some shock. Like Morgana, she wore a black dress, although this one was clean and not covered in mould. She also wore black combat boots and glasses, and she had a tattoo of an ankh on her right index finger.

I went straight to Amelia and embraced her. Her skin was cold to the touch, as always. "It's been too long," I said.

"Has it?" she asked. "I've been travelling the world. Time seems different when you're travelling."

"And what have you seen of the world?" I asked.

"It's mostly been cemeteries like this one," Morgana said, stepping off the monument and taking a glass of wine offered to her by a fey. "That's why we brought you here. We need to talk."

I wanted to lift a hand to fondle her tangled hair, because old habits die hard. I managed to restrain myself, though. "I thought you were in Paris because you sensed what happened at the library, not me."

"We're here because we sensed chaos finding its way into this world," Morgana said. "You're here because when we came to this city, we noted you sleeping like some urchin under a bridge. I assumed you were connected with that chaos so I had Puck fetch you when things played out."

"You weren't the ones that put me under that bridge?" It was the sort of mischief that the faerie might enjoy.

"However you got there, I'm sure you have only yourself to blame." Morgana took a sip of her wine, drawing my gaze to her lips. "Now tell me what happened at the library."

"He killed an angel," Puck said. "With a flaming sword."

"How novel," Morgana said.

"His folio birthed the angel." Puck pointed at the book I still held. "And then the angel left the world in a flood that drowned the library. It was most entertaining."

"That's more peculiar than novel." Morgana eyed the book.

"I was looking for Alice," I said. "That somehow prompted the chaos you sensed, although I don't know how or why."

"Alice," Morgana said softly. "We have heard whispers of the events concerning Noah and the Sunken City."

I didn't bother asking how she knew that, for there had been all manner of strange survivors of that battle. "Then you must also know that Alice was lost there," I said instead.

"A shame," Puck said and leapt up onto the monument, perching atop it like some crow. "She was the only one of your kind that wasn't a dreadful bore."

"Those same whispers said she was lost along with a book." Morgana stepped closer, and I retreated the same distance. I didn't want her to take the copy of *Through the Looking-Glass* like Puck had.

"This isn't it." I put the book behind my back. "She had God's bible at the time, after we had wrested it free of Noah. It was damaged in the battle and created a whirlpool that sucked in both Alice and the bible. I don't know where it took her. I've been searching for her ever since."

Morgana studied me for a moment. "Well, I'm sure she'll turn up," she finally said. "Like so many of your acquaintances, she has a habit of appearing at the most opportune moments. And the most inopportune as well."

I felt that madness from the library bubble up inside me again, out of nowhere. I dropped the book and lunged at Morgana, grabbing her by the throat and carrying her back. I slammed her against the wall of the ossuary, in between the carvings of the mournful dead.

"What are you playing at?" I demanded. "For I doubt it's simply a coincidence that you happen to be in Paris at the same time as I was mysteriously deposited here."

Mustardseed leapt to his feet far quicker than an old man should have been able, and Cobweb came my way, but Morgana waved them off. "I had nothing to do with any of what has befallen you," she said. "I swear on our daughter's life, such as it is."

"You're telling me the White Knight wasn't your doing?"

"I've consorted with many a knight in my time," Morgana said. "But I'm simply not the type for white knights. And I didn't have Puck fetch you because of whatever mischief you've found yourself in this time. You're here because there are things you need to know about Amelia."

"Tell me." I kept Morgana pinned against the ossuary. I knew better than to give her any chance to escape.

"For one, she has an unnatural obsession with places like this." Morgana gestured at the cemetery. "She constantly disappears from the court wherever we travel. We've learned to look for her in abattoirs and graveyards. It's like she prefers the company of the dead to our own. It troubles the court. And it troubles me."

I glanced at Amelia, who wasn't paying any attention to us at all. Instead, she was looking away from the scene, deeper into the cemetery. As if something more interesting had caught her attention.

"What of it?" I asked. "Every young person goes through a phase where they are obsessed with death."

"But does every young person know the secrets of the dead?" Morgana said.

"What kinds of secrets?"

"Show me the respect you would any other queen and I'll tell you."

I hesitated, then managed to force down the rage and suspicion that churned inside me. I released Morgana and she dropped to the ground.

"I don't respect any queen or king," I said. "Not unless they earn it, and most do not."

Morgana took a deep breath, then smiled at me. "I thought I had earned your favour many times over throughout the ages," she said. A worm wriggled in her mouth, but that just drew my attention back to her lips.

I shook my head to clear my thoughts. "Amelia," I said.

Morgana sipped her wine again, which she'd managed not to spill when I lifted her up and then dropped her. "Amelia has some sixth sense for the dead. She knows their names and what fate befell them. Among other things."

Puck grinned at us from atop the ossuary, revealing a mouthful of broken teeth. "The knowledge they carried to the grave. The things they did and the things they wanted to do."

Morgana nodded. "Maybe it is a semblance of your grace, corrupted by her death. I don't know. But it is not of the nature of the faerie. And it grows harder to persuade her to leave these places. She is increasingly disinterested in the worlds of the living."

I took the glass from Morgana's hand and drank some of the wine. I wondered if the faerie had any stronger spirits with them.

"I fear death is trying to reclaim her," Morgana said.

"Perhaps it already has," Puck murmured, gazing off into the cemetery.

I turned and didn't see Amelia. She had disappeared among the graves.

"You see?" Morgana sighed. "She does this sort of thing all the time. Some would say it reflects poorly on me as a mother, but we both know who is truly to blame."

I handed the glass back to Morgana and then went after Amelia. I found her standing on a nearby path, scanning the cemetery.

"The dead are disturbed," she said. "Can you feel it?"

I couldn't feel anything but the mad grace inside me from the angel in the library. It made me want to crack open all the crypts around us to see what I would find. I decided it was best not to share such thoughts, though. "Maybe they don't appreciate our presence. Both the faerie and I have been known to disturb the dead before."

"This is different," she said.

I nodded and considered the graves for a time. If they held a secret, they didn't seem willing to share it with me.

"What Morgana said was true then?" I asked. "You can talk to the dead?"

"I don't talk to them," Amelia said. "I know them. Sometimes I think I belong more to their realm than this one."

I wasn't sure what to say to that. I've never been much of a father. So I asked her the question that was on my mind instead. "Is Alice among the dead?"

Amelia didn't say anything for a moment. I became aware of the intense silence of the cemetery. She sounded weary when she finally spoke again. "I don't yet know her to be among the dead."

"And I can't find her among the living," I said. "So Alice is neither dead nor alive." She was a little like da Vinci that way.

"Alice is unknown," Amelia said.

"But just as lost as ever." I sighed.

There was movement at one of the graves then. A weathered statue of a man dressed in robes lying atop the grave sat up and turned toward us. "That is truly unfortunate," he said. "I was hoping you would lead us to her."

I didn't recognize the statue, but I knew that voice before he'd even finished speaking.

The angel Gabriel.

A PLAGUE OF ANGELS

I ran back to the others, pulling Amelia after me. Maybe I would have tried my luck with Gabriel had I been on my own, but I didn't want to risk Amelia's safety. Although I might have run anyway, as Gabriel had always beaten me when we'd tangled in the past.

"Tell me you brought more than wine," I called to Morgana.

She looked past me, then sighed at the sight of Gabriel lumbering along behind us still in statue form. "Is there nowhere you can go without attracting trouble?" She nodded to the fey, and they produced knives and skewers from the picnic baskets.

I doubted anything the faerie had would be able to harm Gabriel in his current state, but sometimes you just have to make do. I grabbed a wine bottle from a fey and took a long drink, then flipped the bottle around in my hand to use like a club.

Gabriel came to the edge of our group and then stopped. He didn't even look at the others. "It doesn't have to go the way it usually does," he said to me.

"I take it you two are acquainted," Morgana said to Gabriel, stepping around Amelia to stand at my side. "But I don't believe I've had the misfortune of meeting you before."

"Gabriel here was the muscle for a group of angels that called themselves the Ridden or something like that," I said. "They imprisoned the gorgon Mona Lisa and were trying to use her as a weapon in their war with some other faction, until I came along."

"The Risen," Gabriel said. He lifted a glass of wine to his lips and took a drink. I hadn't even seen him take the glass from anyone. A neat trick that. But he was undoubtedly saving his best for what was still to come. "And you wouldn't have been able to interfere if Alice hadn't helped you escape the prison we'd put you in. If not for her, this entire world would be under our domain now."

"Not all of it," Morgana said.

"The glamour that Oberon created and you inherited hardly matters," Gabriel said. "Especially given it has mostly faded."

"Why don't we take an interlude in the glamour then to see just how much it has faded?" Morgana's voice was hard enough that I reflexively took a step away from her. It was a tone that had usually been reserved for me over the years.

"I thought I'd seen the last of you after things went to hell inside da Vinci's *Last Supper* and Mona Lisa escaped," I said to Gabriel, trying to keep the situation a conversation rather than a battle.

Gabriel fixed me with an unblinking stare. "I'll admit your little move with summoning that Egyptian god to aid you nearly worked. But he was not the first god I have faced over the ages."

I wanted to be surprised, but I just couldn't manage it. Gabriel always had been one of the tougher angels.

"I didn't summon him," I said. "He was stalking me. It's a long story."

"We need to put all of that behind us," Gabriel said. "We have larger concerns."

"I'm not any more interested in the wars of your kind now than I was before," I said. "And whatever your interest in Alice, it ends here, today. Leave me and her alone, and I'll let you be. If not, I'll use your grace to help me find her."

Puck clapped at that, and Cobweb and Mustardseed fanned out to either side of me. But Gabriel just took another drink of wine.

"Haven't you grown weary of all this?" He waved his free hand at the ossuary. "The endless dead and their meaningless existences. Life after life after life of nothing."

"If you don't like it, maybe you should try hanging out in one of the cafés instead," I told him. "Although you may want to change your appearance first. Even the French draw the line somewhere."

"This entire world is just as much a graveyard," Gabriel said. "And we are all trapped within it. You along with the rest of us."

"Never mind the cafés," I said. "You've clearly spent too much time with the philosophers there."

"But we can change the world. We can breathe new life into it."

"You know, I've heard many people say that over the centuries. Yet they never seem to change the world for the better. I know all about your plan to make a new Heaven on earth. But I think the last thing we need is another Heaven, let alone any angels at all."

Gabriel shook his head. "Let me point out that even if you could best me, I'm of more use to you alive than dead."

"And let me point out it's foolish of you to have come alone," I said, stretching a little before we got on with it. Maybe with the help of the faerie I'd finally be able to beat Gabriel once and for all.

He crushed the glass in his hand. "Who says I'm alone?"

And just like that I knew we were undone.

Deeper in the cemetery, maybe thirty metres to the left of the ossuary, another stone angel dropped off the roof of a crypt with a thump I felt despite the distance and started making his way through the graves toward us. A marble woman with dead flowers draped over her shoulders came at us from the other side. I heard sounds behind us, like rocks grinding against each other. The sculptures on the ossuary were coming to life.

"Perhaps we were mistaken earlier," Morgana said, raising an eyebrow. "Maybe *this* was the impending chaos that drew us here."

I could sense all the angels myself, or at least the grace within them. Normally I would have noticed them long before now, but the grace from the White Knight was still twisting and churning within me. I wondered if Gabriel were behind it – if he had used the White Knight to distract me.

"A very nicely laid trap," I said. "How did you know I'd be here?"

"We didn't," Gabriel said. "But we know your daughter is a creature of the dead and does not stray far from the cemeteries and tombs of this world. Just as we knew you would eventually seek her out again. We have been hiding in graves and crypts around the world, waiting for you to show up once more."

"I told you we needed to talk," Morgana said to me.

"All right, we'll do that," I said. "Once we've dealt with this plague of angels."

"About time!" Puck cheered. He somersaulted off the top of the ossuary and landed beside me, then pulled a rusty butcher's knife from his pants.

Gabriel glanced at Puck, and I took advantage of his momentary distraction to spin and grab the book from the ground, where I had dropped it to grab Morgana. There was another stone angel behind us, a woman in robes who had stepped out of the ossuary scene, but she just watched me and did nothing.

I'd been in situations like this enough times over the years to know how it would end: with me buried in one of these graves or in some forgotten place or another. If it had just been me, I might have been willing to stick around and fight anyway, just for the chance to kill Gabriel.

But it wasn't just me.

Cobweb flicked her right hand at Gabriel, and the insects covering the earth around her crawled, writhed and scuttled toward the angel. It was an impressive feat considering they were all dead – impressive and more than a little disconcerting.

Gabriel didn't seem at all disturbed, though, and strode forward without hesitation – only to fall into a pit that opened up underneath the insects. I didn't hear his heavy body hit the ground, so it likely wasn't an ordinary grave or some other hole.

"I take it that was your work?" I said to Morgana.

"Yes, but the glamour won't hold him long," she said. "He'll find his way back."

"Let's be about it then." I pulled Amelia in the only direction without angels, and the faerie and fey followed although Puck lingered at the end of the court.

"I thought we were going to fight," he protested.

"I suspect you'll have your chance yet," I called back, which cheered him a little.

Unfortunately, Morgana was right about the glamour not holding Gabriel. It felt like we'd been running for only seconds before his shadow passed over us. He landed on top of Chopin's grave and folded his stone wings back to wherever he was hiding them as he perched on the head of the statue adorning the grave. Euterpe, the muse of music. At least she wasn't another of the angels. I didn't think she was anyway.

"You are trying my patience," Gabriel said.

We veered past him. The tomb of Jim Morrison was to our left, that of the painter Géricault to our right. I didn't hesitate – I made straight for Géricault's grave. It seemed more like a Géricault moment, after all.

Gabriel hopped down and grabbed the last of the fey trailing behind us, the one who had carried the tray of wineglasses. He slammed her into a nearby crypt, hard enough to crack the stone. Something inside her cracked just as loudly, and when Gabriel dropped her she didn't move.

"Don't mistake my charity for weakness," he said.

I didn't bother pointing out he'd probably done the fey a favour. I was too busy looking for a way out as the angels closed in. They were flanking us, an angel with a pitted stone sword on one side and another holding a violin like a club on the other.

Then Amelia stepped forward and pointed deeper into the heart of the cemetery. "This way," she said.

"We need to get back into the city," I said. The angels didn't like to make themselves too widely known these days, so there was a chance they'd leave us alone if we could reach someplace busy, with too many witnesses. It was a small chance, granted, but those were my usual odds.

"Trust me," Amelia said. "This is my world."

I hesitated a heartbeat or two, then nodded. We continued on into the cemetery, pursued by the angels.

"One of these days I'm going to end you just like I did the White Knight back in the library," I yelled back to Gabriel as we ran. "Who was he anyway?"

"He was not one of the Risen," Gabriel said. He walked after us, seeming to be in no particular hurry. "He was an aberration."

A bronze dog came from our left, pushing us away from our path. No doubt someone's faithful hound in some past life. Puck shoved one of the fey into its path, but the hound simply bounded above the fallen fey. Cobweb was ready for that, though, and a cloud of dead insects lifted from the ground suddenly and converged on the hound, blinding it. It crashed into the side of a crypt and fell to the earth, the insects swarming its face. We continued on.

"You know I can't keep all your little cliques straight," I said to Gabriel.

"I believe he was not even an angel at all," Gabriel said. He probably could have leapt into our midst, but he appeared content to let us go farther into the cemetery, away from curious eyes.

"And I believe he was," I said. "I've killed enough of your kind in my time to know."

"There," Amelia murmured, nodding at a path ahead of us that curved to the right.

"There have been other aberrations like him," Gabriel said. "In libraries around the world. All infused with a holiness they should not possess. All connected to the texts that tell Alice's tales. And perhaps another book."

Now I started to put things together. "You're looking for Alice because you think God's bible is linked to whatever's happening."

"Alice disappeared with God's bible," Gabriel said. "And now strange yet miraculous things occur that somehow involve her. This is no burning bush that needs to be interpreted. We must find Alice and retrieve the bible before it's too late."

We came to Molière's grave then, a raised stone casket on four pillars, and Amelia pulled me to a stop. She turned in a slow circle, scanning the surrounding area as the faerie caught up to us.

"Please tell me you have a plan in mind," I said.

"Hush," Morgana said. "We have learned to trust Amelia when it comes to matters of the dead."

"It's around here somewhere," Amelia said. "I can feel it."

"You can enlighten me at any time," I said.

"Our way out of here," Amelia said. "It lies in one of these tombs."

Gabriel strolled through the aged crypts toward us while the other angels converged on us from the sides. We were surrounded.

"What exactly do you think is going to happen if you don't find Alice and the bible?" I asked Gabriel.

"I tell you with all honesty that even the angels don't know," Gabriel said, standing on the other side of Molière's casket. "But a holy text as powerful as God's bible cannot simply be abandoned, for it has the power to undo the world. We must have faith that we will find it."

"You'll understand why I'm not a big believer in faith," I said.

"There is little about you I care to understand. But know that I give you my word as an angel that I will not betray you if we join forces in the search."

"And I know your word is only good until we find Alice or the bible, and not after," I said across the grave. "Just like I know that the angels are probably the last creatures on this world or any other that should have God's bible. I think I'll keep looking for Alice on my own."

"You seem to think this is a negotiation," Gabriel said. "But as usual you are wrong."

"What are you going to do, kill me?" I shrugged. "You know that won't stop me for long."

"Not you," Gabriel said. "I'll kill everyone you've ever loved instead. Starting with your abomination of a daughter."

And with that he leapt over the casket.

THE BOLTHOLE

I'd fought so many angels over the ages that I'd lost track of the number. Sometimes I had a sword or gun or some other weapon at the start of the fight. Often I didn't. I've learned to improvise.

I tossed the *Looking-Glass* to Amelia and then used both hands to rip a marble cross free from a nearby grave. The cross was the length of my arm, so I had to use more of the White Knight's grace to manage it than I liked. But I was hoping to replenish that in a minute anyway.

"Freedom for the first one to silence him," Morgana shouted, and the fey surged toward Gabriel.

He grabbed the first two and smashed them into Molière's casket, then tossed aside their still bodies. He didn't even change expression. He'd had a lot of practice killing people.

The fey kept coming, though, as if eager for death. Maybe they were. Gabriel offered them one way to escape Morgana's court, after all.

I joined their mob as Gabriel began to smash them down, one after another. They were distraction enough that I was able to come out of the crowd and bury the cross in his chest. I put some more grace into the blow, to strengthen the cross, and I had a mad vision of shattering him to pieces, then doing the same to Molière's grave and all the other graves around us. Instead, the cross sank into Gabriel's chest like an axe would have buried itself in flesh. It would have killed me, let alone any mortal person. But the angels aren't like us. Gabriel kicked me to the ground with a blow that knocked the breath from me. Then he pulled the cross from his body and stepped forward.

Mustardseed came at him from the side, moving with surprising speed given his aged body. He smashed his bottle in Gabriel's face, shattering the glass and staining Gabriel with wine that made it look as if he'd cut open the stone angel. Gabriel was as unmoved as when I had struck him. He lashed out with the cross and sent Mustardseed flying across the cemetery. I heard bones break with the blow. The faerie struck an ivy-covered tomb and then fell to the ground. A ragged ring of red smoke escaped his lips, and then he was still.

I heard Morgana cry out somewhere, but I couldn't tell if it was in anguish or rage. Then Puck and Cobweb were at my side, taking hold of my arms and pulling me away from the fight.

"That damned angel is worse than a bandersnatch," Cobweb said.

"Please tell me the bandersnatch isn't another fictional character come to life," I said. Because if it was, I didn't want to meet it. Although such things often weren't up to me.

"Maybe it's not real here," Cobweb said. "But it's real somewhere."

"All the terrible things are real somewhere," Puck said with a giggle. "It's how they become terrible."

They dragged me into a long crypt where Morgana waited, and then I had enough strength to stand and push them away.

"Quickly, before your wretched friend reduces my court even more," Morgana said. "Amelia has found us a bolthole."

I peered into the darkness and saw Amelia at the other end of the crypt. She had shoved the book into one of her pockets and was pushing the lid off another stone casket, this one smaller and less grand that Molière's.

"Follow me if you haven't yet grown weary of life," she said and then climbed into the casket and disappeared from sight.

Morgana gave Gabriel a long look, then crossed to the casket. The other faerie followed her while the remaining fey ran at Gabriel. He'd single-handedly taken out half of them already, and he struck down more with the cross as I watched. The hole I'd made in his chest wasn't even slowing him down. There was no real way for the fey to defend themselves. Nor was there any way for them to hurt him. They were a diversion and nothing more. And even now the other angels were coming to join the battle, closing in from all directions.

There was nowhere else to go, so I closed the door of the crypt. I thought about sealing it with some grace, but it wouldn't hold long anyway. Not against that many angels. I joined the others at the casket and saw the wooden stairs hidden inside, leading down to an earthen tunnel.

"And where exactly does this go?" I asked. I wasn't sure descending underground and potentially getting cornered was an improvement on our situation.

"There's only one way to find out," Morgana said and shoved me down the stairs.

The tunnel appeared to have been dug by hand, but it was shored up with wooden beams at regular intervals, so it seemed stable. It was high enough that I didn't have to stoop, although my shoulders brushed against the side walls. Some of the beams were newer – they weren't as faded and dirty as the others. Which meant someone was maintaining this tunnel.

Amelia leaned against one of the dirt walls, catching her breath. "We shouldn't linger," she said. "This passage is not stable."

Morgana stepped past us and breathed out a cloud of fireflies that flew down the tunnel, illuminating it. Morgana and the faerie followed them, and Amelia and I trailed behind. The cries of the fey faded away.

"Someone please tell me this doesn't just lead to a secret crypt," I said. "I hate secret crypts."

"The main tunnel ends in the basement of a nearby apartment," Amelia said. "It was originally dug by grave robbers who were after some of the dead buried here. One of those dead objected to their scheme and added them to the cemetery. Others have discovered the tunnel over the years and used it for their own purposes. Most recently, a government minister has been using it to visit a spirit he's infatuated with. The spirit barely notices him, but he still comes here several nights a month to seek it out."

"How do you know all that?" I asked.

"I just do," Amelia said. "I know places like these."

I was beginning to understand why Morgana was concerned.

A crash echoed from behind us. The angels hadn't bothered opening the door and had simply knocked it down.

"They'll pursue us into the depths of Hell itself," I said.

"Yes," Amelia said. "Unless we find another distraction for them."

We came to a spot where the tunnel branched in two. A skeleton in rags lay at the junction. Its bones had been heavily gnawed by rats, or perhaps some other creatures. Morgana and the other faerie paused and looked down at it, then at Amelia.

"This way," Amelia said, stepping into the left branch. "Let the grave robber lead them the other way."

I admit it took me several seconds before I understood.

"Right," I said. Then I used the last of my grace to raise the skeleton from the dead. I didn't call its soul back into the body because I didn't know who the dead person was. I could maybe have tracked down the soul given enough time, but we had only minutes before the angels caught up to us. I had to settle for merely animating the skeleton.

It rose from the ground and stood there, waiting. I laid my hands on its shoulders and turned it to face the other branch of the tunnel, then gave it a push to get it started. Morgana waved the fireflies down that way, and the skeleton lurched after them, clods of earth dropping from its bones. With any luck, the angels would sense the grace in the dead grave robber and follow him. Hopefully by the time they caught up to the skeleton and realized their mistake we'd be out of our tunnel and disappearing somewhere in the city.

We went around a bend and into the darkness. I put my hands on the walls on either side to feel my way along. The beams of wood here had been replaced with stone arches. I felt the spongy texture of mushrooms under my fingers.

"This isn't the main tunnel, is it?" I whispered to Amelia.

"The grave robbers tried to dig a second tunnel in case they needed an emergency escape," Amelia said. "Only they ended up in the grave before they could finish it – it's a dead end."

I grabbed her arm and pulled her to a stop. "Then why have we come this way?"

I thought maybe we could turn around and run back to the other tunnel in time. Maybe we could even beat the angels out the other end of it. But then I heard the thunder of stone feet pounding on the ground. The walls and ceiling shook – the angels were following our distraction. We were trapped.

Amelia pulled away from me and nodded at Morgana, who now stood before a waterfall of mist that fell from the ceiling and disappeared into the floor. It gave off a greenish glow, which helped me realize what was happening.

"We're in the glamour," I said. The faerie were taking us to their realm.

"But not far enough yet," Morgana said. "Those murdering angels may still find us if we don't quicken our pace." Puck and Cobweb stepped through the mist and disappeared. Morgana held out her hand to us. Amelia took it, then offered her hand to me.

I took my daughter's cold, undead hand and followed her and the faerie queen into the mist, leaving the angels and the dead behind.

A GLAMOROUS ESCAPE

We walked along the tunnel for maybe a minute or two and then the mushrooms in the walls began to give way to bricks. A trickle of water flowed along the ground at our feet, quickly growing to an ankle-deep stream.

"What did Gabriel mean back there?" I asked Morgana as we made our way through the water. "About Oberon creating the glamour?"

"Oberon did many things," Morgana said. "And eventually paid the price."

"Was he some sort of god?" I couldn't imagine how else anyone could create something like the glamour.

Morgana laughed at that. "He was one of the first faerie of our court. No more, no less. There were others like him. Now there is me."

We arrived at stairs leading to an elevated walkway with a railing on one side. There was graffiti everywhere, but nothing I could decipher. I climbed up onto the walkway and kept an eye on the water as I did so, half expecting to see one of the angels come out of it.

Instead, a body came floating down the tunnel. It took me several seconds to recognize it as Mustardseed. Morgana kneeled down to catch him in her arms, and the others gathered around her.

"Bring him with us," I said, starting back down the stairs to rejoin them. "If I can find more grace, I can raise him from the dead."

Amelia stepped away from the others to block my path. "It's not really Mustardseed's body. It's more the idea of Mustardseed."

Morgana drew Mustardseed closer to her and kissed him on the lips.

Then she passed him to Cobweb, and then Puck, who each did the same. She turned and released Mustardseed into the water. He drifted down the tunnel and disappeared into the mist we had left behind. The faerie stood staring at that mist for a long moment.

"It won't be long before they figure it out and find a way to follow us," I finally said.

"Then I recommend we don't linger," Morgana said.

The faerie left the water and followed me up the steps. I saw that Morgana now had a grey streak in her hair that hadn't been there before.

We carried on and after a time the ceiling was bricks, too. And then there was a manhole cover above us, light shining through its holes and metal rungs ascending one side of the wall.

Puck scrambled up the ladder first, moving disturbingly like a spider, and pushed the manhole cover to the side. The sounds of traffic echoed throughout the tunnel as he pulled himself through the hole above us and disappeared.

Cobweb climbed up next, then Morgana. Amelia stood there a moment, gazing back the way we had come.

"Are they pursuing us?" I asked.

"I can't say," she said, and I knew she was looking back at the cemetery, not for the angels.

Cobweb peered down at us from overhead, a grey sky the colour of wet newsprint above her. "We've found a ride," she said, "but it's not going to wait around all day."

Amelia climbed the ladder and I went up after her and dragged the manhole cover back into place behind me. It was only when I straightened up and glanced around that I saw the ride that Cobweb meant.

It was a red double-decker bus, on a street lined with row homes. I realized right away we were in London. I should have known from the sky. There were no other cars on the street, but that wouldn't last. The doors of the bus were open and Puck was standing beside the driver, his knife at the man's throat. Two passengers stood in the back on the lower level, a man and a woman. They had their phones in their hands but weren't using them. Their eyes had the glazed look of the fey – Morgana must have charmed them.

"Come aboard then and let's figure out where we're going," Morgana said, stepping into the bus.

"If this is in fact London, then I already know where to go," I said. "And it's probably best I go alone."

Morgana turned back to me. "Whatever it is you're after, you'll have a far better chance of succeeding with us. In fact, I suspect that without us you'll have no chance at all."

"I'm going to find Alice before the angels do. And you have lost enough of your court." I couldn't help but look at Amelia, who had collapsed onto one of the bus seats.

"They'll come for her whether you're with us or not," Morgana said. "Because they know she is your weakness. Better for us to stay together to protect her."

I thought things over a moment, but Morgana was right. I climbed aboard the bus and shouldered my way past Puck, then pulled the driver from his seat and sent him down the stairs. He stood there on the street, staring up at me with a dazed expression instead of running like any sensible person would.

"Those two as well," I said, nodding at the passengers in the back.

Morgana glared at me. "You have robbed me of all my fey. Again. Who will serve me now?"

"You can travel with me or you can travel with them," I said. "But not both."

She regarded me a moment, then sighed and waved a hand toward the back of the bus. "When did you develop such a conscience?"

"I'm trying to make up for all the things I've done," I said.

"Fine, but you're going to have to play their part in my court."

The two passengers blinked several times and then stared at us as if truly seeing us for the first time.

"Leave while you can," I told them. "And don't even think about calling anyone."

I had a look at the top level while they scrambled off the bus and ran up the street, after the driver who had come to his senses as well. There was no one else aboard, which was a small mercy.

The bus lurched forward several times as I went back down the steps. I found Puck behind the wheel. The others had taken seats and were clutching the poles around them as if they were afraid of what would happen next. Which wasn't an unreasonable fear where Puck was concerned.

"If he keeps freeing our fey, we'll be as bad off as the Chaos Court," Cobweb said with a scowl at me.

"Hush," Morgana said.

"Do I even want to know what the Chaos Court is?" I asked, but Morgana said nothing else.

I didn't ask any more questions then, because Puck slammed his foot down on the accelerator and the bus took off down the street. We turned at an intersection, and suddenly we were on a busier street with other vehicles that swerved to avoid us. The air filled with the sounds of horns and cursing drivers.

"So what now?" Morgana asked.

"The same as before," I said. "I keep looking for Alice until I find her."

"A most comprehensive plan. And where do you intend to look next?"

"Take us to the British Library."

"Not a library!" Puck said, with what sounded like genuine dismay.

Morgana gave him a look that silenced him, then turned her attention back to me. "You think Alice is there?"

"I don't think she's anywhere in this world," I said. "But Gabriel said there were others like the White Knight, using Alice's tales to enter our world from somewhere."

"So there may be another of those books at the library?"

"Even better. The British Library has the original manuscript of the very first Alice tale ever written. If there's something strange happening with the books, maybe the manuscript is the answer."

"This library could be a place of great power then," Morgana said and settled into her seat.

"All libraries are places of great power," I said. And that was what had me worried.

SPECIAL COLLECTIONS

We left the bus in the parking lot of the London Zoo at Regent's Park and walked the rest of the way to the British Library. It took nearly an hour and by the end of it the faerie were grumbling about having to trudge around like common beasts, until Morgana threatened to turn them all into uncommon beasts. Although she joined them in frowning at the sight of the angular, squat building that was our destination.

"It looks more like a factory than a library," she said. "Or perhaps a prison."

"I've been in prisons that were more entertaining than this place looks," Puck muttered.

"Where is the splendour of the library of Xanadu?" Morgana asked. "Or the endless drama of Genghis Khan's library?"

"Alice took me to Xanadu once, to help stop a sorcerer there," I said. "Believe me when I say the library is not so splendid after you remove the enchantments. Also, libraries have likely changed since you last set foot in one."

"That's the trouble with your world," Morgana said. "It's always changing, but rarely for the better."

A murder of crows flew overhead as we carried on to the library's courtyard, as if some omen.

"Do you have any grace left?" Morgana asked, watching the crows. "Perhaps you should alter your appearance."

"I want the librarians to recognize me," I said.

"At least you're consistent in your madness."

I entered the library first and stood in the entrance hall for a moment, taking it in. A small line of people stood at the reception desk before me. There was a hall to my right and a short set of stairs to my left, leading up to an atrium with tables and benches where people worked on laptops or were bent toward each other, engaged in quiet conversations. Skylights in the ceiling high overhead filled the area with natural light. Escalators at the rear of the atrium climbed to the different levels of the library beyond, while more stairs spiralled up with a landing at each of the floors.

I nodded at the others through the glass doors of the entrance. They came in one after another, except for Amelia, who remained outside. She sat on a bench by a statue of Isaac Newton hard at work on some formula or another. Morgana and I had decided it was best to have someone remain outside if my plan went sideways, which was more than likely. I had her keep the copy of the *Looking-Glass* in case the librarians had some way of sensing it.

"I expected more gloom and musty old texts," Cobweb said.

"They're trying to make libraries more welcoming these days," I said.

"Whatever for?" Morgana asked as she stepped to my side.

We headed deeper into the library, past a row of busts of old men set in the wall to our left. Some of them were vaguely familiar to me – perhaps we had met at some point in the past. We took the escalators to the next level and got off at the King's Library, the glass tower that stretched up from the subterranean depths of the building and through the levels overhead. Thousands of ancient books from the library of King George III sat on shelves behind the glass, but I barely gave them a glance. They weren't why we were here.

"Perhaps no one has recognized you after all," Morgana said.

As if on cue, an alarm began to sound throughout the library. An automated message played over the public address system, asking library patrons to please exit the building in an orderly fashion. As if the British knew any other way.

"I stand corrected," Morgana said. "Where is the manuscript? We had best find it quickly."

"I don't know," I said. "They probably locked it up in one of their special collections after what happened the last time I was here."

"Of course. Well, take us there then."

"I will. As soon as I figure out where it is."

Morgana let out a long sigh, one I had heard too many times before. "I may as well have let Puck come up with a plan."

"I would have used more fire," Puck said.

We slipped past people heading for the escalators and travelled deeper into the library. I found the stairs to the lower levels and took them. I figured whatever special collections area held the manuscript would likely be underground for security measures. We made it all the way to the Magna Carta exhibit before the librarians found us.

The Magna Carta manuscripts were on display in glass cases lining a wall to one side. I really wanted to take the time to give them a good look. That was impossible, though, on account of the man and two women who stepped out of the entrance to the next room, blocking our passage. The woman on the left carried a silver quill in her hand, the one on the right a book bound in scarlet hide. The colour didn't look like dye to me but rather a natural shade. The man wore glasses and pinched a bookmark between two fingers. I could also sense grace beyond them, which meant an angel was somewhere nearby. There was no one else in sight, though, as all the patrons had already left this part of the library.

"I presume those aren't mundane artifacts they're carrying," Morgana said as she considered the librarians.

"I believe we're about to find out," I said.

"Greetings, Morgana, queen of the faerie," the man said, adjusting his glasses slightly as he gazed at her. I decided to call him Specs.

"Do I know you?" Morgana narrowed her eyes at him.

"No, but now we know you," Specs said.

"It's the glasses," I said. "They must give him some insight into us."

"I had already figured that out," Morgana said.

"As representatives of the Bibliognost, we request to know the nature of your visit to our sanctum," Specs went on. "Especially in the company of the one known as Cross."

Morgana took a step back and eyed the passageway the librarians had come through. "What is a Bibliognost?" she murmured to me. "Is it anything like a bandersnatch? Because if it is . . ."

Puck grinned at the mention of the bandersnatch, which made me think I really did not want to encounter it.

"*Bibliognost* is an ancient word for someone knowledgeable about books," I said. "Although I'm guessing their Bibliognost probably has more knowledge than most." Maybe it was the angel I sensed.

"That's fine then because we're after a book." Morgana snapped her fingers at me. "What's it called anyway?"

"*Alice's Adventures Under Ground.* The original manuscript that Lewis Carroll wrote for Alice Liddell." I didn't need to tell them it was the inspiration for *Alice's Adventures in Wonderland.* They were librarians, after all.

"That's the one," Morgana said. "Fetch it for us and we'll be on our way."

The librarians looked at me for a long moment. It was the woman with the scarlet book who finally broke the silence. "That text is no longer available for public viewing. You should know that, given the way you damaged it the last time you were here."

"I wasn't the one who damaged it," I said. "That was Alice. And given her relationship with the book, I'd consider it more of an edit. But none of that matters. We need to see it and right away."

The librarians spread out. They didn't look at all worried, which gave me a bit of concern. Librarians can be a dangerous lot, even if they don't have a secret angel hidden away somewhere.

"We must insist that you accompany us to the Bibliognost," Scarlet said. "She has questions to ask of you before she responds to your request."

"I'm afraid we don't have time for that," I said.

"And I'm afraid you don't have a choice," Quill said.

"You may want to reconsider that," I said and nodded at Puck.

He spun toward the display cases holding the Magna Carta, and now there was a hammer in his hand. I wondered what else he had stashed away in his pockets. He swung the hammer at the glass, but of course it just bounced off. The Magna Carta wasn't going to be protected with regular glass. I didn't think he'd be able to harm the manuscripts, though. I just wanted a distraction.

"Do you really think –" Scarlet began, but she didn't get the chance to finish because I lunged at her. I didn't have enough time to cover the distance between us before she raised the book and started to read aloud. The air started to chill instantly – so it was one of those books. Thankfully, she didn't get to finish what she was reading – a large centipede soared over my shoulder and into her mouth, causing her to choke.

Sometimes the faerie were actually handy to have around. Sometimes.

Quill slashed her namesake in my direction, as if writing there, and a spray of ink spat out from the quill. I wasn't sure what it did, but I didn't want it touching me.

I'd made it close enough to Scarlet that I was able to grab her by the arm and yank her forward, using her as cover. She tried to spin around, and for an instant I thought perhaps she was attempting to get away. Then I realized she was trying to shield the book.

Too late.

The ink struck her and the book alike, burning its way into both. Then there was a flash of light in every colour imaginable – and a few that weren't – and I was thrown back against the display cases by a stinging, cold force. The only time I'd felt something similar was when I'd fought a demon ghost in an abandoned monastery in the Pyrenees a few centuries back. The room filled with words floating through the air, although they weren't in any language I recognized. They melted their way through the walls and the glass cases, although luckily none of them hit the Magna Carta manuscripts. Dozens of words melted their way through Scarlet as well, opening holes in her I could see right through. Her blood spattered the floor, and the smell of her insides was strong. Most people who find themselves with holes in their body try to cover those holes with their hands. But Scarlet just flailed for the book that was no longer there, then fell to the floor.

Cobweb cursed and clutched at her left arm, where a tumbling word had taken a chunk of flesh. Another word had gone through Puck's side, but he just grinned like he enjoyed it. Morgana was unharmed but was several feet to the side of where she had stood only seconds ago. I suspected she had worked some magic to keep out of harm's way.

Specs lifted the bookmark now, but he pointed it at the wounded woman instead of any of us. She froze in mid-convulsion and didn't even draw breath.

"Nice trick," I said. "What does that do, stop time?"

"You're about to find out," he said, swinging the bookmark around to me.

"Why are you pointing that at him rather than me?" Morgana said, and I heard that familiar charm in her voice.

Specs stared at her, blinked several times and licked his lips. His hand with the bookmark drifted in her direction.

"Oh please," the other librarian said, readying her quill again. "Do you really think you're going to stop us with a little enchantment?"

She was too far away for me to rush her, so I cast about for a weapon I could use. That's when I saw what Puck was doing.

"I don't know if we're going to stop you," I said. "But he might."

Both librarians followed my gaze and froze nearly as still as the woman on the floor at what they saw.

Puck had his arm halfway into the display case housing one of the manuscripts. He hadn't broken the glass, though. Instead, he had somehow slid his arm *through* the glass, leaving it intact. His hand hovered mere inches above the manuscript. He leered at the librarians.

"We can keep fighting, and maybe you win, maybe you don't," I said. "But either way the thing you're trying to protect probably gets damaged and maybe even destroyed. Or you just let me see the manuscript we came here to see and then we'll be on our way."

"We save the Magna Carta so you can steal *Alice's Adventures Under Ground*?" Specs asked. "That sounds like trading one evil for another."

"Believe it or not, we're actually friends of libraries and librarians alike," I said.

"I'm not," Puck said, which earned him a look from Morgana.

"Well, I am," I said. "And I'm not looking to steal anything. I just want to track down a friend, and I think the Alice manuscript may be the key to that. Once I've had a look at it, we'll be on our way and you can put it back wherever you hide it."

The two of them exchanged a look, but we all knew it wasn't much of a decision to make.

"Call him off," Quill said.

"Puck," I said.

Puck slid his arm a little deeper into the display case. His fingers brushed against the manuscript. "Are you sure you don't want to let them know how serious we are?"

"*Puck,*" Morgana said.

"All right." He sighed and withdrew his arm. The glass remained intact once his arm was out of the case. He shook his head sadly at the manuscript. "We could have changed history."

I nodded at the fallen librarian. "If one of you has something that can heal her, now is probably the time."

Specs slid the bookmark into a pocket and knelt at the woman's side. He pulled a folded piece of paper from another pocket and unfolded it. It was covered in handwriting that I couldn't make out from where I stood. He placed the paper over the largest of the holes in the woman, and the ink swirled and then ran to the edges of the paper. The paper itself melted into the woman a little, sealing the wound.

He looked at Quill, who was still keeping an eye on us. "It'll keep her alive for a bit longer, but we don't have much time."

She secreted the quill away into her clothing without me seeing where she actually put it. I was more than a bit relieved they didn't seem to want to fight anymore.

"Let's hurry up and get this lot to special collections and then out of this library forever," she said.

THE REVELATION BEAST

Specs picked up Scarlet and carried her in his arms while Quill gathered the remains of the red book. They took us down a hall and through a door marked for staff only. There was another hallway behind the door, this one lit by flickering fluorescent lights every five metres or so. The air smelled stale, as if it never circulated here.

The hallway disappeared around a corner at either end, maybe fifty metres away in each direction. There were a couple more doors in the walls, but the librarians ignored them. Instead, Specs stepped into the shadows between the lights and pulled a different bookmark from his pocket. This one was golden and had an illustration of a black skeleton key on it. He placed the bookmark against the wall and a section of the wall pulled back and slid silently to the side, revealing a new doorway. Uneven stone stairs on the other side descended into darkness.

"Those bookmarks seem pretty handy," I said. "Maybe we can work out a deal to trade for them."

"They don't function outside the library," he said. "And even if they did, I'd sooner burn them than give them to you."

I probably would have felt the same way in his position, so I just nodded and followed him down the stairs. I leaned close to Morgana as we descended.

"How did Puck do what he did back there with the display case?" I asked. "Was that some glamour trick?"

"I have no idea. We aren't in the glamour here." She reached behind us and hauled Puck closer by the ear, as if he were some misbehaving child. "What mischief are you up to now?"

"I don't know," Puck said, wincing but also laughing at the same time. As if he enjoyed the pain. "I just got the idea in my head, so I tried it. And it worked!"

"Yes, but how did it work?" I asked.

Puck shrugged. "How do you do the things you do?"

"I kill angels and use their grace," I said. "But I don't think you're capable of that."

"You don't know what secrets I have," Puck said with a sly smile.

Morgana twisted his ear until he yelped. "No, but I will find out," she said.

The librarians eyed us over their shoulders but said nothing. We went down the stairs for another five minutes or so and then emerged into a large chamber.

The walls and floor were more rough stone, and I got the feeling the entire place had been carved out of some existing mass of rock. The glass column of the King's Library occupied the middle of this chamber, descending from the ceiling and the library overhead and continuing into the depths of a great pit in the centre of the room. Narrow bridges stretched across the pit and connected to a catwalk circling the King's Library, and more stairs spiralled down at the edges of the pit. The area was dimly lit with a soft glow that came from the glass column itself. There was a withered corpse bound in white chains propped up on the other side of the glass directly across from us, as if it were standing guard inside the tower.

"You never got around to finishing the basement?" I asked.

"We built the library overtop of an existing site," Specs said as he laid Scarlet on the ground. "Although it was used for very different purposes in its time."

I took a moment to study the fallen woman. Her eyes were closed and she was pale and still. She was still breathing, though, so there was that at least. I hoped she would make it, for I had no ill will toward librarians. Quite the opposite, in fact.

We crossed to the pit and peered into the depths. It seemed to stretch down forever, and the King's Library with it – level after level of bridges connecting to more catwalks positioned around the column, the stairs eventually disappearing into a distant vanishing point.

"How many special books do you have stored away here?" I asked.

"So many even we are unable to count them," Specs said. "A spirit once told us our collection rivals that of the Forgotten Library."

"Let's not talk about that place," Morgana and I said at the same time. Cobweb muttered a curse, and Puck shuddered.

Specs gave us a curious look. "Something we should know?"

"It's a long and different story," I said. "Now where is the manuscript?"

"We will need the archivist to secure it," he said. He walked across the bridge in front of us and over to the King's Library, to the corpse that was there. He leaned close and whispered into the glass, and then the corpse turned and shuffled around the corner of the tower and out of sight.

"Your archivist is dead?" I asked.

"Not dead," Specs said. "Preserved."

"Death seems a better fate than being trapped in some library for eternity," Cobweb said, making a face.

"I have always imagined that paradise will be a kind of library," Specs said.

"I appreciate a good Borges reference, but I don't think this is the sort of library he imagined," I said.

"And when was the last time you talked to Borges?" Specs muttered.

"Oh, enough with the name-dropping," Morgana said. "We get it. You both have large literary credentials."

I wondered if the archivist was going to fetch the angel whose grace I continued to feel everywhere around us. Instead, it came back with the manuscript and passed it through the glass to Specs, although it didn't shove its arm through like Puck had back in the Magna Carta room.

"Seems everyone knows that trick but me," I said.

Specs came back across the bridge to us. He had put on white gloves without me noticing. They appeared to shine with their own light as he held the manuscript so we could see it.

It was a simple bound manuscript with the title *Alice's Adventures Under Ground* intertwined with vines and flowers on the cover. It didn't look like much, but I felt drawn to it anyway. I took a step forward before I even realized what I was doing.

The faerie didn't seem as captivated by it as I was, though.

"That's it?" Morgana asked. "It hardly seems worthy of all the legends."

"Sometimes the best books have the simplest covers," I said and nodded at Specs.

He opened it with those white gloves and revealed the dedication page, which read as follows: *A Christmas Gift to a Dear Child in Memory of a Summer Day.* He turned the page again, and I had a glimpse of an illustration marking the first chapter, a drawing of one girl reading to another, lines of elegant handwriting covering the rest of the page.

Then the Revelation beast erupted from the book.

It was a black serpent-like creature with a long body that snapped out of the pages like a striking cobra. It had lizard-like legs with vicious-looking talons on the ends. And heads – it had many heads, like a hydra. Seven, in fact, which is why I immediately decided to call it the Revelation beast. The heads resembled those of different reptiles: a snake, a lizard, a turtle and so on. But that was hardly the oddest thing about the creature.

The truly curious thing was the fact the beast was wearing the shredded remains of a black suit. Judging by the fabric, it was likely of nineteenth-century vintage. It also had around a dozen pocket watches swinging from the remains of the suit, the glass shattered on each and the hands frozen.

A crocodile head lunged at me, its jaws snapping shut just a couple of inches from my face. I stumbled back, away from the beast and the book that had birthed it. The smell of the creature followed me – the stench of rotting meat that made me gag a little.

And then I saw the book *did* still hold the beast, which was likely why the crocodile head hadn't quite been able to reach me. The creature's long, serpentine tail disappeared into the page, the words written there swirling around it. The Revelation beast scrabbled its claws on the floor, gouging out chunks of stone as it tried to reach me, but it wasn't able to pull itself entirely free of the book. It was as if something was clinging to it from the other side.

"Welcome, little fishes," the crocodile said in a rumbling voice that carried through the cries of the librarians. So maybe they'd been right in not wanting us in the library.

The fact that the book still held the Revelation beast didn't stop the other heads from acting. The one that looked like a Komodo dragon struck at Specs, latching on to his head with its jaws. He let out a muffled scream and dropped the book, scrambling desperately for a new bookmark. The turtle head lashed out and caught his arm, and then Spec's cries ceased as the two heads ripped him apart. His insides hit the floor with wet splats, and blood showered me.

"Where's your Borges now?" Puck cried, leaping past me to strike at the creature with his hammer. At the same time, Cobweb threw a ball of insects bound together by old spiderwebs. It hit the snake's head and completely engulfed it, while Quill stepped back to give herself some room to use her weapon.

The beast lunged forward again, and its tail slipped free of the book a few inches more. The crocodile head opened its jaws wide, but now Morgana was at my side whispering to the creature. The crocodile paused and turned to look at her. She kept on whispering and raised a hand to its cheek, as if caressing a lover.

Then the turtle head came at me around the side of the crocodile. *"Come and join the dance!"* it cried in a high voice, and I recognized the words once more. The heads were uttering lines from *Alice's Adventures in Wonderland*, as if the Revelation beast were another of Lewis Carroll's characters. It was just like my fight with the White Knight.

A spray of ink from the quill cut through the turtle's beak, slicing the end right off. The turtle reared back with a screech of pain and the severed shard of beak dropped to the ground and hit the fallen book, where it sank into its pages and out of sight. I sensed grace spilling out of the beast, like the White Knight all over again, although I wasn't close enough to do anything about it.

"We need to force it back into the book," I said. "Before it frees itself completely."

"And how exactly do we force something into a book?" Morgana asked, still stroking the crocodile head.

The archivist joined the fight at that moment. It came flying from the direction of the King's Library – the glass wall still intact despite the fact that the archivist had passed through it. And the archivist *was* flying. It had sprouted leathery, mummified wings to match the rest of its body. I realized in the instant before it crashed into the Revelation beast that it must have been the angel I'd sensed before. It wrapped one of its white chains around the neck of the Komodo dragon and began to wrestle it down, back toward the book.

"This is why we avoid libraries," Morgana said, shaking her head. "Too many strange characters."

But even as the archivist tried to force the beast's head back into the book, the creature continued to work its tail free. It seemed as if it were almost ready to slip out now, and then the Revelation beast would be able to move around the room at will. And no doubt beyond the room.

I stepped back to the remaining librarian. "I don't suppose you have another of those quills?"

"I think you've caused enough trouble." She lashed out with the quill again, spraying more ink into the battle. This time, though, the turtle sank what was left of its beak into the archivist's shoulder and pulled the angel down as a shield. The ink cut through its wing, which tumbled to the ground near me, smoking. I breathed deep of the heavenly grace it released, and felt a bit of power within me again. Maybe enough to try one thing.

The archivist didn't seem to notice the loss of its wing. It wrenched the head of the Komodo dragon down farther and forced the head into the book. Like the tip of the turtle's beak, the Komodo dragon sank into the pages and disappeared. From where I stood, I could see the ink swirling around the place it had entered, like a whirlpool.

But it was only one head, and the rest of the Revelation beast was still there. It thrashed its tail wildly, trying to break free of the book that held it. Morgana backed away from it, pulling Cobweb with her. Puck capered around the scene, laughing and striking at the Revelation beast and archivist alike with the hammer. The weapon was stained with dark blood – he must have scored a few hits. The crocodile blinked several times, then snapped its jaws as if trying to clear its thoughts and came after us.

"*Oh dear, what nonsense*," it hissed.

"Everything about this is nonsense!" Morgana said.

I wasn't so sure of that, though. I was starting to see some connections.

It didn't seem like the archivist would be able to carry the fight on its own. The Revelation beast was too strong, even for an angel. The snake had managed to free itself of the webs enough that it bit into the archivist's leg, while the turtle rammed its broken beak into the angel's side. The archivist was already moving slower as it lost blood and grace alike.

"Give me the quill," I said to the librarian.

She didn't even look at me as she prepared to strike again. "I already told you –"

"I think I know how to end this," I said.

She paused and studied me for several long seconds, long enough for the Revelation beast to shred the archivist's other wing.

"You may as well let him try," Morgana said. "As much as I hate to admit it, his ideas do occasionally work."

"And sometimes they make things worse," Cobweb said.

Morgana nodded. "It's admittedly a coin toss."

The librarian looked back and forth between us, then finally nodded and handed me the quill. "The word that powers it is *creo*," she said.

My Latin was rusty, but I still knew enough to remember that it meant *create*. Which was fitting for what I was about to attempt. I took the quill and swept it through the air. At the same time, I sent some of the angel's grace I'd breathed in through my fingers and into the quill.

"*Creo*," I said.

The ink that came out this time was darker and thicker than before. And there was more of it. A giant wave of it, in fact. It swept into the Revelation beast and the archivist, knocking them both to the ground, and then formed a whirlpool around the book – a whirlpool that sank into the book. The Revelation beast was caught and dragged around by the churning ink. It struggled to break free and clawed at the stone floor, but it could not escape the pull of the whirlpool.

"*Begin at the beginning and go on till you come to the end!*" the turtle cried. Then it plunged back into the book as quickly as it had leapt out.

The ink flowed into the pages after it, and the whirlpool began to shrink. The archivist, who had fallen outside of the whirlpool, got to its feet and dove into the whirlpool without hesitation.

"What's it doing?" I said. "We've trapped the beast."

"The archivist is making sure the creature doesn't come out again," Quill said softly.

Then the archivist was gone as completely as the Revelation beast. The ink flowed into the book after them, until there wasn't a drop of it left. The book lay on the ground beside what was left of Specs. His glasses were cracked now, and he stared sightlessly at the King's Library tower.

Quill knelt beside him and half reached for him, as if she wanted to try to put him back together but didn't know how. I knew the feeling well.

"Sorry," I said, trying not to look at Specs. "This wasn't what I intended."

"And you call yourselves friends of libraries," Quill said.

"Not me," Morgana said.

"I would be content if this is the last library I ever see," Cobweb said.

"Actually, they're kind of growing on me," Puck said.

Quill whispered in Specs' ear. Then she gently pulled off his gloves and put them on her own hands.

"You're just going to put it back on the shelf?" Morgana asked. "Shouldn't we burn it like your kind always do with the dangerous books?"

Quill lifted the book so we could see it. The archivist's white chains were wrapped around the book now, linked together in such a way that I could see no beginning or end.

"The book has been bound," Quill said.

"For a time anyway," I said. I wasn't sure how long those chains would hold.

"And I do not see Alice anywhere," Morgana said, surveying the chamber. "We battled the beast for nothing."

"Perhaps we should keep trying," Puck said. He licked his lips as he stared at the book.

"It wasn't for nothing," I said. "It proved Gabriel was right. There's still some connection between Alice and God's bible. That creature was straight out of one of Alice's tales and the bible combined. And it was full of grace."

"Maybe that angel brought it to life from the book," Morgana said.

"For what purpose?" I asked. "The angel sacrificed itself to bind the beast."

"You know how angels are," she said with a shrug.

"That doesn't explain the White Knight," I said. "Or the others that Gabriel mentioned. I've seen this sort of thing before. The bible is damaged and leaking power. And wherever it is, it's got something to do with Alice for it to manifest like this. If we can find the right book, we find Alice."

Morgana folded her arms across her chest and narrowed her eyes at me. "So we travel to every library in the world, battling monstrous beasts like the one we just faced, until we randomly stumble across the one we need?"

"I doubt we'd survive many more battles like that," I said. "We need to know what we're looking for."

"Well, if it's not the original manuscript, then what is it?" Morgana asked.

I thought about the Revelation beast's last words. "*Begin at the beginning*, it said. What if that book isn't the beginning of the Alice tales?"

"It is very much the original manuscript," Quill said. "We have ways of determining such things." She took the quill from my hand as if offended by my question and then went to Scarlet's side. Thankfully the other librarian was still breathing.

"But maybe we're looking for the wrong original manuscript," I said.

Morgana turned to Quill. "Do you have any more of those healing pages? I fear he may have taken a blow to the head during the battle."

"There *are* rumours of a lost manuscript," Quill said, gathering Scarlet in her arms. "But there are often such rumours with significant texts. It doesn't mean there is another manuscript."

"What if it's not even that dramatic?" I asked. "Maybe all we need to look for are Lewis Carroll's earliest notes for the Wonderland stories."

"Who is this Lewis Carroll you keep babbling about?" Morgana asked, and Quill stared at her with an expression I can only call horror.

"The author of that tale and a few others," I said, nodding at the book. "Although his real name was Charles Dodgson."

"Only a mortal could have that many names and all of them be dull," Morgana said.

"What kind of notes?" Puck asked. "As in secret correspondence shared by co-conspirators?"

"I just mean the ideas he wrote down as he conceived of Alice's adventures," I said. "Every writer begins a tale with random ideas they jot down somewhere. In a journal or index cards or even on scraps of paper."

"Those would be invaluable and under heavy guard," Quill said. "But I don't know of any library that has such a collection. And even if they did, no one will share such a text with you after today. I will ensure that. Now leave this library."

"Maybe they're not in anyone's collection because they've never been found," I said. "Tell me where the book was written and we'll trouble you no more."

"Christ Church college, Oxford," Quill quickly said. "It's where Lewis Carroll spent most of his life and first came up with the Alice tales."

"Then that's where we're going next," I said and headed for the stairs.

"And where will we look for these mythical notes if even the librarians don't know of their existence?" Morgana called after me.

"I don't know," I said. "But I'll take the entire place apart brick by brick to find them."

I would take the whole world apart to find Alice.

A CURIOUS DISCOVERY IN CHRIST CHURCH

We went back outside the library to where Amelia waited. She was seated on the same bench, only now she cradled a dead crow in her hands and gazed into its black eyes. I wondered if it was one of the crows we had seen earlier.

"We didn't find what we need here," I told her.

"That's certainly one way of putting it," Cobweb muttered, wiping at the blood on her clothing.

"We're going to Oxford," I continued. "The sooner the better."

Amelia nodded like she'd expected that. "I have some friends in Holywell and Wolvercote. It would be good to see them again, if we can."

"It's not a social visit." I tried not to think about what kinds of friends she might have in cemeteries like the ones she had named.

Amelia took the crow over to a nearby planter and set it down in the earth. "Did you know crows have funerals for their dead? They come from all around and observe the fallen crow for hours."

"They also have sex with the dead," Morgana said.

"Crows are wise," Amelia said, smoothing down the bird's feathers. "They know there is much to be learned from the dead."

"Let's see what we can learn from our own dead," I said.

First, we needed to find a way to Oxford. It was only a few hours away, but we couldn't take the usual forms of transit. The Royals who ruled over this land would definitely be aware of our presence after the events at the library. They would be looking for us – me in particular. I had a very long history with the Royals, and I was in no hurry to renew our acquaintance. The transit stations would be watched. And Gabriel and the other Risen would be looking for us as well. Hell, for all I knew the Royals and the Risen could be working together.

We split up and walked the street outside the library, looking for a car to steal. I made my way up one side and tried the doors of the vehicles parked there, but they were all locked. Then Puck drove up in a food truck that sold pita sandwiches from the looks of it.

"You couldn't find anything less noticeable?" I asked.

"It comes with food. And drink." He pulled a half-empty bottle of whisky from the glove compartment.

There were no better alternatives, so we climbed aboard the food truck and headed for Oxford. The day was fading into evening by the time we arrived, the grey clouds overhead darkening to those deeper shades of grey that can only be found in England.

We left the food truck parked on the side of High Street, near Oxford Castle. Hopefully, if anyone came looking for us, they'd start there. The castle was the sort of place that historically had attracted trouble, with its role in civil wars and the plague deaths that had happened there. Some said ghosts still walked its grounds, although I'd learned that nearly every historical site in England was haunted by spirits.

We made our way across Oxford to the long outside wall of Christ Church and managed to join a tour group that was just entering, slipping in among their ranks unnoticed. The tour took us into the grassy quad at the centre of the college, where the guide carried on about the differences between Norman and Gothic architecture for a time. He pointed out different features on the surrounding buildings every few seconds, which seemed to excite him more than anyone in our group.

I turned in a slow circle and considered the wings of the college. "I can't feel any grace nearby," I said softly. "We'll have to do this the hard way and search every room."

"Maybe not," Morgana said with a frown. "For I can sense something."

"What is it?" I followed her gaze toward the great hall, but I saw only more stone walls and stained glass windows.

"I don't know," she said. "There's a strangeness about this place. Yet familiar at the same time."

"I feel it, too," Cobweb said, also staring at the great hall.

"Like memories of the night before when you've had too much ale," Puck said.

I turned to Amelia, to see if she felt whatever they were sensing, but she shook her head. Whatever it was, it only affected the faerie.

"It's the only thing we have to go on until something else shows itself," I said.

The guide began to talk about the library in a nearby part of the campus, which caused the faerie to scowl all at once. We broke from the group and entered the college, heading for the great hall.

I kept my eyes on the windows. I still had memories of the time Anubis had used a similar window to spirit away the body of Will Shakespeare from the Holy Trinity Church in Stratford-upon-Avon to who knew where. He'd done so on behalf of the Royals, who really didn't want me getting close to Shakespeare again. I hoped they didn't have anyone hiding in these windows, or anywhere else in Christ Church.

There were more tourists inside, but they busied themselves photographing the architectural features and paid no attention to us. They likely would have been less enamoured of the place if they'd been here during its earlier days. History is always less thrilling to those who have to live through the drafts and vermin. And the plagues.

We eventually found our way to the great hall, a room of high vaulted ceilings and more stained glass windows. Long rows of tables and chairs filled the room, and paintings of old men covered the walls. They had been important characters in the college in their time, but now they were the anonymous dead to everyone but the tour guide, and perhaps Amelia.

We paid them little attention because we were drawn to the pictures at the far end of the hall. There was an exhibition on the wall there, hazy photographs of young girls and drawings of fanciful characters. A rabbit in a checkered jacket, standing on its hind legs and looking at a pocket watch. A dodo bird leaning on a walking stick and conversing with a baboon. A large striped cat perched in a tree, with a wide grin. A flamingo wielding a croquet mallet. I recognized them immediately as illustrations by John

Tenniel, the original illustrator of the Wonderland books. The memories of the dead may fade, but their works live on.

Morgana let out a sharp breath as she stared at the exhibition. I studied the illustrations in search of what she saw there.

"I'm still not feeling any grace," I said. "What exactly is it you're sensing?"

Morgana ignored the drawings, though, and instead stepped over to a photograph of three girls standing in front of a forest. They were young, the oldest girl being eight or nine and the other two perhaps five or six. They hung on to each other as if they were one and smiled at the camera in a way that I could only describe as mischievous.

"It's the Liddell sisters," I said. "The girls that inspired Lewis Carroll to create the Alice tales."

"Those aren't girls," Morgana said. "They are changelings."

A MEMORABLE LETTER

I stared at the girls in the photograph and they smiled back at me.

"Changelings as in faerie?" I asked.

"Are there other kinds?" Morgana asked.

Cobweb let out a low whistle as she studied the photo, while Puck cackled so loudly that tourists throughout the hall turned their heads our way.

"I remember them," he said. "They were always getting into the most wicked trouble. One time we all went to the circus together and they freed the bears from their chains, and then –"

"The sisters were *your* subjects?" I asked, turning to Morgana.

"Don't be ridiculous," she snapped. "We are high faerie. I would never allow changelings and their like into my court any more than I would allow pixies or brownies. No, these girls, if you can call them that, are from the Chaos Court."

I looked to Amelia, to see if maybe she could help me understand what was happening, but she just shrugged.

"It's before my time," she said.

"I thought you were queen of the faerie," I said to Morgana.

"I am the queen of *my* faerie," she said. "Which are the only faerie that matter."

"Explain it to me like I don't understand," I said. "It shouldn't be too difficult."

Morgana sighed. "As almost everyone knows, except for you it seems, there are many different courts of the faerie. The Chaos Court, the Drowning Court, the Moss Court – more than I can be bothered to name, for they are all beneath my concern. Think of my court as those of your kind who live in castles, while the other faerie are more like those who dwell in huts in the woods."

"What's the name of your court?" I asked.

Morgana stared at me. "You mean you don't know? After all this time?"

"How would I know?"

"You always have been rather simple. My court is the Court of the Veil. It has always been named that except for when it wasn't. And no, I'm not going to explain the name to you."

I turned back to the photo of the girls. "Where are they now then?"

"I haven't the slightest notion, nor do I care," Morgana said with a shrug. "We haven't seen any other faerie for ages."

"They're dead," Amelia said, studying the sisters. "They have been for some time. The Chaos Court is no more in this realm."

"That trick of yours is getting a little unnerving," I told her.

She slumped into a nearby chair. I wondered how tired she was, given all we'd been through so far. "Would you prefer I don't use it?" she asked.

It's true what they say: Children are never easy.

Morgana wandered down the wall, turning her attention to the Wonderland illustrations. "I suppose it explains these curious drawings. It's the sort of nonsense the changelings would inspire. Perhaps it explains your Alice's curious nature as well."

"You think Alice is a faerie?" I asked.

"You really did take one blow too many to the head," Morgana said. "Alice is very much her own creature and unlike any other I have encountered before. But if the sisters are connected to that book she escaped from, it could be that they had a role in it. Or perhaps some of their essence simply slipped into the tales about her and helped bring her to life."

I didn't know what all of this meant, but I knew it meant something. I also knew time was running out – it wouldn't be long before someone realized we were here.

"Where can we find their court? Are they in your glamour?"

"Please," Morgana said. "The Chaos Court did not create a lasting glamour like some, but instead created realms within the chaos. Such as the Wonder Lands, which the tales of Alice seem based upon. Maybe the sisters revealed a few of the secrets about that place. But I don't know if the Wonder Lands yet exist, for nothing persists in the chaos. The glamour of the Chaos Court may have faded away over the ages, as surely as the sisters."

"We need to find Carroll's notes now more than ever. But I don't think we're going to discover them here. We need to find wherever it was he wrote when he lived in this place and see what secrets it contains." I headed for the exit.

"And where might that be?" Morgana asked as she followed along.

"I don't know," I admitted as we left the hall. "But someone around here likely has the knowledge."

We descended a wide staircase and found another group of tourists. A guide was talking to them about the high vaulted ceiling, which apparently had been in some film or another. Morgana stepped straight to him and placed her hand on his arm. She gave him a smile, and I felt both jealous of the man and sad for him at the same time. "Lead us to the chambers of . . . what was his name again?"

"Lewis Carroll," I said.

"Yes, lead us to the chambers of Lewis Carroll," Morgana said.

The guide stared at her and his eyes had the cloudy look of the fey now. He wandered down the stairs, casting a look back at Morgana every now and then to ensure that we were following. None of the other tourists complained. In fact, they were quite excited about the prospect of seeing where Carroll had lived.

As it turned out, there wasn't much to be excited about. The guide led us to an unremarkable room filled with some stuffed couches and a couple of tables and chairs. A chess set made of crystal playing pieces sat on a side table near the fireplace, which now held a monitor and video game system. A baby grand piano was set to one side. Another table on the other wall had a microwave and some packets of tea and spoons. A framed painting of Carroll hung over the fireplace, but that was the only sign this room had ever been anything of significance. It was nothing more than a study room.

"We want the *private* quarters of Lewis Carroll," I said, but the guide just nodded dreamily at Morgana.

"This was once the room of Charles Dodgson, aka the writer Lewis Carroll," he said, pointing at the painting. "As well as Einstein and other notables. It's used now as a common room for the residents, who will hopefully be inspired by those who graced this space before them."

The tourists made soft cooing noises and set about photographing every object there. I cast about but didn't see anything resembling old papers or notebooks.

"Well, this is certainly disappointing," Morgana said. "And I don't even know why I'm disappointed."

"I'm sorry," the guide said, wringing his hands. "Let me take you to the tower and show you the bell. It has a very interesting history of –"

Morgana waved him off and came to my side as the others of our group wandered the room. "Shall I have him tear the place apart brick by brick as you suggested?"

I nodded at the painting over the fireplace. "What about him? Was Lewis Carroll anything special like the girls? Another faerie perhaps?"

Morgana barely even glanced at the painting. "He's just another dull fey, no doubt fallen under some enchantment. Perhaps we should find his grave so you can do your little trick of talking with the dead, to see what he knows."

Puck sat at the piano and began to hit keys, seemingly at random. The discordant notes that filled the air matched my confused thoughts. I stepped to Amelia as she considered the painting.

"He is buried far from here, in Mount Cemetery," she said. "And there is nothing in the grave with him."

"Maybe the girls then?" I asked.

"Their graves are even farther away," Amelia said. "And empty."

"So where do we go next?" Morgana asked. "For this room is certainly lacking the import we seek."

I thought things over as Puck continued to hammer the keys, as if he were trying to find notes that least accompanied each other.

"The library," I finally said, for nothing else came to mind.

"No," Cobweb breathed.

"It's always the libraries with you," Morgana said. "And never the taverns or dungeons."

"I don't think Lewis Carroll was the tavern type," I said. "And I'm pretty sure this place doesn't have a dungeon."

"You'd be surprised at all the places that have dungeons."

We found an exit and made our way to the smaller quad next door, where the first tour guide had taken his group. Three of the buildings were identical brown structures that had clean lines and grids of windows interspersed with decorative columns that were a nod to classical architecture.

"It's like they are courthouses trying to pass as Greek temples," Morgana said. "Only without the orgies."

"They're mostly student housing, so I don't know about that," I said.

I didn't pay those buildings much attention, though, for it was the fourth one that interested me. It was the same neo-Palladian architecture as the others, only it had more columns and was mostly white in colour, as if to distinguish itself from the other buildings. I already knew it was the library for I had come here looking for Alice not long after she had first disappeared. This time I had an idea of what I was looking for, though. Maybe.

We went inside and up a flight of stairs to the Upper Library, a long hall with high windows and even higher ceilings. The hall was lined with old wooden bookshelves filled with books even older than the shelves. Glass-topped tables with special exhibits ran along the middle of the room, and there were a few tables scattered about with students studying at them.

I glanced at the nearest display case and saw it contained a copy of *Philosophiæ Naturalis Principia Mathematica* by Isaac Newton. It was the original binding, judging from the floral roll and gilt edges, and so probably priceless in more ways than one. But it had no value for me at the moment.

"These look to be of some interest," Morgana said, stopping at another display and peering inside.

We all gathered around the case and saw what appeared to be draft title pages for *Alice's Adventures in Wonderland* that were mostly experiments in typography, as well as a collection of letters from Charles Dodgson to other people whose names I didn't recognize. I scanned the letters, but they were mundane stuff – an invitation to a friend to come see a new catalogue at the library, and a complaint to the post office about some ambiguity in their rules. One of the letters caught my eye, though, because of its brevity and curious addressee.

My dearest self, if you fancy to write a memorable tale, then place this letter amid the Elements. Regards, Charles Dodgson.

"I'm getting that strange feeling again," Morgana murmured, looking around.

"From the case?" I asked.

She turned to peer down the length of the library. "There is something peculiar over there," she said, and the other faerie nodded.

We moved down the rows of books until Morgana stopped before a section of shelves. "It almost feels like the glamour here," she said. "But different. As if it were some other glamour."

I studied the bookshelf and saw several volumes of commentary about Homer's *The Odyssey*, a copy of Aeschylus's *Tragedies* and a matching set of *Poetae Graeci*. All the usual sorts of books you would find in a library like this.

Then I saw it. The Homer books all looked identical, a deep brown in colour with gold-leaf printing on their worn spines. One of them was covered in a thick layer of dust, though, as if it hadn't been touched for decades, if not longer. I reached out and pulled it from the shelf.

But the book I held was not the one that had sat on the shelf. Instead, it was a green volume with cursive writing on the cover in a colour I could only describe as ice. It was like one of those moments in a dream, where reality changes. The title of the book read *The Elements of Fancy.*

"A secret book," Cobweb breathed.

"Is it what we seek?" Morgana asked.

I opened the book but the pages inside were blank.

"Perhaps the notes are in invisible ink," Puck said. "We could try burning a few pages to see if any words appear."

"Can you do that trick again that you did at the British Library?" I asked him.

Puck grinned at me. "What do you want me to steal?"

"Bring me the letter that Dodgson wrote to himself," I said.

"That's it? A letter? I mean, surely this place has some skulls or –"

"Just the letter," I said.

Puck sighed and slouched back to the display case. He reached his hand through the glass and pulled out the letter. He raised it to his face, reading it. Even from our distance I could see it was upside down.

"You still don't know how he's able to do that?" I asked Morgana.

"Puck is always hiding secrets," she said, shaking her head. "But not usually anything like that. He's been up to mischief."

Puck brought the letter back and handed it to me. It felt brittle to the touch, and I worried about it crumbling away with age.

"*Place this letter amid the Elements*," I said, reading the words on the page again. Then I slipped the letter in between the pages of the book and waited.

The book remained unchanged in my hand. I felt no surge of grace or other magic.

"It didn't do anything," I said, flipping through the pages again. They remained as blank as before.

"I wouldn't say that," Morgana said. "I think it did *something*."

There was a doorway in the middle of the bookshelf now. It was a plain wooden door that would have barely caught my notice, if not for the fact it had magically appeared in a bookshelf in the library of Christ Church. I stepped closer to the door and studied it. I could see the books shimmering behind it, as if the door were spectral in nature.

"It's a glamour," Morgana said. "But not a glamour of our making."

We didn't have time to dwell on the door's origins because it wouldn't be long before someone else noticed it. I stepped forward and took hold of the handle. It was cool to the touch, and wet. I caught the scent of lavender. Then I opened the door.

There was a small study on the other side, a room maybe three metres by three metres and lined with more bookshelves. A wooden desk and chair occupied the centre of the room, carved with fanciful characters. I recognized some from the Wonderland books, but others were unknown to me: a flock of flamingos playing croquet, a fish-man wearing a suit and glasses, a crocodile building a house with a hammer and so on. There were papers scattered atop the desk, along with a quill and an inkpot. A worn rug covered the stone floor, its edges embroidered with flowers and plants that looked familiar yet strange at the same time. Everything was damp, and I smelled salt water now instead of lavender.

We stepped inside and I closed the door behind us to make sure no students or librarians followed. I suspected no one knew about this place, judging from the amount of dust on the book I had used to summon the door. I wanted to keep it that way. Hopefully the door would no longer be visible once we were in the room. That's how secret doors usually worked.

I stepped over to the desk and peered into the inkpot. It was empty. I examined the quill without picking it up – I'd learned my lesson about such things. It was a raven's feather, but the light caught it in such a way that it gleamed with the colours of the rainbow. That in itself was curious because there was no source of light in the room, yet shadows danced in the corners as if there were invisible candles somewhere.

"This was created by the Chaos Court, wasn't it?" I asked.

"The room is their glamour but not the books," Morgana said. "They must have been brought in after its creation."

"Why is it so damp?" It was as if the place had been flooded at some point in the past.

"I don't know," Morgana said. "They are curious creatures. It's really not worth thinking about why they do what they do."

I studied the books on the shelves. They were mainly old history and philosophy texts in the same vein as the books in the library outside this room. I nodded at the desk. "What about the quill?"

"A faerie creation, although not one of any note," Morgana said. "The ink, on the other hand . . ." She stepped closer and peered down into the inkpot. "I'm not certain. There is something more to it."

I handed *Elements* to Amelia and went around to the other side of the desk. The seat of the chair was worn, the armrests faded to a different shade than the rest of the chair. It had seen some use in its time. I wondered how often Dodgson had sat here, dipping his quill into that faerie ink in the name of Lewis Carroll. The trick with the letter suggested it was his study. So what exactly had he created here?

The drawers on the left contained only more papers and another quill, all as damp as everything else in the room. I let them be without touching them and tried the drawers on the right.

The top drawer held more letters, but the ink had run so much I couldn't read a word on any of them. I was beginning to think this trip was a dead end. Then I opened the bottom drawer.

There was a journal inside, bound in dark, unadorned leather. I took it from the drawer and turned it over in my hands, inspecting it. There was nothing written on the front or the spine and it was damp like all the other books. Yet I felt a bit of grace.

"Is that what we came for?" Morgana asked, eyeing the journal. "It doesn't look like much."

I had no response, for when I opened the journal and began to flip through it, I saw water had washed away words and drawings on the pages, just like it had everything else in the study. Lines of notes and sentences had become waves of ink, while illustrations had been turned into ponds of it. I could see the ghostly shapes of figures, with strange limbs and bodies, but I couldn't make out what they had once been.

Until I came to the last page.

The ink was crisp and clean, as if it had just been drawn. And the page was dry while the rest of the book was wet. There was a simple illustration drawn on the page, in the style of Tenniel's original Wonderland drawings. But it was no image of Wonderland I had ever seen before.

It showed Alice amid ruins, stone blocks jumbled all around her. Alice looked like she always did in those illustrations, only she was drawn in colour rather than black and white. She fought an angel erupting from a book at her feet, grappling with it and obviously trying to force it back into the book. I didn't recognize the angel, but they were legion, after all.

I recognized the book, though. It was God's bible. The bible that Alice had been holding when the whirlpool had taken her in the battle with Noah at the Sunken City. The book we had wrested away from Noah to stop him from ending the world. What price had she paid for that?

Alice turned her head to look at me. "Too late," she said, and then she was still again.

"Perhaps you really can't judge a book by its cover," Morgana murmured.

I glanced at Amelia. "You said Alice wasn't dead, right?"

She nodded. "I've never known her to be among the dead. She is somewhere else."

"Then I think I know where she is." I stared back down at Alice fighting the angel. "She's in this journal."

A FADING GLAMOUR

I set the journal down on the desk and grabbed a random book off the nearest shelf. I began to flip through its soggy pages, scanning the watery ink.

"How could that ridiculous girl be in this journal?" Morgana asked. She poked the illustration of Alice fighting the angel, as if trying to nudge her free of the page.

"I'm not sure," I said. "Maybe the same way Gabriel and the other Risen hid Mona Lisa in the *Last Supper* all those years ago and trapped me in a different painting. It was Alice who rescued me from that one after all." And maybe saved the world in the process, for who knew what the Risen might have done if they had managed to unleash Mona Lisa upon their enemies before I freed her?

I checked the room, but nothing had changed since I'd taken the book from the shelf. I put it back and picked up the next one. It was just more waterlogged pages with nothing legible as well.

"And she's nowhere to be found in this world. That would explain why everything here is wet and smells of the sea. When she vanished at the battle of the Sunken City this is where the whirlpool took her. In there." I pointed at the notebook. "Or maybe she took herself there."

"You think she was looking for a place to hide," Morgana said.

"She was wounded and probably wanted to lay low," I said, moving on to the next book. "What better place than where she was born? Because if I'm right, that journal is where Lewis Carroll made the first notes about the Alice stories – the same stories she escaped from."

"A secret journal hidden away in a secret glamour that the world has forgotten about," Morgana said, nodding. "Yes, I can see the appeal of that."

"You can just travel in and out of books?" Puck asked. "Can you teach me that trick? There's a few books I would like to explore." The leer on his face told me exactly the nature of those books.

"I don't have that ability, but Alice must," I said. "She's a character who came from a book, so why not seek sanctuary in one?"

"It doesn't look very restful, though," Morgana said. "Unless I'm misinterpreting what she and that angel are doing."

I took another book from the shelf, but it was the same as the first two. This wasn't going anywhere. But I had to try.

"She must still have God's bible with her," I said. "But it's damaged and its power is likely leaking out and taking form, as it has before. The angel she's fighting is probably no more a real angel than the White Knight or the Revelation beast."

"So she has found refuge within her own tales, but the bible's creatures are using those tales to escape into our world," Morgana said. "This is a particular sort of madness even for you."

"Alice is trying to stop it, though," Amelia said, joining Morgana to study the illustration.

"Why isn't she coming out now that we're here to help?" Cobweb asked, lifting the journal to squint under it as if Alice might be hiding there.

"I don't know," I admitted. "Maybe she can't."

I reached for the next book on the shelf, but my fingers passed through it. The title on the spine was still legible enough that I could read it: *Principles of Philosophy* by René Descartes. "Or maybe there's some other reason. Because it doesn't appear to be the only curious book in here."

Morgana came to my side and peered at the book. "It's not these ridiculous texts. This glamour is fading."

"What do you mean 'fading'?" I asked. I reached for a book on the next shelf but wasn't able to grasp it either.

"The Chaos Court created this room, but they are no more. Without them to power the glamour, it will slowly cease to be."

"How long do we have?"

"It's not a glamour of our making, so I can't say. I suspect that if it's survived this long, then it probably remains in some sort of limbo when not in use. But the longer we remain here, the more it will fade."

"We need to take the journal somewhere safer." I went back to the desk.

"That may not be wise," Morgana said. "If the journal is part of this glamour, I don't know what will happen to it if we remove it. It could lose all its power or even fade away entirely."

I stared at Alice fighting the angel on the page before me. Morgana didn't have to point out that if the journal disappeared, then Alice might be gone forever.

"We need to find a way into its pages then," I said. "We'll rescue Alice and bring her out ourselves."

"But you said we can't travel into books," Puck said.

I nodded. "We'll need a little help with that part."

"Let me guess," Morgana said. "Another of your questionable acquaintances."

"There's only one person I can think of that could manage it," I said. "Da Vinci."

The problem was I didn't know if he was alive or dead.

A FERRYMAN

We left the secret room and returned to the library. The same students that had been there before were still studying at their tables, while a librarian was busy returning books to a shelf at the other end of the hall. None of them paid us any attention, which struck me as more than a bit lucky.

"Is there a reason no one has noticed us enter and leave a secret room in plain sight?" I asked Morgana.

"It's most likely a part of the glamour," she said. "It seems the Chaos Court didn't want that room to be found."

I took the letter from *Elements* and the book's colours faded, turning back into the dusty Homer tome once more. The doorway faded in the same manner, leaving just the shelves before us.

"That raises the question of what the Chaos Court were doing with Lewis Carroll at all," I said. "Why create that room for him and give him the magic ink and whatever else he used to write the Alice tales?"

"Who can say with creatures like that?" Morgana said, making a face. "They're like Puck – full of mischief. I sometimes wonder if he is a changeling foisted upon me by their court."

Puck grinned, then furrowed his brow as he tried to figure out if Morgana was complimenting or insulting him.

"We'll likely never know," Morgana went on. "It may be one of the mysteries of the world. Like da Vinci's whereabouts. Unless you happen to know where he is these days?"

I slipped the book back into its place on the shelf. "I haven't seen him in centuries. He could be anywhere."

"So we're back to where we started," Morgana said. "Only my court is much reduced since you stumbled into it." She lifted a hand to her head and fingered her streak of grey hair.

"That wasn't my fault," I said. "And we're not exactly back where we began. I know someone who can help in our search."

I gave Puck the letter to return to the display case, and I kept an eye on him to make sure he did so. We were going to need that letter in one piece when we returned here. A librarian turned away from a shelf just as he was pulling his arm out of the display, and she paused and gave him a look. Puck opened his mouth as if to say something, but I grabbed him and led him toward the stairs.

"I don't want anyone to notice us," I said. Not when we were so close to rescuing Alice.

"We could make her a fey," he said, eyeing the librarian. "Maybe she knows of other secret chambers in this wretched place."

"And maybe we should leave you in that secret chamber, where you can't cause any more trouble," I said.

The idea of being stuck in a room of books was enough to shut him up and we left the library without any further incident. At least nothing I noticed anyway.

We found a cab on one of the streets outside and took it to the coastal town of Folkestone. The driver was reluctant to leave Oxford, but Morgana blew him a kiss and he fell asleep. I drove the cab into an alley where Puck and Cobweb laid the driver beside a trash bin. Morgana wanted to bring him with us, in the trunk, so he couldn't tell anyone what had happened to him, but I told her it was best no one else knew where we'd gone. The cab firm would track the vehicle down by GPS, but I didn't bother sharing that with her. I was trying to do the man a favour by leaving him behind.

The sun was setting by the time we arrived in Folkestone, and it turned the sky bloody. I hoped it wasn't a portent of things to come. We made our way to the docks and found a fishing boat I knew. The captain was a weathered old man named Coal who was missing a few fingers and his left eye. He'd once told me his mother had named him after Cole Porter but didn't know how to spell the name.

He was sitting on a rail, drinking a bottle of rum and watching the darkening sea when we walked up. He almost didn't recognize me, for it had been some time.

"A place like this, I can hide him away where no one will ever find him," Puck said with a grin. "Then his boat is ours."

"Harm a hair on his head and I'll hide you away," I said. "He's a friend."

I stepped to the side of the boat and waited, for I wasn't about to set foot on this vessel without permission. Coal stared at me for a long moment, then whistled in surprise and waved me aboard.

I motioned at the others to stay where they were and stepped on to the boat. Coal offered me the bottle as I sat on the rail beside him and I took a long drink. The rum was cheap and strong, which was exactly what I wanted at that moment.

"You haven't aged a damned moment since I saw you last," he said.

"I suppose I'm just cursed that way." I handed the bottle back.

We watched the day fade into evening for a time, passing the bottle back and forth until the first stars showed themselves.

"I'm guessing you need to be ferried somewhere without attracting too much attention again," Coal said.

"I wish I were a better friend," I said. "I should have stopped by with my own bottle long before this." It was the least I could do given I was the reason he'd lost his eye.

Coal shook his head as if he knew my thoughts. "If not for you and what you did that day, I wouldn't be able to look upon those stars with my one good eye. Or upon yourself, for that matter." He glanced at the others. "Although I'm not sure what to make of your friends."

"Me neither."

Coal chuckled at that. "So you haven't changed the company you keep then. Good. Life is too short to waste it among those who have never lived. Now, where can I ferry you this time?"

"Just get us to the coast of France and we can take it from there," I said.

Coal grunted and squinted out to sea again. "I can do that. If you promise to someday tell me what you're up to."

"Someday," I promised.

When we were done the bottle, he waved the others aboard and we set out to sea. He stepped into the wheelhouse on his own while the rest of us stumbled into the galley and laid down on the benches in exhaustion.

"Are you going to tell us our destination?" Morgana asked. "Or is this another of those times you're making it up as we go?"

I closed my eyes instead of answering and quickly fell asleep. I dreamed I was back in Noah's ruined, sinking ark, searching through his library for Alice after we had stopped him from ending the world. But I couldn't find her no matter how many books I went through.

It was still dark when Coal woke me. He had made coffee for all of us, and we drank it in silence before heading back out on deck. We were perhaps a kilometre off the coast of France, drifting near a small cove. The lights of cities shone in the distance on either side, so I put us somewhere between Calais and Dunkirk.

"I've prepared the raft," Coal said and nodded at the rear of the boat, where an inflatable covered life raft trailed behind us, connected to the boat by a rope.

"I can bring it back to you and then swim to shore on my own," I said.

"No need," Coal said. "Just be sure to drag it ashore with you and hide it somewhere. I don't want someone stumbling across it and thinking there's a missing sailor out here."

"And what if you run into trouble on the way home and need it?" I asked.

Coal grunted. "I've led a good life. If I meet my end helping the one who gave me that life, then so be it."

"Until next time then."

"Until next time," he agreed. "And it'll be your turn to bring the bottle then."

I pulled the raft close and held it while the others climbed in, and then I joined them. Coal untied the rope and cast it to me, then waved and went back to the wheelhouse without a backward glance.

"You two seem like you have a story," Morgana said, watching him go.

"We do," I said. "But it's not a story I'm going to share with anyone who wasn't there."

And with that I grabbed an oar from the bottom of the raft and set about taking us to land as Coal headed back out to sea and faded away.

A VISIT WITH AN OLD FRIEND

We dragged the raft up onto the beach, which was mostly small, smooth stones with the occasional empty beer can mixed in. The stones stretched all the way up to some bushes, where a trail led to a road. There was no place to put the raft, so we lodged it in the edge of the bushes and weighed it down with some of the bigger stones, and then Morgana did a trick with the glamour to hide the raft so well even I couldn't see it.

We climbed up to the road and walked for maybe a kilometre when we came across a car parked on the shoulder, the engine still running and the front wheel against the roadside barrier. The driver was asleep at the wheel, snoring and unharmed and smelling of wine.

"I suppose you have some meaningless objection to letting me have him, too," Morgana said.

I pulled the man from the car and stretched him out on the earth on the other side of the barrier. He barely stirred – he must have had a lot to drink before he'd got behind the wheel. He was lucky I didn't let the faerie have him as punishment for being so reckless.

"What kind of queen am I supposed to be if I don't have servants for my court?" Morgana asked.

"A queen who isn't imprisoned in the dungeons of the Royals," I said, getting behind the wheel. "A fate that will be easier to avoid if you're not travelling with a noticeable entourage."

"They wouldn't dare." Morgana joined me in the car. "They know what happened last time we were at odds."

"Maybe," I said as the others got into the back. "But as you said, your court is reduced now. And the angels are looking for us as well, remember? Or do you have a treaty with them, too?"

"I suppose it's just as well," Morgana said. "The French have never been very good at following orders."

I was careful not to hit the accelerator too hard as we left the man behind, for I didn't want to shower him with rocks. Hopefully someone would offer him a ride once he woke. And if not, then he'd think twice before driving drunk again.

As it turned out, he hadn't finished all of his wine. A half-full bottle sat in a cupholder, much to the delight of Puck and Cobweb, who took turns passing it between them in the back seat. They didn't offer any to Amelia, but she didn't seem interested anyway. I hadn't seen her eat or drink yet, and I wondered if she even needed sustenance.

Morgana watched the countryside as we travelled and twirled her patch of grey hair around a finger. "Once I ruled this entire land. And now look at me. Reduced to scurrying about in a drunkard's stolen vehicle, to who knows where."

"I'm pretty sure France had other leaders," I said. I'd been under threat of execution from enough of them, after all.

"But they answered to me," she said. "For each and every one were under my spell."

I couldn't argue with that. I said nothing else and focused instead on trying not to listen to Puck and Cobweb in the back as they sang a song about a promiscuous goat. I wasn't entirely certain if the goat was made up or not.

We drove the car to Paris and left it on a street in the 2nd arrondissement when it ran out of petrol. Morgana complained about returning to Paris when we had so recently fled it, but she grudgingly accepted my argument that it would be the last place the angels would be looking for us then. I don't know if she believed that any more than I did, though. We walked the rest of the way to the Louvre and arrived just as it was opening for the day. I stopped the others in the courtyard, to one side of the long line of people forming near the glass pyramid that served as the entrance to the museum.

"I should have known this is where you'd bring us," Morgana said. "Do you really expect me to set foot in such a place after what happened at the British Library?"

"I expect you to wait for me in the garden," I said, waving in the direction of the nearby Tuileries. "If I go in alone, maybe there's a chance I won't be recognized this time."

"A truly cunning plan," Morgana said. "And if the unthinkable does happen and someone notices you?"

"Then it'll be good to have reinforcements nearby," I said. "Just try not to add any fey to your court while you wait."

"That will depend on how long you take," Morgana said.

We parted ways there and I joined the line into the museum. I broke from the crowd once inside to enter the gift shop, where I bought a sketchbook and a pencil kit. Then I made my way to the Denon Wing.

Most people were there to see da Vinci's *Mona Lisa* – the painting, not the gorgon – or Delacroix's *Liberty Leading the People*. They jammed into the display rooms in such numbers you couldn't even see the paintings from the entranceways. Which was fine with me because it meant they left other works in the wing relatively free of crowds. And it was one of those that was my reason for being here.

I headed straight for the massive Daru staircase, which held multiple landings and connected different parts of the museum. It was one of those places that had taken decades to complete and could hold hundreds of people. Today, though, there was fewer than a dozen going up and down the stairs on their way to other parts of the museum. Most didn't even linger more than a few seconds to look at the headless statue of a winged woman at the top landing. If they'd known what she really was they wouldn't have lingered at all but would have run screaming from the museum.

Her name was *Winged Victory of Samothrace*, although I just called her Victory. We had a history of sorts.

I leaned against the wall where I was out of the way and opened the sketchbook and pencil kit. The light came through the windows overhead and fell on Victory in a way that created interesting shadows. I did my best to capture them as I sketched. I've become a passable artist over the ages, but I'm no da Vinci. I do have a few other tricks, though.

I had little grace left within me, but there was enough for a trickle, which I let flow through my fingers and into the pencil. If I'd had more, I could have raised Victory from her eternal slumber, like I had the last time I'd been here. But this time I had to try something new. Thankfully, it worked.

I drew a decent rendering of Victory and a bit of the surrounding landing, and then I filled in the statue's head. I used lighter strokes, barely even visible on the paper, so that the head was ghostlike. It was a woman's face, surrounded by serpents for hair, for Victory was a gorgon. Or had been in her prime anyway. It was hard to say what she was now.

I wasn't sure if I'd got it right, because I couldn't remember the exact number of serpents on her head. They're always moving around, so it's hard to keep track of them. But it must have been close enough, for she turned her face to look up at me from the page.

"Hydra," she said, using her pet name for me, and the snakes all hissed. Maybe in greeting, maybe not. She glanced around the page and the half-drawn landing. "What strange realm have you summoned us into this time?"

"I'm afraid I can only manage a sketch this visit," I whispered. "And even then, not for long. We'll have to save the pleasantries for another day."

"That is just as well," she said, smiling and revealing fangs streaked red with blood even though I'd only drawn her in shades of grey. "We generally prefer to skip the pleasantries ourselves and move on to the more enjoyable parts of those who seek us out."

I glanced around the staircase, but so far no one was paying me any attention. Or maybe they thought I was just another crazed artist and were politely looking the other way. I put it at even odds.

"Actually, it's not you I seek," I said. "It's Mona Lisa."

The snakes lashed out at me, and I swear they came out of the paper a bit before falling back down. "Again? It seems like just a breath ago that you came in search of our lost sister."

I nodded. "And I found her, although Judas stole her away. You left out the part about them being lovers when you told me of her."

Victory smiled. "Would it have changed anything?"

"I don't know," I said. "But I'm looking for da Vinci now. I'm hoping you or Mona Lisa knows his whereabouts."

"We have not seen da Vinci for ages. Not since we walked the earth in our glory and rage."

"And what about Mona Lisa? Is she there in your head with all of you now? Maybe she can tell me how to find him."

That was why Victory kept referring to herself in the plural. The gorgons shared consciousness somehow, even in death. Except for Mona Lisa when she had been hidden away in the *Last Supper* by the angels. I was hoping for a little goodwill from the gorgons now for rescuing her from that fate.

"What would you have of da Vinci?" Victory asked, studying me.

"He taught the angels how to move in and out of paintings as if they are real places."

"They are real places," Victory said. "Have you learned nothing in all your lifetimes?"

"I need to do something similar and find a way into a book." I pointed the pencil at the sketchbook. "Much like this one. I'm hoping da Vinci can help."

"And what do you seek in your book?"

"It's a long story. Let's just say Alice is trapped in there and I'm going to free her."

Victory took a moment before speaking again. "Our sister is not with us. When the angels tore her away, it was for eternity. She walks the earth again, thanks to you, but she is lost to us."

"Damn it." I sighed, just as a woman wearing a lanyard that marked her as one of the museum staff came up the stairs. She gave me a look, so I tapped the sketchbook with my pencil as if I were frustrated by the drawing. "This is not turning out the way I had hoped," I said. "Why can't anything ever be easy?"

Victory laughed at that, a sound that was like hyenas battling over a bone. The woman with the lanyard must not have heard it, for she continued on her way.

"Perhaps you would prefer to change places with us," Victory said. "Then you might understand the true meaning of hardship."

I nodded. "Apologies. I wasn't thinking of your situation."

"It's not entirely unpleasant." She smiled again. "Our current state has given us much time to think on what we will do once we are free again."

"I'm pretty sure I don't want to know about that," I said. "So let's get back to Mona Lisa. Do you know where she is at least?"

"Of course," Victory said. "She did visit us here after you freed her, so we are grateful for that. She has sought sanctuary in the Great Dismal where none can find her unless she so wishes."

"The swamp in the US? That seems a strange place for a gorgon to hide."

"No, the elder wasteland with all the ruins of castles and trolls in the mountains and those delightful little biting bugs." Then she paused as one of the snakes leaned close to her ear and hissed in it. "Ah, your kind have a different name for it now. The Scottish Highlands."

"Mona Lisa is hiding away in the Scottish Highlands?" That made a sort of sense, as the highlands were sparsely populated and a big enough area that it would be hard to find anyone there. Which did not make things any easier for me. "I don't suppose you know *where* in the Scottish Highlands?"

Victory shrugged. "All we know is that she has made her lair in an abandoned keep surrounded by a field of the dead."

"Well, how hard could that be to find?"

"You do seem to have a talent for seeking out the dead."

I took a deep breath before asking the next question. "Is she alone?"

"She is lost to us, but she is not alone," Victory said.

I tightened my hand so hard on the pencil that I snapped it between my fingers. "Judas."

"She remains with the trickster. They have corrupted each other with love."

"Judas knows nothing of love. He is a creature of hate."

"Is he that different from you?" Victory eyed me.

"He condemned all of humanity to a meaningless existence when he got Christ killed," I said. "And he condemned me to an eternity in this body. I don't think I've done anything quite like that."

"Perhaps not yet."

"And he killed Penelope and Amelia."

"The wife of Odysseus? I thought her before your time."

"A different Penelope," I said. "This one was born of an angel and was my only true love. Amelia was our daughter. Until Morgana ripped her from Penelope's dead body and gave birth to her anyway."

"Why would she birth another's spawn?"

"Maybe because she wanted to find a new way to torment me. Or maybe because she cares for me in her own way. Maybe both. It's a complicated relationship."

"Perhaps our sister and Judas have their own complicated relationship," Victory said.

I mulled that over. It was true that Judas and Mona Lisa did have some sort of strange feelings for each other. After all, when the angels had trapped Mona Lisa in the *Last Supper*, Judas had tricked me into finding her so that I would free her where he could not. I had seen the love they had for each other when they fled the painting together, which Mona Lisa had turned into an apocalyptic hellscape with her powers. If I hadn't been so busy battling the angels left behind in the painting, I would have hunted them down. But they escaped and disappeared, and I was distracted with other things, such as saving Amelia from that *Hamlet* ghost and stopping Noah. It had been a busy few years.

"Judas is a creature of a different time," Victory added. "Like ourselves."

I wasn't sure if she was referring to her and her sisters or me and her, but a thought distracted me then anyway. "Why haven't they freed you?"

"Mona Lisa will liberate us when she is ready. And she will restore us to what we once were. We look forward to finally meeting you in the flesh then, hydra."

"No offence, but I think I'm going to be busy elsewhere that day," I said.

But Victory wasn't listening. Instead, she turned her head to the side and peered off the page. The snakes all turned in that direction as well, hissing and spitting black venom.

"What is it?" I asked. I looked in the same direction, but I saw only the empty stairs leading up to the next level.

"We are not the only monstrosities in this place," she said. "There is another like us coming."

"Another gorgon?"

"No, another creature trapped in stone and magic." Her snakes waved at her body, as if gesturing.

Then I heard it. The sounds of heavy footsteps coming down the stairs. Stone treading on stone.

"Any idea what it is?" I asked.

But the grace had run out and Victory was silent now, just a sketch on paper once more. I ripped the page from the sketchbook and crumpled it into a ball that I shoved into my pocket, then dropped the sketchbook and pencils to the step. No doubt some poor art student would be able to make use of them.

The creature came down the steps then, and I saw her fully: One of the statues that had come to life in the Père Lachaise Cemetery. The woman made of marble with dead flowers around her neck.

No, not a woman. An angel.

A man and woman in matching jackets came up the other stairs. They kept their eyes on Victory and barely glanced at the stone woman they passed. That told me she had cast some sort of sleight to make herself look normal. To everyone but me anyway. She wanted me to see her for what she was.

I left Victory behind and headed back the way I had come. The angel followed me, walking at the same pace. She didn't close on me, but she didn't lose any ground either. Maybe she was waiting for the rest of the angels to arrive. Or maybe whatever she had planned, she didn't want to do it in the museum.

I made my way back outside the Louvre to the courtyard. I lingered a bit near the pyramid, until I saw the angel still following me. She moved through the crowd in a straight line toward me, and people moved to one side or another to let her pass. No one gave her a second look, though – there was definitely magic at work.

I headed for the thickest part of the crowd, where there was a fresh wave of people lining up to enter the museum. I moved through them and changed direction a couple of times, hoping to lose the angel, before I slipped away. I crossed the Place du Carrousel and went by the Arc de Triomphe du Carrousel, which had attracted a number of obviously confused tourists who thought it was the much larger and grander Arc de Triomphe on the Champs-Élysées. If you must know, you can tell them apart by the statue of Peace riding in a chariot flanked by golden angels atop the smaller Arc de Triomphe near the Louvre. That and the dead buried under the larger Arc de Triomphe. I hurried into the Tuileries Garden, hoping the statues of golden angels were just statues for a change.

I carried on down the Grande Allée that crossed the Tuileries, to the large octagonal pool at the end. The pool was surrounded by chairs for tourists and locals alike to relax a bit. I found Morgana and all the others there except for Puck. They were sitting on a cluster of chairs, Morgana and Cobweb eating croissants.

"I have such fond memories of this place," Morgana said to me as I walked up. "Do you remember that time we found ourselves cavorting in this very pool together?"

"I remember you drowning me in this pool," I said. "When I was serving in the Swiss Guards during the revolution and you led the crowds into the garden to hunt us down."

"Such lovely memories," Morgana murmured, gazing at the pool.

"You were drunk," Amelia said, closing her eyes. "Or you could have escaped. You were always drunk then."

"We don't have time to reminisce," I said. "The angels have found us again."

Morgana got to her feet and glared back the way I had come. "I'm tired of running," she said. "I would like to drown some of the Fallen in the pool now. They need to learn the wrath of the faerie queen."

I shook my head. "Maybe in its glory days your court could have stood against a handful of angels. But not now."

Cobweb stood and stepped over to me. She gave me a look that said she had taken offence at my words, even if we both knew they were true. "Perhaps our glory days are yet to come," she said. "What better way to find out than to test ourselves against a court of the Fallen. Or perhaps even yourself, if you challenge our queen again."

"I know all your tricks," I told the faerie. "But I don't think you can say the same of me."

"Oh, enough of your posturing." Morgana sighed. "Both of you. Just tell us you found what we came here for."

"Not exactly," I said and shared what Victory had told me. By the time I was done, we all saw the stone angel walking along the Grande Allée toward us.

"Call Puck from wherever he is and let's get out of here," I said.

"I'm right here." Puck was at my side, holding a rolled-up canvas in his hand.

"Where did you get that?" I asked him. I hoped he had simply paid some street artist for a self-portrait, even though I knew better.

"I found it in there," he said, nodding at a nearby building at the edge of the park. It was a long stone and glass structure, with more tourists lined up to get inside. "They had pictures hanging up all over, where anyone could just take them."

"The Orangerie," I said. "Are you saying you walked into a world-famous gallery and took a picture from the wall?"

"I was bored." Puck shrugged. "And you know I can't help myself when I'm bored."

"He really can't," Morgana said.

"Please tell me it's not one of the Monets," I said.

"It's just some plants," Puck said. He unrolled the canvas with a snap of his fingers, and I saw a ragged section of one of Monet's *Water Lilies*, maybe a metre by a metre – a small fraction of the overall painting. It looked like Puck had torn it from the canvas with his fingers rather than carefully cut it free.

"We can't take that with us," I said. "Every curator and government official in the world will be looking for it."

"You always ruin the fun," Puck said and tossed the scrap of painting into the pond.

I scrambled in after it, grabbing it from the water as fast as I could. That was when I saw the angel had reached the other side of the pool already. She stepped onto the water – not into it – and began to walk across. None of the other people sitting around the pool noticed her any more than the museum crowd had.

"Time to go," I said and laid the scrap of wet canvas down on an empty chair. Hopefully the gallery staff would find it soon enough. With any luck, they'd even be able to repair it. I still had a bad feeling about it, though. There was no doubt I was going to take the blame in some way for what Puck had done.

Amelia had managed to drift off to sleep during all this, so I shook her awake and pulled her from the chair, then led us out of the garden and to the nearby Seine. We hurried down some steps to the path alongside the river, where there were a number of boats tied to a dock. One of them was a long tour boat, meant to take a few dozen passengers up and down the Seine to see the sights of Paris. Personally, I've always found the alleys of Paris to be home to the best sights, but to each their own.

We climbed onto the boat, where Puck ripped the control panel apart and stuck his hands into the wiring inside until the engine started. I undid the ropes and then he took us out into the water, blowing the horn as we went. The angel came down the steps and stood at the river's edge, watching us go. I waved at her but she didn't wave back. Angels never did.

Every time I visit Paris, something like this happens.

A RIVER CRUISE

We cruised down the Seine in the tour boat, past the town of Vernon, where for a time I'd made a living as a smuggler of religious artifacts. I had my own booth in a tavern where people brought me bloody shrouds and preserved fingers and eyeballs in jars and the like. I delivered the ones with some power to an archbishop named Borromeo in Rome, who stored them away for safekeeping. I even gave him a white bible that a demon swore had been one of Gabriel's holy texts. The insides of the bible had been burned, but the ash still held the shape of the pages, so I figured it had probably belonged to someone special if not Gabriel. Borromeo thought it best such things were not left free in the world, and I was inclined to agree with him. I was even more inclined to take his coin.

From there we travelled past the ruins of Château Gaillard, where I'd hid out after the Templars caught wind of my smuggling escapades and came for me. Coincidentally, that was around the same time Borromeo mysteriously died and was then canonized by Pope Paul V. I got to know the pope a little when he hired me to organize the Gunpowder Plot, during which I learned he had sold many of the religious artifacts I'd given to Borromeo. He'd used the proceeds to finance the completion of St. Peter's Basilica and to pay off some blackmail debts. If you only knew the things I did about the saints.

We next cruised through Rouen, where the three spires of the Rouen Cathedral were visible even from the river. I'd once fought a Valkyrie atop one of those towers, when the Vikings had raided Rouen back in the ninth century or so, but that was not the memory that lingered when I saw the cathedral.

"Do you remember that time we were struck by lightning while we consorted in the spire?" Morgana asked, gazing at the cathedral.

"Maybe we could reminisce about that another time," I said, trying not to look at Amelia.

"I remember that!" Puck laughed and pointed at me. "You had to flee into the night naked as the spire burned down. The flames singed the very hairs off your arse."

"And how would you know that?" I asked.

"Because I watched the whole thing hidden away as a gargoyle," Puck said with a leer.

"You weren't very well hidden if I knew you were there the whole time," Morgana said.

"That explains why I couldn't find my clothes," I said. "And here I thought all these years that the lightning had blown them out of the spire."

"I try to live my life like lightning would," Puck said.

We left Rouen and the memories behind and I found a padded bench to lie down on and rest. I closed my eyes for a time and dreamed of Alice once again, this time on that journal page. She turned her head to look at me, and then the page caught fire and burned up, and there was nothing but ash in my hand.

When I opened my eyes, it felt like it was only a few minutes later but someone had covered me with a blanket and the boat was rocking heavily from waves that were too strong for the Seine. I sat up and saw mist all around us. I could tell from the bit of water that was visible that we were no longer on the river.

"How are we in the ocean already?" I asked.

"I was bored so I moved us along a little," Morgana said from another bench nearby. She was building a house of cards beside her with a deck she had found somewhere. It was more of a palace really, with multiple wings and a large courtyard.

I stood and studied the waters. "I don't know that we should be making the crossing in a riverboat. Glamour or not."

"I took care of that, too." She nodded to the port side of the boat.

As if on cue, a sailboat drifted out of the mist then, heading our way. It was in rough shape, listing to one side, the hull stained with age. The sail was loose and torn, little more than rags. I saw no sign of anyone on board.

"It will take us the rest of the way," Morgana said as Puck steered us toward the ship. She dropped the remaining cards onto the palace she had built, and the whole structure collapsed. "And we'll be less likely to draw attention when we arrive."

I wasn't so sure about that, but it didn't seem I had a say in things at this point anyway.

Cobweb leapt onto the ship, which was named *Rachel*, and caught the end of a rope Puck threw. She pulled the two vessels together, close enough we could all step across and onto the deck of the sailboat. Puck was the last and left the riverboat's engine running when he came across.

"You should turn everything off but its lights so it's less of a hazard," I said.

"Sometimes I think you don't even know me." He pushed the boat away with a foot. We watched it motor off into the mist.

Cobweb managed to get the sailboat's engine running despite the fact it looked as if it hadn't been started in decades. I stepped into the cabin to have a look around and found it as empty as the rest of the ship. It was ankle-deep in water, though. I went through the cupboards until I found a half-full bottle of rum, the label of which had long peeled off, and a couple of glasses. I took them back to the deck, poured a generous splash in each of the glasses, then handed one to Amelia while I kept the other to myself.

"And where is mine?" Morgana asked.

"It's your ship," I said. "I figured if you want a drink, you know where it is."

She gave me a look and then sat at the prow, like some sort of figurehead. Cobweb took the wheel, while Puck climbed up the mast and swung about like a crazed gymnast, looking for land.

We sipped the rum for a time, which tasted like fire and burned the same. Amelia took the *Looking-Glass* from her pocket and offered it to me. I'd forgotten she was still carrying it with everything that had taken place since the cemetery.

"You keep it for now," I said. "It seems to bring me trouble when I have it."

"Why not get rid of it then?" she asked, nodding at the sea.

"We may have need of it yet. There are still too many unknowns."

Amelia put the book back in her pocket and I considered the mist for a time.

"How did you know I was drunk when Morgana drowned me in the pool in the Tuileries all those years ago?" I asked.

"Perhaps it was just a guess." Amelia smiled. "The odds would be in my favour."

"Fair point. But you also knew the exact right tomb to lead us to in the cemetery so we could escape Gabriel and the others. If I didn't already know you, I would suspect that maybe you're some sort of angel of death like Azrael."

"Azrael's not really dead, you know."

"I think you may be wrong there. I remember killing him quite clearly, because of just how hard it was to cut off his head with a sword. I had to use three swords, in fact, because they kept breaking."

"Azrael was created to be undying. He'll be back. And when he returns, he will come looking for you."

"Hmm." I took a bigger drink this time. "I'll be waiting for him then. And I'll just have to kill him again."

"Maybe. Death changes Azrael, so each time he returns he is a different angel."

"I know a little about that."

She didn't say anything else for a time, so I just waited. There wasn't anything else I could do, after all.

"I think for most people death is like the mist that surrounds us," she eventually said. "The living can't perceive what lies on the other side. Neither can the dead. But I'm different. I can't see the mist. Or rather, I can choose to ignore it."

"You can see the dead?"

She hesitated a moment before answering. "It's not that I see them exactly. It's more that I know them. For instance, there are thirty-seven lost souls beneath us at this very moment, on the ocean floor, trapped in the wreck of a frigate that sank when Noah's ark passed too close. They are doomed to haunt that shipwreck until their bodies rot away and their bones finally crumble to dust, freeing their damned souls. I don't need to see them to know they are there, as sure as you are standing beside me now."

I peered down into the darkness of the water. What was there to say to that?

"Sometimes I think they are the lucky ones," Amelia said.

"The drowned sailors?"

"Them and those like them. For eventually they'll be free of this world and remain fully in the realm of death. While I'm forever pulled between both worlds because of my very nature."

She stared down into the water then and didn't speak again. I knew our conversation was over.

I emptied the rest of the bottle into my glass because it had been one of those talks. Then I joined Morgana. She was dangling her feet over the rail. I almost did the same, until I remembered the dead beneath us. I sat cross-legged instead and offered her my glass.

She held up a bottle of wine in her right hand. I hadn't seen any wine in the cabin, so maybe she had produced it using one of those glamour tricks.

"It seems we have left your kin behind," she said.

"The angels are not my kind," I said.

"Sometimes I wonder," she said and drank from the bottle.

I leaned against the rail and gazed back along the length of the sailboat. Amelia remained where I had left her, and Puck continued to cast about for land at the top of the mast. Cobweb stared back at me as she stood behind the wheel, with an expression on her face I couldn't read. The ocean faded into the mist behind the sailboat. If the angel still pursued us, I didn't know where she was. But then I didn't even know where we were at that moment.

"I'm sorry about Mustardseed," I said.

"We are less without him," Morgana said. "And I will speak of it no more."

"Then I'll change the subject. I've been thinking about the angel and what it wants."

"Clearly it wants us," she said. "Or at least you. No doubt the angels from the cemetery and more are scattered across your usual haunts, waiting for you to show up."

"Maybe. But she didn't make much of an effort to chase me down."

"Perhaps she knew she would face the wrath of the faerie queen if she did. For you are my pet, not hers."

"Or maybe she wasn't trying to catch anyone," I said.

"You think she's just watching? Why show herself at all then?"

"Because she wanted us to run."

Morgana took another drink from the bottle and thought that over. "What if there was some object of import at the museum that she did not want us to find?"

"Trust me, there are many objects of import at the Louvre. But I think Victory would have known if what we needed was there. No, I think the angel wanted us to run for another reason."

"You think they're following us."

"Maybe they want to know where we're going." I downed the rest of the rum in one swallow. "Or maybe they're herding us somewhere."

THE FIELDS OF THE DEAD

The engine on the *Rachel* gave out some time later, just before we drifted out of the mist to find ourselves in the outer reach of the harbour at Inverness. Cobweb and Puck took paddles from the cabin and brought us in, under a bridge that hadn't been there the last time I had visited this place. It was slow going as Puck kept paddling in the opposite direction whenever Cobweb wasn't looking.

Eventually we reached the marina and I climbed up onto a dock and secured the sailboat to a cleat. By the time I was done, the boat was taking on water from somewhere. It was visibly rising around the feet of the others as they stepped up onto the dock themselves. I suspected the boat would sink within minutes.

We left it behind, a mystery for others in the marina to decipher, and made our way to the nearby parking lot. There were a handful of cars scattered across the lot, and I assumed the owners were either asleep in one of the other boats or out at sea somewhere. I tried the doors on them until I found one that had been left unlocked. I checked the glove compartment and under the seat for keys but couldn't find any, so I hotwired it. We headed out of Inverness as the sun turned the sky golden with the new day's promises. I almost felt calm for once. Of course it didn't last.

"So where do we find Mona Lisa?" Morgana asked, wrinkling her nose at the smell of the ancient car. "Hopefully she has found a castle to set up court in. Or better yet, a pub."

"I have no idea," I said. "If you want to lose yourself and not be found again, the highlands are a pretty good place."

"We just wait for the angels to show us the way then? That won't end well."

"If they knew exactly where she was, they wouldn't need us. They must think we can find her." I looked at Amelia in the rear-view mirror.

"And then they move in," Morgana said.

"It's what I would do if I were in their place," I said.

"Let's hope that will never happen," Morgana said.

"Victory said Mona Lisa was in an abandoned keep surrounded by a field of the dead," I said to Amelia. "Can you find them?"

Amelia closed her eyes for a moment, then nodded. "There are caves full of bones to the north. Beyond that are the remains of a tower like a hand reaching for the sky. The ruins you seek are forgotten in the wilderness past both of those."

I thought for a moment. "The Bone Caves and Ardvreck Castle. They are no more than a few hours' walk from each other. There are many glens around them that could hold hidden ruins." I knew the area well because of past misadventures there. I'd used those very caves to dispose of a number of bodies in my wayward past, and I'd helped reduce the castle to little more than a broken shell of what it had once been. But I saw no point in sharing that with anyone – I was trying to be a different man these days.

We drove across the bridge we had sailed under earlier and along a highway bordered by gentle hills and light forest that in turn gave way to farmers' fields. The houses and other buildings gradually began to fade away, replaced by lochs and waterfalls. The land grew more desolate as the hills turned into small mountains, which began to rise higher the farther we drove. The traffic dwindled away, and there were long stretches where we were the only vehicle on the road. The lochs grew longer and no doubt deeper, and the clouds grew more troubled overhead.

It was a little before noon when we reached what was left of Ardvreck Castle, which wasn't much. We first passed the remains of a crumbling stone house on the shore of Loch Assynt, and then saw the lonely broken spire on a peninsula jutting into the loch in the distance. I parked the car at a viewpoint between the two and we all got out. There were no other cars at the viewpoint or anywhere along the road. I turned to Amelia, and she gazed up the hill that rose beside the loch. The top of it was shrouded in mist.

"There are many dead that way," she said.

"Let's see what they're hiding then." I started up the hill.

The slope was gentle but long. We climbed up through the heath, going around the carpets of purple and pink heather so as to not leave too much of a trail. The ground became rocky as we moved into the mist, the heather giving way to fields of moss and then to nothing but the odd hardy shrub. The faerie went up the hill like it was a simple stroll across a flat plain, but Amelia kept lagging behind and we had to wait for her a number of times.

"We'll find a place to rest soon," I said, but the look she gave me said she didn't believe that any more than I did.

We reached the top of the hill but could see little of the glen on the other side, on account of the mist having turned into a dense fog there. We made our way down into that fog and found the slope covered with a field of mountain everlasting plants growing among the black pebbles and small boulders. There was a small loch at the bottom of the hill but no man-made structures.

We continued on like that for some time, winding through the hills in the fog that grew ever thicker around us, until we could barely see a few metres in any direction. We stopped at one point to drink water straight from a stream that trickled down the side of one of the slopes. It was as cold and clear as any water I'd ever drank. It was while I rested on a large flat rock that I heard it: the crunch of pebbles higher up the hill, from the direction we had just come. It was not unlike the sound of the stone angel's feet on the stairs in the Louvre.

"We're being followed," I said.

"Again?" Morgana peered up the slope. She had heard it as well.

"I think it's more like still."

"Perhaps we should stand and fight," Cobweb said. "It's a fitting setting."

"Yes," Puck said. He picked up a rock in his hand and weighed it, as if to see if it was appropriate for braining someone. "We could add whoever it is to the dead, wherever they are buried. They're no doubt lonely out here."

"They are buried in the glen over the next hill," Amelia said. "And they have forgotten about such worldly things as loneliness."

We pushed ourselves back to our feet and climbed over the next hill and down into the glen, which was a few hundred yards across and filled with the yellow flowers of alpine hawkweeds. It would have been very idyllic if not for the corpses that began to pull themselves from the ground all around us.

THE FAERIE COURT IS FURTHER DIMINISHED

Scores of the dead ripped themselves free of the earth in that slow, laborious way of their kind. That gave us time to head toward a jumble of rocks. The bodies pulling themselves from the ground had obviously been dead for centuries, as their clothing was little more than rags, and the state of their bodies was no better. Most were skeletons, although a few still had strips of leathery, mummified flesh hanging from their skulls like tangles of hair or clinging to their ribs like decorative sashes. Judging from the weapons in their hands and the lack of coffins or other burial containers, these dead had fallen on a battlefield. Whatever animosity they'd had in the past had been forgotten, though, as each one turned toward us as they stood.

"Amelia, is this your doing?" Morgana asked as we ran for the rocks.

"I know the dead, but I don't have dominion over them," Amelia said.

"It's not her," I said. "It's the angel."

Sure enough, the stone woman who had followed me from the Louvre stepped out of the fog behind us then, walking in that same unhurried pace as before. I briefly wondered if she had walked across the ocean like she had the pond, then put it out of mind. I could figure it out later if we survived.

The weapons of the fallen soldiers had been corroded by the ages spent in the earth but still appeared formidable enough. They had more or less equal numbers of claymores and poleaxes. There were a few with bows as well, but thankfully the strings had rotted away on those. One of the skeletal warriors stepped my way and swung its claymore at me, but I ducked under its swing and wrenched the sword free of its grasp.

Puck charged at one of the dead wielding a poleaxe and somersaulted over the warrior's thrust. He landed on the skeleton's shoulders and ripped its skull free, tossing it over his shoulder. Then he seized the polearm and rammed it into the ground, using it to vault over to the rocks. Cobweb kicked the blade out of the hands of another of the dead, then used the sword to parry the blow from a warrior who came at her from the side. She struck back at the skeleton, knocking the claymore from its hands and sending the weapon cartwheeling through the air toward Morgana, who caught it as nimbly as if she'd been born with it in her hands. Amelia simply made her way through the dead – for whatever reason they didn't attack her. It was as if they recognized her as one of their own.

We made it to the rocks and caught our breath for a moment atop them. The dead were converging on us from around the field, several dozen already and more of them shuffling out of the fog. If we didn't move quickly, they would have us surrounded in enough numbers that we might not be able to fight our way through them. And then there was the matter of the angel.

Except it wasn't just one angel now.

The stone angel with the violin from the cemetery emerged from the fog to the east, while the angel with the sword came from the west. I half expected another to come from the north, but instead Gabriel stepped out of the fog to the south and walked up to the first angel's side. He still had that hole in his chest from the cross I had rammed into him, but it didn't seem to bother him any. Typical.

"Look at us trapped in this dying world," he said. "Fighting for causes that no longer matter, if we even remember them. Help us find the bible and we can leave all this behind."

That was when I began to understand what Gabriel really wanted.

"You're not searching for the bible because you think it'll harm the world now that it's damaged," I said. "You want the bible because you think it can help you *escape* this world, don't you? Maybe even get you back into Heaven?"

"And what would the sin be in that?" Gabriel asked. "I am a creature of Heaven, yet I am marooned on this world, where the inhabitants strive for nothing more than better ways to murder one another and become even more depraved. A world where all the other gods and creatures like us have died out and only their ghosts remain. You are of this world, so I understand why you fight for them. But what is there for the angels? How long until we wind up as just more statues in some museum?"

"You strike me as the type that would be just as miserable in Heaven," I said. "Maybe you need to make your own meaning of this world, as I do."

"And what meaning do you find in this forsaken place that can possibly redeem it?" Gabriel asked.

One of the skeletons jabbed a pickaxe at me, but I knocked it aside easily. We couldn't carry on with this forever, though.

"For starters, I'm not looking for Heaven." I told Gabriel as I glanced around. "Because as far as I'm concerned it doesn't exist anymore. I just want to make the world a better place as best I can."

"Well, either way we need to find God's bible and repair the damage you have done to it," Gabriel said. "Help us do so or join the dead."

"We'll make our own way, thanks." I leapt off the rocks and into the dead, and started chopping down one of them with my claymore as I landed. Its neighbours turned to me, but then Puck was there, on my left, flailing so wildly with the poleaxe that I had to duck under it. He felled another three of them, which gave Amelia enough room to pass through the gap. Then Morgana was on my right, deflecting a knife thrust meant for my side. Cobweb brought up the rear, parrying the strikes of three different dead so quickly I could barely track her blade. The faerie were no strangers to swordplay. We headed to the north, away from the angels.

"I should have left that cemetery with my court the moment Puck brought you to us," Morgana said to me. "I am so weary of you involving us in affairs that are not ours."

"I think whatever it is the angels have planned for the world may have some small effect on your lives," I said.

"We were before the world began," Morgana said. "And we will be after it is gone – if you don't get us all killed first."

"Let's work on staying alive then."

We hacked our way to the bottom of the hill and then started up it, but it was slow going. More of the dead came down the slope toward us, impeding our progress even more. I chopped the arms off a warrior in front of me, then kicked him away and glanced around.

The angels had halved the distance between us. They weren't moving any faster, but they didn't need to. The horde of skeletons was slowing us down enough that they would catch up to us in another moment. Gabriel smiled at me, as if confirming my thoughts, and ripped a sword free of a nearby skeleton, tearing its arms off in the process. He swung the two-handed weapon about like a child's toy.

"Perhaps I'll raise up your companions from the dead like this lot," he called to me. "So I can strike them down again over and over in front of your eyes. Perhaps then you will truly understand the futility of this world."

"Damn it, we're trapped," I said to Morgana, as she fended off two poleaxes. A third got through her guard and scored her side, before I hacked the weapon in two. "Can you get us out of here in the glamour?"

"The angels are too close," she said. "They would just follow us wherever we go. Our only chance is to find some sanctuary where we can hold them off."

Another skeleton nearly ran her through from behind then, its blade knocked aside at the last second by Cobweb's desperate lunge. One of the dead Cobweb had been fighting took advantage of the moment and drove his sword through her right calf. I cut the skeleton in two with my claymore, but the damage had been done. Cobweb cursed and nearly fell but managed to keep herself upright by jamming her sword into the ground and leaning upon it.

"Come, lean on me," Morgana said, holding out her right hand while she waved her sword to keep the dead at bay.

But Cobweb pushed her away. "You go. I will hold them off to buy you time."

"You'll be buying your own death in the bargain," I said. But she was right.

"It's the long fade to oblivion or the glorious death now," she said and grinned at Morgana. "At least this way you have a chance to escape and the faerie court can live on for a time longer."

Morgana swore, then nodded once. The situation was as clear to her as to the rest of us. "The glamour will be less without you."

Cobweb gave her a thin smile. "The glamour will go on, though, if you persist." Then she took a deep breath, pushed herself up off the sword and turned to face the angels and the dead coming at us from behind.

"The only way past me is over my dead body," she said and spat on the ground.

"That's what I was thinking anyway," Gabriel said, walking forward.

Puck moved to stand beside Cobweb, but Morgana grabbed him by the shoulder and shoved him the other way. "Clear us a path," she said, her voice hard again.

Puck hesitated, then nodded and set about dismembering the skeletons in front of us. Morgana gave Cobweb one last look, then turned away and joined Puck.

I kept our flanks safe, cutting down a warrior on the right with an overhead swing and then, with the same swing, chopping out the legs from underneath a warrior to my left. The momentum of the swing spun me half about, and I saw what happened with Cobweb.

She waved her sword in a circle over her head, and insects flew up all around like a biblical swarm. They trailed webs behind them, so many and so thick that they caught the dead and the angels both, entangling their limbs. Then Cobweb slumped down and swayed in place, as if the move had drained her of most of her energy.

The webbing stopped the dead from being able to attack us for a moment, as they struggled to pull the webs from their eyes or disentangle their limbs. We moved forward and quickly cut down a dozen in front of us, revealing a gap in their line that we surged through.

I saw a shape looming out of the fog above us then, the crumbling ruins of a small keep atop the hill. Much of it had collapsed, but for one tower about three storeys high and a section of wall around the front gate. The gate was open, with only a thin line of skeletons between us and it. We made quick work of them. I turned back to Cobweb.

Gabriel ripped free of the webbing that the dead still struggled with and strode toward the slumped-over faerie who seemed almost asleep. Then Cobweb threw herself forward, despite her damaged leg, and thrust her blade straight at Gabriel's stomach.

The angel let Cobweb strike him. The blade connected with his stomach and shattered on the stone. Gabriel ran Cobweb through with the claymore. He lifted her overhead, and Cobweb slid down the blade with a cry, one echoed by Morgana. Gabriel stared into Cobweb's eyes for a moment, then nodded. "Not a bad death for one of your kind," he said. He tossed Cobweb and the blade aside and started after us.

"I will see that you never find Heaven again!" Morgana screamed at him, but Gabriel remained as stoic as ever.

The webs melted away from the dead and the other angels, but Cobweb's sacrifice hadn't been in vain for we had broken free of the attack. We rushed up the hill and were almost at the gate of the keep when I saw shadows move within the ruins.

"There are more inside," I said. I threw myself to the left of the gate and put my back to the wall. "We make our stand here."

The others joined me, and we waited with weapons ready as the dead charged toward us, the angels following.

And then the dead began to burst into flame, one after the other.

MONA LISA

Within seconds all the dead were aflame. And these were no normal flames. They burned so hot the skeletons crumbled to ash before our eyes, their swords and poleaxes melted away, the trampled grass and flowers under their feet flared up, and the very earth itself seemed to catch fire.

And then, as the dead fell to their knees and came apart, she came out of the ruins.

Mona Lisa.

She looked much the same as the last time I'd seen her, when I'd helped her escape from *The Last Supper* where the angels had imprisoned her. She wore the rags of a dark dress that did little to hide her mutilated flesh. Smoke poured from her empty eye sockets, darkening the air. Melted wire still pierced her lips where the angels had tried to bind her into silence. The hair on her head was a mess of writhing snakes like Victory, only these snakes were made of the same fire that was now burning up the dead that the angels had raised. Some of those snakes turned our way and spat blue flames at us, and for a second, I thought we were about to join the dead. The flames just licked at us, though, enough to scorch the skin of my arms, before withdrawing. The air smelled like the whole world was burning.

Mona Lisa walked a dozen paces farther down the hill, striding through the smoking ash with bare feet that belonged more to a bird of prey than anything human. The last of the dead burned away before her, and she cast her gaze upon the angels.

But Gabriel and the others did not advance toward her like the dead had.

Instead, they retreated back into the fog without another word. And then the world was still again except for the crackle of the last few flames dying out.

"Wonderful," Puck breathed. "Can you show me how to do that?"

Mona Lisa turned and stared at us with those empty eye sockets. Fiery snakes darted out of them and then disappeared back inside. When she opened her mouth to speak, her fangs were bloody.

"It will be the last sight you see if you don't have a worthy reason for disturbing us," she said, and her tongue flickered with more fire.

I knew I'd never look at that painting of her the same way again. I stepped forward. "I'm really hoping you remember me."

She considered me for a moment. "We know you, hydra." Then she turned and strode back into the ruins, grinding little bits of fallen stone to rock under her feet.

"She doesn't seem particularly welcoming," Morgana said. "Are you sure about this?"

"Not at all," I said and followed Mona Lisa. After a few seconds, I heard the others walking slowly behind me.

The interior structures of the keep had mostly collapsed, as had the walls. Only the tower remained standing, and even then, part of its back wall and the top floor had fallen away. There was an open door in the ground floor of the tower, and Mona Lisa made for that now.

"Why did you bring the angels here?" she asked over her shoulder. "We have no wish to see any of their kind ever again."

"It wasn't our intention," I said. "They tracked us and then sprang an ambush with all those dead warriors." I scanned the rubble, which was wreathed with smoke, but I didn't see signs of anyone else.

"And what do they seek?" she asked.

"We're both searching for a friend of mine," I said. "Someone not unlike yourself. But I suspect we have very different ideas of what we'll do when we find her."

Mona Lisa paused in the tower's doorway without turning around. The flames of her hair lit up the room inside, which was as empty and barren as the rest of the place. "Another gorgon?"

"Someone trapped against their will." I didn't bother getting into the details as she didn't seem particularly patient.

"We are not trapped anymore," she said.

"Thanks to me."

"And Judas."

I sighed. "Yes. And speaking of Judas, where is he?"

"You may accompany us. The others remain here." She stepped inside the tower, shadows dancing crazily on the other side of the doorway.

I paused. "If I don't come out, then you all get the hell away from here," I said to Morgana.

She sat on a jumble of fallen stones and gazed back out the gate, at the battlefield. The only body that remained untouched by the flames was Cobweb. "If you don't come back soon, I'm coming in after you no matter if it's straight into Hell itself. I'll not lose another member of my court today."

I didn't waste my breath arguing with her. I strode into the tower and saw a staircase spiralling up the walls, but it ended in empty air overhead because of the collapsed back part of the tower. Another staircase descended into the depths in the middle of the room, and Mona Lisa went down these steps now.

I followed her and found myself in what had once clearly been a dungeon. The stairs ended in a large chamber with an old wooden table and a couple of battered but sturdy chairs. There was a weapons rack on one wall, mostly filled with spears but also holding a few swords. Beside the weapons rack was a long shelf with pegs that held a number of tools used for torture. There were whips and flails of varying lengths and weights, irons for branding and some knives that looked very sharp despite their age.

The other three walls were lined with cells, although the barred doors of each had been ripped free and cast upon the floor. The insides were barren, void of any furnishings, and the walls and floor were scorched, as if some great fire had raged in each. They were all empty except for the middle one in the far wall, which Mona Lisa now stood before. In that cell a naked man hung suspended from manacles attached to spikes driven into the wall. His flesh was a bloody ruin, as he'd obviously been flogged for some time, and his breathing was so ragged he seemed near death.

But he grinned at me despite his sorry state, and I recognized him instantly.

It was me.

JUDAS

Except the bloody, maimed figure hanging from the manacles in this forgotten dungeon in the middle of nowhere wasn't me, of course. And I sensed no grace from him, which meant he wasn't another angel in disguise. So there was only one person he could be. Or rather, one abomination.

Judas.

"Hello, monkey," he said and spat blood my way. "And here I was thinking we'd never meet again."

I grabbed a sword from the weapons rack without even thinking. "Maybe this is the last time we meet." But something about the way Mona Lisa turned in my direction gave me pause.

Judas chuckled. "Somehow I don't think so."

"Has the veil been lifted from your mind? You've finally seen the truth about him?" I asked Mona Lisa.

She stepped into the cell and grabbed Judas by the hair, twisting his head to gaze into his eyes even though she had no eyes of her own.

"We know him," she said. "We know him like we have never known him before. Like we have never known anyone but our sisters."

"You won't mind if I cut off his head then and bury it far from the rest of his body."

Mona Lisa smiled. "Perhaps one day, when we are done with him. But that time is not today." And with that she wrenched Judas's face up and kissed him.

I looked away – it was a scene I couldn't bear. I wanted to bury the sword in Judas. I wanted to make him suffer in all the ways he had made me suffer over the ages. Maybe I couldn't get past Mona Lisa to strike him down. Then again, maybe I could. But if I gave in to what I was feeling, I'd have no way to rescue Alice. They say love hurts, but sometimes it hurts others the most.

Mona Lisa shoved Judas's face away from her, as if she were disgusted by him. Her lips were bloody and mangled. Kissing a gorgon was a dangerous affair even at the best of times.

"Why are you torturing him if you're still lovers?" I asked.

"You don't need to know," Mona Lisa said, turning back to me. "Now, why do you think we can help free your friend?"

"I don't think you can," I said. "But I think da Vinci can."

Mona Lisa considered me for a long moment. "Da Vinci is dead."

"We both know that's not true. Hell, all three of us probably know that's not true."

"I tried to corrupt him, too, but he's always been much stronger than you," Judas said. He shrugged in his chains. I didn't respond because he was right.

Mona Lisa shook her head. "Whatever his state, we have not seen him in centuries. We don't know his whereabouts anymore. But one of his lovers may."

"I imagine all da Vinci's lovers died some time ago," I said.

"Perhaps not his angel lover," Mona Lisa said.

I wasn't expecting that revelation, and it must have showed on my face for Judas laughed at me. "Poor Cross. Everyone has a lover but him. It must be maddening."

I tightened my grip on the sword, then forced myself to turn and put it back on the weapons rack. "Tell me what you know of this lover."

"It is not much," Mona Lisa said. "Da Vinci hid himself away with Raphael on a secret island named Isola Malcontenta, near Venice, as the other angels did not approve of their union. We visited them there once, for we have our own history with the island. He had built a small manor with a library and a studio for his experiments. Perhaps he is still there. Or perhaps the angels who followed you here already found him and Raphael."

"What kind of secret island exactly?" I asked, for I'd learned the importance of such a question over the ages.

Mona Lisa turned her head and gazed at the wall, as if looking into a distance I couldn't see. "It is a place in between worlds. You can only find it on a night of storms and madness, and even then only when someone has drowned nearby."

"Oh, that kind of secret island," I said.

"It's a desolate place where nothing grows and the living fear to set foot," she continued. "We were very happy there until heroes came with their delusions of immortality and changing the world."

"I thought the gorgons lived on one of the Greek isles."

"Do you remain in one place when you are hunted?" Mona Lisa stepped out of the cell. "Now, whatever debt we have to you is paid. You saved us once, that is true. And we have saved you. The next time you intrude upon our domain, we will not be so forgiving."

I'd learned everything I could from her, but still I hesitated. "I have one more question." I looked at Judas. "Why are you masquerading as me?"

He licked the blood from his lips. "Abuse me with one of those flails and I'll tell you," he said.

I reached out and pulled a long flail with heavy straps from a peg without even thinking about it, and I took a step toward him.

Mona Lisa's snakes reared up and hissed at me. "We will allow you one blow upon Judas. But only one."

I stopped myself from moving any closer, for I knew that if I struck Judas once I would not be able to stop myself from striking him again.

He rolled his eyes at me. "Oh, stop pretending you're civilized and give in to your base urges. Use that flail on me until you have scoured every inch of flesh from my bones. Become the animal you know you are inside."

"You're not why I'm here." I closed my eyes and pictured Alice trapped in that book.

"Send in Amelia then," Judas said. "For I know she waits outside. Surely she wants to meet the monster that killed her mother. The monster that killed her. And ruined you in the process. Maybe she'll do what you cannot."

I opened my eyes, but Judas was still there, still masquerading as me. I dropped the flail to the floor and went back to the stairs. I paused at the bottom step.

"When all this is done, I will find you again," I told him. "And I will kill you when that time comes."

Judas smiled at me as he hung there in his manacles.

"I'll be waiting for you," he said. "I'll always be waiting for you."

A TROUBLING JOURNEY

I rejoined the others and together we left the ruins. I saw Cobweb's body was gone from the battlefield. Streaks of grey had spread through Morgana's hair – she looked more weary and worn than I had ever seen her.

We trudged down the hill on the opposite side from which we had come, into a landscape of more fog and broken boulders. I told the others what I had learned as we walked, although I made sure not to look at Amelia as I did so. I wasn't sure how she would react to Judas being so close, and I didn't know if I'd be able to stop myself from going back to end him if that's what she wanted. But I couldn't risk another confrontation with Mona Lisa. Not until I'd found a way rescue Alice anyway.

We made our way through the hills until the fog eventually faded, revealing another desolate loch stretched out beneath us. Thankfully, we seemed to have lost the angels for the time being. I wasn't sure if they were still interested in following us, or if they had shifted their attention to Mona Lisa. I had a feeling they'd be in for a surprise if they tried to get any information out of her. She had no love for angels these days.

We came across a small house and garage tucked against the shore of the loch partway down its length, but no smoke rose from the chimney despite the ever-present highlands chill. We invited ourselves inside by having Puck break a kitchen window and climb through to unlock the door for the rest of us.

The place must have been a vacation home for the fridge was empty and the beds were all bare of sheets and blankets. There were enough cans in the cupboards that we were able to make a soup to feed us all, though. I checked the garage while the others were finishing and found an old van. A couple of minutes of searching turned up a key hidden inside a worn tire leaning against one wall. I was able to start the van after a few tries. We had a vehicle again.

We lingered only long enough for me to wash the dishes and put them away. Morgana went outside and stared at the loch. I let her be.

If Puck was upset by the loss of one of his kin, he didn't let on. He wandered the house juggling knives he had taken from a kitchen drawer.

"We should burn the place down so there's no evidence we were here," he said.

"Burning the place down would be a pretty good sign we were here," I said. "At least to those who are looking for us."

He made a face but didn't argue the point, instead settling for slashing up the mattresses. I didn't try to stop him – compromise is important sometimes.

I drove once more, for I didn't want Puck behind the wheel again. I took us north for a while, then along a lonely road across the highlands to the east. I chose not to go back the way we had come in case Gabriel and the others were waiting for us. I pulled the van into a seaside town by the name of Dornoch around the same time the van used up the last of the gas, and we ended up coasting into the parking lot of a restaurant that had no sign as the sun eased into the waters on the horizon. It was no doubt the sort of place favoured by locals, which meant the food would likely be good.

Puck left to scout the area for a petrol station that might still be open while the rest of us went inside the restaurant for coffee and whatever they had to eat. Luckily, it was one of those places that offered all-day breakfast. I ordered extra of everything, figuring it was going to be a while before I had the chance to sleep again.

Morgana ordered an extra portion as well, but set it aside at an empty place on the table.

"Do you want to talk about what happened?" I asked, even though it wasn't what I wanted. But I'd learned a long time ago that being human means having to face things you'd rather avoid.

Morgana sipped her coffee and gazed out the window. "I've lost two members of my court, to say nothing of all the fey this misadventure has cost me. The only thing I want to talk about is how we can leave you to your quest without the angels coming for Amelia."

"They'll come for her as long as they're after the bible," I said, trying not to look at Amelia. "Because they know she's my weakness. And we're talking about Alice here. Remember how she helped when the *Hamlet* ghost was killing your court? You'd have no one left by now if not for her. Including yourself. And if I recall correctly, it was you who put Amelia at risk that time."

Morgana turned her gaze to me. Her eyes had turned as black as a raven's. "I know what I have done, and I know what Alice has done. But I won't have a court left at all if this continues."

"Help me until I find da Vinci," I said. "After that I'll have what I need to rescue Alice. Or it won't be possible to save her at all."

"He's right," Amelia said. "The angels will keep coming until they get what they want or they are dead. We're safer with him than without him."

Morgana considered our daughter. "How will we find this secret island of malcontents then?"

"Leave that part to me," I said. "But first we need to find a way back to the continent."

"I've taken care of that part," Puck said, sliding into our booth out of nowhere. He twirled a set of keys on a finger. "I found a boat."

"What kind of boat?" I asked.

"The kind of boat that will allow us to escape your angel kin," Puck said. "Unless you want to order yet more food and sit around here waiting for them."

I visited the washroom and, on the way back, lifted the wallet of a man drinking coffee at the counter. I left a good tip using his wallet, and then we abandoned the stolen van in the parking lot. We walked a few blocks to a small dock, which was lit only by a sole lamppost. Puck led us onto a whale-watching boat that had room for maybe a dozen people, plus a storage area under a tarp at the back. He tossed me the keys and undid the ropes as I started the boat, then he laid himself down on the tarp and promptly fell asleep. I took us out to sea before anyone could notice us. The lights of the Scottish coast slowly faded behind us, until they were little more than stars, and then nothing at all.

I sat behind the wheel of the boat, trying and failing to empty my mind. Amelia came and joined me and we stared out into the night before us.

"How are you doing?" I asked. "Because it's been a rough few days."

Amelia considered the darkness for a time. "I'm the same as always."

"I thought maybe what happened back there might have upset you."

"The battle with the angels? I've been through stranger than that since I came back to life."

"I meant the whole business with Judas. I know it must be difficult to be near the one who killed your mother." And killed Amelia herself, for that matter.

"That doesn't bother me," she said. "For I know he will join the dead one day like everyone else."

"I suppose that's some small satisfaction," I said. "With any luck there will be some suffering involved."

"Death is his release. It's his life that is suffering. Like all of us."

"You've been reading too much philosophy."

"And you haven't been reading enough."

"That's probably on account of the philosophers I've known."

Morgana leaned over my shoulder then and peered ahead of us. "Are we nearly there?"

"I don't think so," I said, for I had yet to see any lights in the distance. "Unless maybe you want to create another glamour to move us along."

She shook her head. "I must rest before I can manage such a thing. And it takes more effort now that . . ." She didn't finish and returned to the cabin, but I knew what she meant to say.

Now that Cobweb was gone.

I put it out of my head. There was no cost I wasn't willing to pay to rescue Alice.

Sometime after that Puck sat up and yawned, then stood and stretched. He gazed out at the ocean, but there was still nothing to see.

"I suppose this is as good a place as any," he said and pulled the tarp to one side.

There was a pile of bodies underneath. What I had taken for storage was actually six dead people. Two of them were young men in matching yellow jackets, while the others were middle-aged men and women in different rain jackets. A couple of them had slit throats, while the others bore stab wounds to various parts of their bodies. The older men and women had deep cuts in their hands – they'd died trying to defend themselves. Or each other.

Morgana came out of the cabin and sighed at the sight. "Not again."

"What the hell have you done?" I asked, staring at the dead.

"I found us a boat," Puck said. He dragged one of the men in yellow over to the starboard side and shoved him over. The man fell into the water and disappeared in the wake behind us.

"You couldn't have chosen another boat?" I asked. "Maybe one without people on board?"

"Why bother?" Puck asked. "I'd already found this one."

I turned to Amelia, who hadn't turned away from the front of the boat. "Did you know about this?"

"Of course," she said.

"And you didn't tell me?"

"Would it have made a difference?"

When I looked back at Puck, he was tossing the last body overboard.

"We should make better time now that we're lighter," he said.

"If you murder anyone else, I'm throwing you overboard," I said.

Puck grinned and opened his arms wide, as if in invitation. Morgana stepped between us.

"Enough," she said. "Both of you. We need to focus on keeping ourselves alive. Or have you forgotten the angels that pursue us?"

"I haven't forgotten them or Alice either," Puck said and fixed me with a look. "And do you really think you can save her all on your own, without us? Without me?"

I had no answer to that, so I sat back down and waited for some sort of light to materialize in all the darkness.

AN ACQUAINTANCE OF QUESTIONABLE CHARACTER

Thankfully the rest of our trip was less dramatic. We made our way across the ocean to Stavanger, Norway, a journey that took two days and every ounce of the containers of extra gasoline I found in a storage bin. We left the boat at a dock much like we had the sailboat in Inverness, only this boat didn't sink. Maybe it would have been better if it did after what had happened aboard it. I'm not as superstitious as most sailors tend to be, but even I thought the boat was likely cursed after this.

From there we travelled by train down through the continent, from Oslo to Berlin and then into the south of Germany. We rented a car in Munich and drove it to Milan to hopefully throw off any possible pursuit. It reminded me of the time I'd been pursued by a pack of werewolves on almost the exact same route after I'd killed their leader in a bar fight. I'd finally managed to shake them when I'd found Alice in a dead man's library and she had taken me into the stacks and out into an abandoned sanitarium in New York. I had to deal with a troubled spirit that followed me out of the sanitarium, but trust me when I say it was better than a pack of angry werewolves.

We left the car in Milan near Castello Sforzesco, which had been one of the largest fortifications in the area when it was built in the fifteenth century or so but was now a museum. That's the way with most of history. It happened to be some sort of international fashion week in the city when we arrived, and the streets were filled with large groups of people in suits and dresses that looked as if they were out of some fable. They seemed vaguely disturbed whenever we passed, as if they could smell us from our days of travel but not quite see us.

We boarded a new train at the Milan station, which was a curious mix of architectural styles that some would call art deco or art nouveau, but which I liked to think of as post-fascist. Morgana and Puck had some personal history with the place – they started reminiscing about the time they had taken over one of the secret rooms in the station for a full year, when the faerie court numbered in the hundreds. I had my own memories of the station involving a train and a fugitive SS officer who turned out to be an angel. Or maybe he had been a demon. Sometimes I had trouble telling angels and demons apart in my memories.

We arrived in Venice in the early afternoon. It was a sweltering day with a clear sky, and the cafés and canals were full of tourists taking photos of each other. I tried to stay out of their shots as best I could and led us into the labyrinth of Venetian streets and courtyards, until the others were lost and I wasn't entirely certain where we were myself. Morgana threatened to leave me to my own devices if I didn't reveal where I was taking them soon. That was when I finally found Nadia.

She was passed out in a cistern in a small courtyard far from the tourist areas, sitting with her back to the fountain that was pouring water down over her. She wore work pants and a shirt so faded as to be no colour at all. Her dark hair was long and hung over her face, but I would have recognized her anywhere from the way her hair moved slightly from side to side, as if in some current.

I stopped at the edge of the cistern and reached over to shake her shoulder. She snorted and waved me away without opening her eyes. There was an empty wine bottle in her other hand.

"You've taken us halfway around the world only to find another drunk?" Morgana asked. "I should have known."

"She's not just any drunk," I said. "She's the only one who can find the currents we seek out there in the lagoon."

Nadia opened one eye to look at me then. "Oh goddamn," she said.

"Yes," I said.

"I thought I'd seen the last of you a long time ago," she muttered. "In fact, I was hoping I'd simply dreamed you up."

"I get that a lot."

She opened her other eye and took in the others. "Looks like you don't need me, though. What do you have here, a couple of faerie and . . . What is that girl?"

Morgana narrowed her eyes as she considered Nadia but thankfully said nothing.

"It doesn't matter who or what they are," I said. "We need your help."

"I don't take tourists around the canals anymore," Nadia said.

"That's good," I said. "Because it's not the canals we're here to visit."

Nadia lifted the bottle to her lips and seemed genuinely surprised to find it empty. "And I'm not interested in helping you with another getaway either. I still can't get anywhere near San Marco without attracting the wrong sort of attention."

"We need you to take us to Isola Malcontenta," I said.

Nadia tossed the bottle aside with a sigh. "You don't even know what you ask."

"Actually, I do."

She met my gaze for a long moment, and I saw some sort of understanding pass across her face.

"Do you remember when I saved you from Foscari's hunters?" I asked. "You know what the priests would have done with you."

"You should have let me die," Nadia said.

"Maybe. But I'm calling in that debt now."

"Foscari as in the doge of Venice?" Morgana asked.

"Several hundred years ago," I said. "Did you know him?"

"In a manner," Morgana said, and Puck chuckled.

Nadia eyed Morgana. "And you? What debt do you owe Cross? For surely no one would accompany him voluntarily."

"I'm just trying to keep him alive so he can repay all that he owes me," Morgana said.

Nadia laughed and turned her attention to Amelia. "What of you, girl? Do you even know who this rogue is?"

"I know him as well as I know the dead you drowned and hid away in the lagoon," Amelia said.

"Well," Nadia said and stared at her for a long moment, the smile frozen on her lips. She stood and stepped out of the fountain, water pouring from her clothes. Her hair drifted around her head. "We should be on our way. It is not an easy journey to your destination."

Nadia took us into an alley that led away from the courtyard in a winding manner that soon had me disoriented again. The alley was so narrow the brick walls touched my shoulders. We went up and down crumbling stone stairs. At one point we stepped over a pile of rags that looked like they perhaps covered a body, but I didn't disturb them and neither did any of the others.

By the time we reached another canal and stepped out onto a sagging sliver of dock, Nadia's clothes were dry. This canal seemed an afterthought, a thin and winding corridor of water bordered by weathered three-storey buildings with shuttered windows. A gondola was tied to the dock, but it was mostly sunk. Only the ferro on the prow and stern were above water. Judging by what I could see of the gondola under the water, it had been down there for some time.

"Do you perhaps have a boat that still floats?" Morgana asked, eyeing the gondola. "For my clothing does not dry as quickly as yours."

Nadia smiled and crouched down on the dock. She dipped a hand into the water and swirled it around for a moment. When she drew her hand back, the water continued to swirl in a widening area. Within seconds it had spread out across the gondola. The gondola rose up, tilting from one side to the other to drain the water within it. Once the interior of the boat was mostly empty, the water below subsided and grew still, and the gondola floated beside the dock. Nadia reached into the water again and pulled an oar out, then stood and leaned on it as if she had grown weary.

"So you're a water nymph," Morgana said. She shook her head at me. "I should have known your plan would involve yet more acquaintances of questionable character."

"I like her," Puck said. He stepped to the end of the dock and peered down into the water. "What else can you raise from the depths?"

Nadia stepped into the stern of the gondola. "The currents are favourable at the moment, but even I can't say how long that will last. Come aboard now or remain behind. It's all the same to me."

We got into the gondola and Nadia took us away from the dock and out into a wider canal, where other gondolas and boats passed us. If anyone thought us a strange crew, they didn't look at us twice to show it. I imagine any local of Venice had seen plenty of strange things in their time.

"Are you sure this thing won't sink again?" Morgana asked as Nadia took us out of the canal and into the lagoon surrounding Venice. Her concern was justified given the water seeping through cracks in the bottom and side of the gondola.

"Everything sinks over time," Nadia said. "But it will get us to your destination. You will need to find your own way back."

"And how are we supposed to manage that without you?" I asked.

Nadia stared straight ahead. "I don't know, nor do I care. As you said, my debt to you is paid with transport to the isle. There was no mention of a return voyage."

She took us past Isola di San Michele, the cemetery island with its high red walls and lush trees, and then past the island of Murano and its glass shops and toward the nature preserve of Stretto Oratteo. A flock of distant birds lifted up out of the marshy land and flew parallel with our path for some time, before breaking away and disappearing into the horizon. By this time the water in the bottom of the boat was a couple of inches deep.

"Perhaps the birds are an omen," Puck said. He pulled a bottle of wine from the back of his shirt and took a long drink.

"Hopefully they're just birds," I said. I had a bad history with omens. I turned back to Nadia, who was watching the birds herself with a frown. "How much farther is it?"

"First we must pass an abandoned island on the port side," she said. "And then a shipwreck on the starboard side. After that, well, the island you seek has never been an easy one to find."

"Hopefully that will make us hard to find as well then," Morgana said.

Nadia's lips tightened into a thin line. "Do I need to know if someone is looking for you?"

"It's the usual crowd," I said.

"Why don't you make yourself useful and bail water so we can reach the isle," she said. "I would really like to be done with you."

I cast about but didn't see any containers. I decided it was probably best to let the conversation be and began to scoop up water with my hands and toss it overboard.

"This moment more than any other sums up your life in this miserable realm," Morgana said and turned away from me to scan the horizon.

We travelled past a small island that was little more than a rock jutting out of the water with a crumbling stone building on it. Probably a monastery or other religious structure – I couldn't imagine why anyone else would want to live on a lonely island out here.

"That's the first marker," Nadia said. She squinted up at the sky. It was nearing dusk now, but the heavens were frustratingly empty. Just like usual. "I can't do anything about the weather, though, and we won't be able to find the second marker without a storm."

"Leave that to me," Morgana said.

"Will a storm in the glamour even count?" I asked.

"I'm the faerie queen," she said. "I have more tricks than just the glamour, you know."

"It's true," Puck said with a laugh, and I felt my old jealousy return enough that I had to look away and out to sea.

The clouds came rolling in from that same direction a few minutes later, and a wind began to raise waves around us. I redoubled my efforts to bail water from the boat, but it didn't seem to do much good. The water was over my feet now.

Puck let out a cheer and pointed to the starboard side, and I saw a broken mast rising out of the lagoon there, with loose ropes hanging from it and whipping about in the wind. I wondered what fate had brought the ship here and if the crew had been trying to find the same island as us. Then the rain began and obscured everything.

Nadia took us deeper into the storm for maybe another hour, although I wasn't certain about the time. Lights began to shimmer in the growing darkness ahead, like will-o'-the-wisps. Nadia leaned on the oar and let the gondola drift.

"The secret Isola Malcontenta," she said.

"Take us in," Morgana said. "Before this boat fills with water and sends us to the bottom."

Nadia stared straight ahead. "There is a price. If we do not pay it, we will break up on the rocks surrounding the island."

"Don't you know where the rocks are?" Morgana said. "I thought your kind knew everything about the water."

"They are more kin to Scylla than normal rocks," Nadia said. "They demand a sacrifice from all who pass, even the gods."

"Well, we have no more use of you if you're not going to ferry us back," Morgana said. Puck grinned and finished off the rest of the wine bottle, then began to flip it in his hand.

"I'll handle the sacrifice part," I said. Everyone looked at me except for Amelia, who gazed down into the water beside the boat.

I stood up and watched the lights shimmering through the storm. "I'll drown myself. Hopefully one of you will see fit to fish me out of the water and drag me to the island. Then you just have to wait for me to resurrect."

"I certainly like that plan compared to the alternatives," Nadia said.

"And how long will it take you to raise from the dead?" Morgana asked. "Because it doesn't seem like you have much grace at the moment, unless you've been holding out on us."

"A couple of days maybe. I can't say for certain. It's different each time." I took a few deep breaths to ready myself.

"Those angels could find us in a couple of days, and I'd prefer not to face them with a diminished court," Morgana said. "The nymph is the better choice."

I saw her point even though I wasn't sure if the angels were the real reason she didn't want me to drown myself. But I wasn't about to let her or Puck do anything to Nadia.

"I didn't save her all those years ago just to betray her now," I said, stepping in front of Nadia.

"Then let Puck do it," Morgana said. "It's in his nature if not yours."

"'Tis true." Puck bowed, as if asking for a dance.

"Take this," Amelia said and put the *Looking-Glass* in my hands. Then she stepped over the side of the gondola. "I'm already dead, after all."

I leapt forward to grab her, but she had slipped beneath the waves. I saw her face rippling in the depths as she looked back at me. Then she drifted down and out of sight.

"No!" I cried. "It should be me." I was dimly aware of an echoing cry from Morgana.

"It's too late," Nadia said, laying a hand on my arm and trying to pull me back. "The sea has accepted her sacrifice."

I tossed the book aside and dove in after Amelia, plunging into the darkness. I couldn't see her, even though she should be right there. I twisted this way and that, desperately trying to find her. I swam deeper, despite my lungs crying out for air. If I had grace, I could have lit up the water to find her. If I had grace, I could have breathed that water in like air and searched for however long it took. But I had nothing.

Then the oar pushed into my back from behind, sending me deeper. And I saw Amelia's pale face drifting beneath me.

I swam down and grabbed her by one arm, then tried to pull her up to the surface. She was heavy, though, as if she were resisting me even though she wasn't moving. I could barely lift her a few feet, and I was so desperate to take a breath, I was ready to open my mouth and fill my lungs with water.

The oar was there again, reaching down toward me. I grabbed on to it with my free hand, and it dragged me back up to the gondola. I pulled Amelia after me.

I broke the surface into a full storm: lightning flashing in the dark clouds overhead, and rain beating down like it was trying to force me back under the waves. I had time for a quick breath, and then Nadia was shouting at me over the edge of the gondola. "Hang on!"

I caught a quick glimpse of the lights of the island, and they were much closer now – maybe a couple hundred metres. I could see the shape of a building when the lightning flashed, and a few stunted trees scattered around it. Then a wave caught us and swept us over some rocks, and sharp edges of stone gouged my torso and legs. I managed to keep my grip on Amelia, though.

The gondola spun about in an eddy on the other side of the rocks for a couple of seconds, and I started to pull myself back into it one-handed. Then another wave crashed over the rocks and hit us sideways and capsized the gondola. Morgana and Puck fell into the water on either side of me while Nadia launched herself gracefully over my head and dived into the wave as it swept past us.

I tried to push the gondola back up, but it had taken on too much water. It sank beneath the waves and kept going, disappearing like Amelia had. Those same waves threw us forward in surges, then tossed us back. The water was so violent I could barely keep my head above it to draw breath. I began to grow weary from the weight of Amelia and I started sinking deeper into the water.

Nadia was suddenly at my side, lifting me up and propelling me smoothly forward.

"The sea is angry now that you have taken Amelia back!" she said.

"I'm not going to give her up," I said.

I caught glimpses of the lights nearly overhead now, of more flashes of lightning, of Morgana lifting her face out of the water, Puck howling with glee at the storm.

Then my feet struck something solid. For a second I thought it was the gondola, that maybe Nadia was bringing it back up for us. But the surface underfoot was uneven and rounded, and I realized that I was stepping on stones. I managed to stand and stagger forward in chest-deep water, and I saw the dim crescent of a beach ahead, with a rock face that stretched up higher, toward the building with the lights.

I lifted Amelia up out of the water and Nadia let go of me. I turned back to look at her, but she was drifting away from me, against the waves.

"Now you are in my debt!" she cried through the crashing surf. Then she slipped under and was gone. She didn't resurface again.

I pushed myself through the waves, which tried to drag me back into the depths, until I was able to throw myself and Amelia down on the rocky beach. Morgana and Puck followed soon after, wading ashore and cursing the ocean, Nadia and me. Morgana was sporting a cut on her forehead, and rivers of blood ran down her face. Puck must have gone face first over the rocks, for much of his left cheek was shredded so bad I could see his teeth through the hole.

They were both alive, though. I turned my attention to Amelia. She stared at the storm overhead for a moment without blinking, then sat up.

I collapsed onto the rocks beside her with relief. "I thought you were dead."

"I am," she said.

"You know what I mean."

I scanned the churning water for Nadia or the gondola, but there was no sign of either.

"I could hear all the other dead in the water calling to me," Amelia said.

"What did they say?" Puck asked as he poked a finger into the wound in his cheek.

"They wanted me to stay with them," Amelia said, which earned a hard look from Morgana.

"Next time let me be the one to sacrifice myself," I said, and Amelia didn't say anything to that.

"I still think we should have drowned the nymph," Morgana said.

"I'm not sure a water nymph is capable of drowning," I said.

The copy of *Through the Looking-Glass* washed up on the beach then, propelled by a wave that left it at my feet. A final gift from Nadia perhaps. I picked it up and saw that it was waterlogged but otherwise intact. I didn't dare open it to see what had become of its contents.

"We should sink that thing in the depths," Morgana said. "For it has brought only misfortune into our midst."

"You never know when you may need a book," I said and handed it to Amelia, who made it disappear into her pocket again.

I gazed up at the rock face that loomed over the beach. I could just make out the top floor of the building overhead. This close, I could see that the lights we had spotted earlier were windows lit by flickering candlelight. A bell chimed once from somewhere else on the island.

"Well, we have reached your Isola Malcontenta," Morgana said. "And it seems we are not alone. So, what now?"

"Now we go up there and find whoever lives here," I said. "And hope to hell they know what's become of da Vinci's lover."

AN OLD FRIEND

We searched the cliff wall until I found a narrow path that wound up through the rock, wide enough for one person. We climbed it, going slow because the path was slick from the rain and because I kept stopping to scan the clifftop above. If someone wanted to ambush us – like, say, a group of irate angels – this would have been the perfect place. But nothing fell upon us and no one showed their face, and eventually we made it to the top and stepped out onto a rocky but more or less flat stretch of land.

The building we had seen earlier stood before us, and I saw now that it was made of stones mortared together. Patches of grass and the odd twisted tree grew around the building, but there was a gap to the right side where there was nothing. We went that way, coming to a well with one side caved in and a wooden bucket swaying in the wind on a rope. Puck stopped at the well and began to lower the bucket.

"I could do with a drink after all that exertion," he said. "Maybe one of you could turn the water into spirits."

"I suspect we can find a drink inside," I said. I stepped around the edge of the building and saw a pair of wooden doors taller than me set into the wall. They had patterns carved into them I couldn't make out from where I stood. I also saw another smaller building to the side, large enough to hold maybe a dozen people, with a leaning cross atop it. A chapel then. The other side of the island was beyond the chapel, with another path that led down and out of sight.

I turned back to wave on the others as Puck reached down into the bucket and pulled out a bone. A human finger bone.

"Well, I guess we're not alone here," he said.

Amelia stepped to the edge of the well and peered down into the darkness. "There's a witch's dozen of the dead down there," she said.

"Some other group that found the island like us?" I asked.

She leaned on the well, and I put my arm out before her for fear that she might fall in. We were all past the point of exhaustion now, and cold and wet on top of that.

"They're from different ages," she said. "I believe they were thrown into the well at different times, each of them separately from the others."

Puck stuck the finger bone into his mouth and chewed on it like a stalk of grass as he contemplated the lights in the windows. "Now I'm really curious about who lives here."

"So am I," I said. "I don't suppose there are any weapons down in that well with the dead?"

Amelia shrugged. "My abilities do not extend beyond the dead, and none of them are armed."

I headed around the side of the building. "Let's see if there are any living we can talk to then."

The path beyond the chapel led down to a sheltered cove. A pier made of more rocks jutted into the water there, and a small boat had been dragged up onto the pier and covered with a worn tarp to protect it from the elements.

"At least we have a way off the island," Morgana said.

"First we have to get what we came for." I turned to the two tall doors and saw they were carved with anatomical renderings of two beings. On the left door was a man, the skin pulled aside on part of his body to reveal his organs and bones. On the right side was an angel, similarly opened up. The man and angel appeared to be the same person, except for the added wings on the right door. I recognized the style at a glance as da Vinci's work. So at least we were in the right place. I opened the doors and stepped through.

There was a dining hall on the other side, with a scattering of wooden tables and benches around a fireplace. Candles flickered on the tables and shelves on the walls. Through the windows I could see lightning flash outside. Two of the tables were occupied by a dozen or so old men in threadbare robes eating stew from chipped bowls. A third table had more bowls of stew and glasses of wine even though no one sat there.

"Welcome!" a gaunt man near the fireplace bellowed as he stood and smiled at us. "We knew from the storm that visitors were on the way, so we prepared extra servings for you. Please join us in our humble feast." He gestured at the empty table with the bowls set upon it. The others looked our way but continued to noisily eat their stew.

It was a strange scene, no doubt about it. But what made it even stranger was the fact I could sense grace in all of the men. So perhaps they were angels in disguise. Except for the fact that I recognized the man that had stood.

"Hello, Borromeo," I said. "It's been a time."

THE ORDER OF THE ANGEL INCARNATE

A sudden silence fell upon the room then, broken only by thunder from outside and a renewed howling of the wind. Borromeo and the men at the tables all stared at me for a long moment.

"Is this da Vinci's lover then?" Morgana asked. "Because if so, I really question his taste."

"No," I said. "But he is a friend of mine." If you could call a partner in smuggling religious artifacts centuries ago a friend. And if you couldn't, then I'd had far fewer friends over the ages than I thought.

Borromeo came over to us, studying me the whole while. He stopped a few feet away. "Cross, is it truly you?"

"In the flesh," I said. I studied him right back, for I could feel the grace even stronger in him now. A grace he had never had before.

He lunged forward and for a moment I thought he was attacking. The other men at the tables must have thought the same thing, for they started to rise. But Borromeo wrapped me in a hug instead, laughing so loud his voice echoed throughout the room.

"By God, you don't appear to have aged a day," he said.

"I could say the same about you," I said. "Which is strange, because you're supposed to be dead."

"It's a long story." Borromeo held me at arm's length, grinning.

"I imagine so, but probably one worth telling anyway." To the best of my knowledge Borromeo wasn't an angel or anything else that could come back from death. Yet here he was, emanating grace just like Gabriel and his kind.

"All in time," Borromeo said. "First warm yourselves by the fire and join us in our meal. Then you can tell us why you are here. I don't think you have journeyed all this way simply to inquire about my health."

We sat at the empty table and Puck began to wolf down the stew as if he hadn't eaten in days. I moved the spoon around in mine, but I couldn't stop thinking about the dead in the well outside. I settled for sipping from a glass of wine instead.

Borromeo sat at our table, across from me. Now that I'd had time to look at him closely, I saw his lips were cracked and bloody, as were his fingertips.

"So tell me, old friend, what brings the son of God to our humble sanctuary?" he asked.

"You have mistaken me for someone else," I said. "For the real son of God long ago left this world."

Borromeo chuckled. "Well, you are here at least. And with companions." He nodded at the others, and his gaze settled on Amelia for a moment.

I introduced Morgana and Puck, though I didn't explain their true nature. I figured if Borromeo had some secrets, it was probably good to have some of our own.

"It's a welcome surprise to find you here," I told him. "But we came all this way seeking another."

"You're trying to find da Vinci," he said.

"We are not the first then."

He nodded. "Many others have tried over the ages, for different reasons. But one thing remains the same: da Vinci is not here. I must tell you that I have not seen him for centuries. Nearly as long as you, in fact."

I sipped some more wine. It was fine stuff that had clearly been aged for some time.

"To be honest, I know it is not so easy to track down da Vinci," I said. "But I was hoping to find his lover, who could perhaps tell us his whereabouts."

Borromeo continued to smile at me for another moment, but it was one of those smiles that no longer reached his eyes. He didn't blink as he stared at me, and I could feel the gaze of his comrades upon me now as well.

"That seems to have struck a chord," Morgana said, swirling the wine in her glass. "It appears we have indeed come to the right place for a change."

Puck seemed oblivious to the sudden change in mood, perhaps because he had lifted the bowl of stew to his lips to drain the last of it. He set it down on the table and nodded at my bowl. "Are you not going to have yours then?" He grabbed my bowl and pulled it toward him before I could answer.

"Da Vinci had many lovers over the years," Borromeo eventually said. "He lived a very worldly life."

"We don't need to speak to them all," I said. "Just the one that he lived with on this island."

Borromeo shook his head and sighed. "I'm sorry to say that you have wasted your trip then. The one you seek is no longer among the living."

"And how would you know that?" I asked.

The smile left Borromeo's face completely. "I was there when the angels killed him."

Puck belched loudly as he finished the last of my soup. "They didn't happen to be stone angels, did they?" he asked.

Borromeo frowned at him, although I wasn't sure if he was irritated by Puck's question or his table manners. "Does their nature matter?"

"Of course it matters," Puck said. "Do you know how much harder it is to stab a creature made of stone?"

Borromeo's companions gave up all pretences of trying to eat and openly stared at us. They were not idle looks of curiosity. I was pretty sure we had found those responsible for the dead in the well outside.

"He speaks the truth," Amelia said beside me. "Da Vinci's lover is no longer among the living. None of his lovers are. But one is not quite dead yet either. He remains torn between life and death, like myself."

Borromeo regarded Amelia again as he took a long drink of his wine. "I see you continue to surround yourself with interesting characters."

"You have no idea," I told him. "And I'm going to need some proof that da Vinci's lover is dead." It wasn't that I didn't believe him, or Amelia for that matter. But if the person we'd come here to find was indeed dead, then

I needed some other way to find da Vinci. His lover was the only clue I had at the moment.

"It may be easier if I show you." Borromeo stood and led us back out into the night, toward the chapel I'd glimpsed earlier. The rain and lightning had eased off, but the wind still scoured us, as if it were trying to force us from the island.

"You are probably wondering how it is that I came to be here with the other faithful," Borromeo shouted over the wind.

"Something like that," I said. "Although I'm mainly wondering how you're still alive after all this time."

"The answer is the same to both questions," Borromeo said as we approached the chapel. The building had a simple, unadorned wooden door that Borromeo unlocked with a skeleton key he pulled from a pocket deep in his robe. "We are the Order of the Angel Incarnate, and we are bound here by a sacred duty."

"Not another angel," I sighed.

"No," Borromeo said. "Not exactly."

He pushed open the door and stepped inside, and I followed him. The chapel was a small, simple room with no windows or other doors. There were two wooden pews, one behind the other, each wide enough to hold maybe three people. The floorboards were worn and uneven, suggesting this place saw a lot of use. More candles burned on shelves, casting flickering shadows about the room. There was a charcoal sketch in a plain wooden frame on the opposite wall, where a cross or even a creative rendering of myself usually hung. None of them are ever accurate, for what it's worth.

The sketch depicted a curious figure – a person with long hair, androgynous in appearance, holding part of a robe away from a bare breast, with an erect penis at the bottom of the image. I could sense more grace radiating from the sketch, and I noted the floor was the most worn directly in front of it.

"The angel Raphael," Borromeo said. "Da Vinci's lover."

A CONFESSION OF SORTS

I stared at the sketch of the angel, trying to place him. Or maybe her. It was sometimes hard to pin angels down into human categories like gender.

"I don't think I've met this one before," I said.

"And you likely never will now," Borromeo said softly, gazing upon the sketch with an expression I could only call rapturous. "For he is dead."

"Well, I'm pretty sure I'd remember if I did it," I said, although that was stretching the truth. There were entire ages I couldn't remember because I'd been drunk for most of them.

"Oh, it wasn't you," Borromeo said as he walked up to the sketch. "The other angels killed him when they learned that he had become da Vinci's lover. Such things are forbidden by their kind. In fact, they killed him on the very spot this chapel now stands."

"I suppose that explains a few things about this island," Morgana muttered. I was inclined to agree with her.

"Forbidden by who exactly?" I asked Borromeo. "Because I haven't noticed God coming around to enforce the rules lately."

"The Risen forbid relations between their kind and mortals," Borromeo said. "They fear it will lead to Heaven becoming even more distant from them." He laid a hand upon the sketch. Immediately I sensed a change in the chapel. Borromeo was tapping into the grace I felt. I readied myself in case he tried something, but he just stood there with his hand on Raphael's breast.

"You seem to know a lot about the angels," I said. "More than most, anyway."

"I was there when the Risen pronounced judgment upon Raphael and da Vinci," Borromeo said. "There was little they could do to da Vinci, because he had many powerful friends. And he was a being of particular ability even then. Raphael, however, was one of them, and they had more leeway with him. So they killed him as a lesson for the others of their kind. And our kind, I suppose."

"That doesn't explain why you're here," I said.

Borromeo dropped his hand from the sketch. "The Risen proclaimed that death was not enough of a punishment for Raphael, for his soul could still find peace in death. So they ripped his soul from his body as he lay dying and bound it to this sketch. His body and soul are now divided and denied Heaven as long as they remain so."

I contemplated the sketch. That explained the grace I felt in it. There was only one problem with Borromeo's story. "But that looks like da Vinci's work to me."

"So it is." Borromeo nodded. "The angels made him create the sketch, for such a thing was beyond even their ability. But you know da Vinci. He is always unlocking the secrets of the world."

"Why would he condemn his lover to such a fate?" Morgana asked. "Does he have faerie blood?"

"Because they wanted to torment him as well," Borromeo said. "And they understand the worst way to torment a human is to give them hope. As long as Raphael's soul remains torn from his body, neither soul nor body can truly die. Raphael persists in some state between life and death."

"I told you," Amelia said.

I stepped to the sketch myself. It didn't have any protections I could see. Someone could just walk in here and take it from the wall. If they could find their way to the island, that was. Standing this close to it, I couldn't help but notice the drop of blood on the floor at Borromeo's feet.

"So why hasn't da Vinci done anything about it yet?" I asked.

"That's where I have a role in this story," Borromeo said. "Raphael's body and soul needed to be kept separate. And each needed to be protected. There were few in the church that could be trusted with such a duty. I was one of those and was given dominion over Raphael's soul. I kept it safe in a secure crypt in Rome for many years. Much like those holy relics you smuggled to me all those ages ago."

"Then why is it here?" I asked.

Borromeo gazed back out the open door, into the night. I used the opportunity to scan his body. I saw the blood I was looking for on the fingertips of the hand that had touched the sketch.

"I became a man of God to be closer to Heaven," he said. "And to help others follow in my path. I did not ever dream that when I set out on my journey, I would encounter an angel. Nor did I imagine I would be responsible for ensuring the lost soul of such a being be eternally denied the same Heaven that I sought. I came to question my cause and those I served."

"I've found that happens a lot with the angels," I said.

Borromeo smiled a little at that, but only a little. "I've since learned I am far from alone in becoming dissatisfied with the rule of angels. I do not have the power to undo what has been done to Raphael. But I thought that perhaps I could prevent worse fates being inflicted upon him. So I fled in the night with the sketch, accompanied only by a few of the faithful that I believed I could trust and who had become as disillusioned as me. We became the Order of the Angel Incarnate and we have hidden ourselves away from the world ever since."

"And the church staged your death to cover up your absence," I said. "Because they couldn't let it be known one of their own had turned his back on them."

"The church aspires to Heaven," Borromeo said. "But unfortunately, it is trapped in this world with the rest of us. Sometimes it must make hard choices."

I nodded. "And the world keeps finding you, doesn't it? Because I'm guessing those bones in the well don't belong to your friends."

Borromeo sat down on one of the pews and considered the sketch. "Others have found us from time to time. Some were searching for Raphael, some for other things. We have protected the secrets of this place and upheld our sacred duty. It is not a light burden."

"And what do you do when you're not murdering people and tossing them into wells?" Morgana asked. "Because this seems like a dreadfully boring place."

"Mostly we pray for forgiveness for our transgressions," Borromeo said. "Or we busy ourselves in the scriptorium."

"Busy yourselves doing what?" I asked.

"Da Vinci left notes from his time on the island. They are written in code. We try to interpret them as best we can. But I'll warn you now, we have found nothing about da Vinci's whereabouts in those notes."

"So that's it?" Morgana asked. "We came all this way and have lost Mustardseed and Cobweb for nothing?"

"Life is sacrifice," Borromeo murmured.

"Maybe," I said. "But maybe not. Where is Raphael's physical body?"

Borromeo laughed. "It will mean your end if you try to find it for it lies at the very heart of the church's power. It is entombed within a crypt buried deep underneath St. Peter's Basilica and is well guarded. Even da Vinci was never able to free Raphael's body from its grave."

I thought things over but couldn't see the next step. I felt heavy with weariness and sat down on the other end of the pew.

"Why are you so desperate to find da Vinci?" Borromeo asked. "He clearly does not want to be found. If he is even still alive."

"I am trying to rescue someone close to me," I said. "And I believe he is the only one who can help."

Borromeo nodded like he understood. "Well, it is too dangerous to venture back out onto the water now. Tomorrow, we will help you on your way back to the world, and perhaps in time you will find what you seek. Tonight, you are welcome to join us in our humble quarters. We have already prepared a room for you."

"Is there more stew?" Puck asked. "And perhaps some wine to go with it?"

"We don't have much on this island, but we always have plenty of that," Borromeo said. "Please, help yourselves. But if I may have a moment alone with Cross before we retire for the evening?"

My companions returned to the dining hall, leaving Borromeo and I with the sketch of Raphael.

"How does it keep you alive?" I asked. "Is it the grace?"

Borromeo chuckled. "How did you know?"

"It's not the first time I've been around a work of art that's had some power to it," I said. "Also, I noticed your fingers started to bleed after touching the sketch. Like some power had transferred between you. Your lips look the same – you've all been kissing it. Is the sketch sentient?"

Borromeo thought things over before answering. "I don't believe it is anything like that," he eventually said. "Although one can never say for certain when it comes to angels. But yes, it has granted us immortality in return for our service. I am often undecided if that is a gift or a curse."

"I know the feeling."

"I imagine you do. Which is the reason I asked you to remain with me for a moment. I do not know how much of the son of God remains within you, but . . ."

"None at all, based on the things I've done."

"And my conscience troubles me for the things I have done." He shifted to face me.

"If you're looking to make a confession, you're wasting it on me," I said. "I've got no channel to higher divinity, and I don't want to hear about your sins."

"Nevertheless," Borromeo said. "If even some trace of my message gets through to whatever created you . . ."

I held up a hand to stop him. "You and your lot are damned. Whatever you've done in the ages since last we met, whatever your original intentions, even Raphael here thinks it's abominable. He's cursed you with stigmata, after all. You bleed when you touch him. I imagine if he could come back to life, you would do more than bleed."

Borromeo stared at me but didn't say anything else.

"There's no need to murder us and toss us in the well after the others. We'll leave in the morning, as you said. And then you can get back to doing whatever it is you do in this place. Just know it's not the secrets of immortality that brought me here. I came in search of an old friend. I didn't find the one I was looking for, that is true. But I found an old friend anyway, and I would like for us to part still friends."

We listened to the thunder and wind for a moment. Borromeo cleared his throat. "I will pray for you," he said.

"It's wasted on me," I said. "You should pray for yourself instead."

He smiled thinly. "I fear it is even more wasted on me."

"I guess I'll see you in Hell then."

And with that I left him there, a cursed priest in an unholy chapel, with only the undead spirit of a condemned angel for company.

A CURIOUS CHRIST

I left the chapel but didn't return to the dining hall right away. Instead, I walked around the side of the main building, toward the back, where I found a small brick structure tucked partway down the slope. It had no windows, only a tall wooden door with the outline of a quill carved into it. The scriptorium.

I knew Borromeo would be lost in his thoughts for some time before he rejoined the others, so I opened the door and went through. I didn't know what I was looking for, but I rarely did.

The room beyond contained a long wooden table with a number of aged stools. Crumbling sheets of paper were scattered along the length of the table, along with a few candles, some journals, a couple pairs of spectacles and a magnifying glass. The walls were lined with shelves that held more stacks of ancient paper, scroll tubes, a few dozen weathered tomes and several inkpots and quills.

I crossed to the table and went through the papers, but I couldn't decipher what I saw on them. One contained hieroglyphs of humanoid figures with wings, seemingly battling other large humanoids that appeared to be made of rocks. The ones with wings were maybe angels, but I wasn't sure about the nature of the rock men. At the centre of the sheet was a sun, and within the sun was a rectangle that was perhaps a book, but again I couldn't say for sure. Another sheet had a mix of squiggly lines and strange melting shapes that repeated in some pattern that I couldn't make sense of. The third sheet was a spiral of bloodstains that seemed to move as I watched it.

And so on. They must have been the notes written in code that Borromeo had mentioned. I didn't spend any more time on them – I wouldn't be able to decipher the codes if the others hadn't.

I wandered the shelves on the walls and felt the familiar tug of grace almost immediately. I checked the inkpots and quills, but it wasn't from them. The grace pulled me farther along until I came to a stack of parchments. The top one was a rough sketch of a plaza I didn't recognize so either it was someplace I had never seen, which was unlikely, or it was an invention da Vinci or perhaps another person had dreamed up. I placed my hand on it, but the grace was not in the drawing. I could feel it beneath the parchment, though.

I slid the sheet carefully to the side to reveal the next one in the stack, a drawing of a catapult launching some sort of fiery shot. I put my hand on that one, too, with the same result. I went through the stack, passing sketches of armour made of diamond and a carriage powered by sails and a ship pulled by whales, until I finally found the source of the grace.

The last parchment in the stack was a rough sketch of angels and saints I had known floating in the sky over a landscape of dead rising from their graves and sinners being dragged to Hell by demons. Christ hung suspended in the air in the middle of the scene, Mary clinging to his side and Saint Peter and John the Baptist hovering nearby. I recognized the sketch immediately as a rendering of *The Last Judgment* fresco, which covered the altar wall in the Sistine Chapel. It had the look of an early sketch – the artist was working out the details of a larger composition. But that fresco had been created by Michelangelo, not da Vinci.

Even more curious was the appearance of the Christ in the drawing. For he didn't look at all like the Christ in the Sistine Chapel version. Instead, he looked much like me, or at least how I had looked when da Vinci had known me.

I laid my hand on the Christ, on myself, and now I felt the grace. It was hidden inside the Christ, but it flowed out at my touch and into my fingers. Just a tiny amount, perhaps enough to turn a glass of water into wine and no more. But enough that I knew there was something special about this drawing. The problem was I didn't know what.

For a moment I contemplated taking it with me, but I quickly abandoned the idea. Someone would no doubt notice it missing and it wouldn't be hard to figure out who had taken it. I gave the sketch one last look and then replaced the parchments atop it.

I wanted to go through the rest of the scriptorium to see if there were any more secrets hidden here, but I was short on time. Borromeo would be leaving the chapel soon, and he would note my absence if he returned to the dining hall and I wasn't there. I went back out into the night, leaving the scriptorium and its mysteries behind.

A MOB OF FAITHFUL

Back in the dining hall, I joined the others in drinking more wine. Borromeo's fellow faithful filled our glasses with bottles of different varieties. The labels had peeled off most or were missing entirely, and they had the sort of battered look that told me they had been rescued from shipwrecks. Still, there's little better than a glass of wine on a stormy night.

We drank in silence as I considered everything I had learned. I had the beginnings of an idea of what to do next, but I didn't like it. There was too much chance of all of us winding up dead this time, so I was hoping another idea would occur to me.

Morgana laid her head on my shoulder and let out a long sigh. "I would very much like to rest my head on a pillow and lay my body in a warm bed," she said, then added in a lower voice, "These monks are trying to get us drunk."

I realized it was true, for there was one member of the order that refilled our glasses before we had even emptied them. And he drank little from his own glass. I made eye contact with Amelia, trying to warn her, but saw she had barely touched her own glass anyway. She was gazing into the fire as if unaware of the room. Puck appeared to have drunk his and her share of the wine combined, though, judging from the glazed and unfocused look of his eyes.

Borromeo returned then and I saw his lips were bleeding. He wiped the blood away with his sleeve. It was an unconscious gesture, as if he'd done it countless times before. I sensed more grace in him now – he'd kissed the sketch of Raphael in the chapel before joining us in the hall.

"Let us retire," he said, looking at no one. "To slumber or prayer, depending on your nature."

He led us through a door on the left side of the back wall and into a corridor lined with more doors. They were all open, revealing small sleeping rooms that consisted of a couple of cots with thin blankets and a washbasin in each.

"Forgive our humble quarters, but we do not indulge in the pleasures of the world here," Borromeo said.

"A pity," Morgana said, giving him a smile I had seen too many times before. "I'm sure we could have a wicked time with you lot. I find your kind are often the most hearty lovers. Must be all that time you spend on your knees."

Borromeo turned away from her. "Rest now, for we will come for you soon enough."

He left us there and entered a room farther down the hall. The other members of the order did the same, shuffling past us to their own chambers. I closed the door and leaned against one of the walls while Morgana laid down on one of the cots.

"What are the odds they are going to try to murder us in our sleep?" she asked through a yawn.

"I wouldn't bet against it," I said.

"We should murder them first then," Puck said. "Like we did with those –"

"I don't want to know about any more of your crimes," I told him. "Besides, I have an idea."

I told them what I had come up with and they considered me in silence for a moment.

Then Morgana shrugged. "You've come up with worse plans."

"Can you think of something better?" I asked.

"Not at all," she said and pulled the blanket over herself.

"I like it," Puck said, climbing into the other bed. "It's mad enough that it may just work."

I turned to Amelia, who was standing in the shadows under the window. "Any thoughts?"

"The worst that could happen is we wind up in the well," she said.

"I appreciate the confidence," I muttered as I slid into the cot beside Morgana.

"It's not your confidence I'm interested in right now," Morgana said, patting me on the leg.

I had to admit I was tempted, but not with my undead daughter in the same room. To say nothing of Puck, who'd snuck into our bed more than once over the years.

"Let's just rest up for what's to come," I said and closed my eyes.

The faithful attacked when the storm had more or less faded to a steady wind. They burst through the door in a mob, swarming the beds. I didn't hear them before they entered. Maybe because of the wind, maybe because they'd had a lot of practice. Or maybe they'd used their grace to conceal any sounds they made as they gathered.

The first couple tripped over the bedsheet I'd stretched between the legs of the two beds. The ones behind them had to step over their fallen comrades, which gave Morgana and me time to roll off the bed and turn it on its side. By the time the faithful reached us we were behind it and using it as a shield.

They all carried rusty metal crucifixes the size of axes in their hands, and they swung them at us like any warrior trying to kill a foe. Like I had tried to kill Gabriel back in the cemetery. I hoped they were just as successful. I kicked the bed forward, knocking the nearest ones off balance. I was able to grab a crucifix from the hand of one man, and I quickly buried one side of the cross in the head of another. He looked surprised in that way the dying always do. No one ever expects to get killed, let alone get killed by a crucifix to the head. I pulled him close and breathed deep of the grace that spilled from his wound.

Beside me, Morgana had managed to wrap the blanket around the head of another faithful and was slowly smothering him while using his body to keep the others at bay. I felt a sudden sympathy for the man, for I remembered the time she had smothered me to death in her bed. I quickly put it out of my mind.

On the other side of the room, Puck was holding his own. He'd kicked the bed into the midst of the mob as we had, but he'd leapt up onto it instead of using it as a shield. He'd found another bottle of wine somewhere and had used it to club the faithful on their heads and shoulders. One of them was on the ground, bleeding from a cut on his head so deep I could glimpse his skull. Puck laughed madly the whole while.

I couldn't see Amelia at Puck's side and I didn't have time to look for her. I could only hope she was where she was supposed to be for this plan to work.

I didn't see Borromeo, either – not in the crowd or even behind them. I wanted to believe it was due to his conscience getting the better of him, that he didn't want to take part in the murder of an old friend. Because the alternative meant he was waiting for us elsewhere.

The men in the middle of the mob managed to pull the dead one away from me, wrenching the crucifix from my grasp as they did so. Then he wasn't dead anymore. He reached up and pulled the crucifix from his head and grinned at me.

"You cannot kill one of the Order of the Angel Incarnate," he said. "For we *are* the Angel Incarnate."

I knew then that one of the others had raised him from the dead. Which is what I had more or less been expecting.

The one that Puck had felled rose up too, throwing himself into Puck's legs and bringing the faerie crashing down to the floor. Puck managed to brain him with the bottle again, but then another man buried his crucifix in Puck's chest.

Morgana let out a cry of rage and started forward, but I threw out an arm to hold her back.

"Time to leave," I said and used a bit of grace to shove the bed into the mob hard enough that it knocked most of them to the ground. Then I pulled Morgana to the window. She climbed through and dropped down and out of sight. I followed her, pausing briefly to look back at the room.

The faithful pushed themselves back to their feet and surged after me. At least they ignored Puck, who lay where he had fallen with the crucifix still embedded in his chest.

I threw myself out of the window and to the rocky ground below, where Morgana and Amelia waited. I slapped my hand on the wall and let the grace flow into it as I went, and the stones came apart from one another behind me. I barely managed to roll out of the way before a jumble of blocks crashed down where I had landed.

The falling blocks travelled down the length of the building and the entire wall tumbled down, bringing some of the roof with it. There were screams and shouts from inside, which grew in number and volume as fires flared up here and there. The flames of the fallen candles must have caught on the blankets and meagre beds and quickly spread. If the faithful had had my kind of experience with grace, perhaps they could have extinguished the flames and even repaired the wall. But I had a feeling they had used grace over the years for little more than granting themselves immortality and healing the wounds their victims inflicted upon them.

I quickly got to my feet and we headed for the path down to the dock. There was a figure standing on it now. I slowed a little as I took in who it was – Borromeo. He stood between us and the boat.

"I'd hoped you were anywhere but here." I sighed.

"There's only one way off this island," he said. "And you are not the first to attempt such an escape." His eyes flicked to the burning building behind us. "Although other efforts have not been so dramatic."

"Out of our way, zealot," Morgana snapped. "Or we'll burn you along with the others."

"I doubt whatever fires you can summon will compare to the flames of Hell that await me," Borromeo said. "But as long as I have grace, I can keep that eternity at bay."

Puck came tumbling down the cliff then and crashed onto the ground in between us. The crucifix remained buried in his chest and his flesh was scorched, but he sat up and grinned at us. He clutched a rolled-up piece of canvas in his right hand.

"You'll have a hard time stealing more grace without your angel," I told Borromeo.

He stared at the canvas Puck held. "This is what you're reduced to, Cross? A common thief?"

"I've always been a thief," I said. "Although Puck was the one who gave me the idea when he stole part of a painting back in Paris."

"You owe me an apology," Puck said. "I will take it in spirits."

"And in my own defence, stealing the bound soul of an angel is hardly a common crime," I added, ignoring Puck.

Puck spat blood on the rocks, then unrolled the sketch of Raphael and considered it. The edges were ragged – he must have torn it from the frame rather than carefully cut it out. I wasn't too worried, though. It was the soul of an angel trapped in the paper after all.

"So you have managed more than most who visit Isola Malcontenta," Borromeo said. "Do you really think I'm going to let you leave with that? I am its sworn protector, and I have never failed in my duty all these years. I even abandoned the very church itself to remain faithful to my vow."

The wind picked up again and the clouds behind him began to churn. It was one of those moments where things could go any number of ways, none of them likely ending well.

Puck tossed the sketch aside casually, but luckily Amelia was there to catch it. He pulled the crucifix from his chest and swung it a few times, spattering Borromeo with blood droplets. "There's only one way to find out," he said. I wasn't sure how he was still standing, given the nature of his wound. It was another of his mysteries.

I stepped past Puck and closer to Borromeo. "If you truly swore to protect the soul of Raphael, you'll let us leave with that sketch. For what you are doing here is not honouring your promise."

"Do you know what I gave up to hide away here for all eternity with the remnant of that angel?" Borromeo said, pointing at the sketch Amelia now gripped. "I surrendered my very life to it!"

"I have no doubt that you stole the sketch and brought it here with noble intentions," I said, keeping an eye on the clouds. I didn't want to get struck by lightning if he called it. "But what you and the others are doing now is no longer protecting it. You're keeping it for yourselves and using its power for your own devices. And Raphael remains sundered and denied Heaven because of that."

Borromeo glared at me but said nothing. I heard shouting from farther up the path. We didn't have much time.

"How many visitors to this island have you killed and dropped down that well?" I asked. "Or thrown back into the sea? Hell, how many have you drowned just trying to keep them away from the island? And for what?"

Borromeo licked his lips and glanced at the sketch again. Still he said nothing.

I stepped closer. "You asked me for redemption earlier. Here is your redemption: Let us pass with Raphael's soul. I will find da Vinci wherever he is hiding in the world, and I will deliver the sketch to him. That will truly be protecting the angel's soul, for da Vinci will know what to do with it. Or you can fight us and continue living the life you have been if you win."

"That's a pretty generous if," Puck muttered behind me.

Borromeo stared at me for a long moment as the clouds continued to churn. The shouting at our backs was closer now. The rest of the faithful were coming. We were out of time.

Then Borromeo stepped aside. "Go with God then," he said. "For he is no longer with me."

"I don't think he's with any of us anymore," I said as we rushed past him.

I glanced back along the path and saw the faithful running toward us, brandishing their crucifixes. Some were scorched from flames, while others were bleeding from various wounds. Maybe from the collapse of the wall, maybe from stigmata. You never could tell with the faithful.

I grabbed the bow of the boat and Puck grabbed the stern, and we dragged it down the rocks and into the water. I ripped off the tarp covering it and Morgana stepped into the boat like it was some sort of royal chariot, then offered her hand to Amelia to help her aboard. I jumped in next, followed by Puck, who waved at the faithful and cackled.

Borromeo stood on the rocky pier and watched us, and for a moment I thought about inviting him into the boat as well. But I could tell from the expression on his face he wouldn't have accepted. His gaze lingered on the sketch, and it was the look of someone laying eyes on a lover for the last time.

I grabbed the oars from the bottom of the boat and shoved them into the oarlocks, then started rowing. The waves crashed against us, trying to force us back into the rocks, as the foremost in the mob reached the pier.

The first dipped his crucifix into the water and started moving it in a circle like he was stirring a cauldron. The second raised his crucifix to the sky and began to shout words that were lost to me in the wind. Maybe a prayer, maybe something else. I decided I didn't want to find out and snapped a little of my remaining grace into the oars and down their length to the water. The boat shot forward through the waves as if we were on a calm lake.

But then a powerful wave surged into us, driving us back a few feet. It was followed by another one. The faithful were using the grace they'd taken from the Raphael sketch much like I was.

A second later there was a bright flash of light accompanied by a deafening crack, as if the world had broken open. We'd been hit by lightning called down by the second faithful. Or rather, Puck had been hit by lightning. He remained standing at the stern of the boat, but the crucifix in his hand was melted and twisted now. Puck himself looked the way one does after being struck by lightning – surprised and uncertain if he was alive or dead. Then he threw up both arms up and laughed.

"Again!" he cried.

"Quit pleasuring yourself and help us escape," Morgana said to him.

"Actually, I'm thinking of converting to their dead god," Puck said. "I haven't had this much fun since –"

Whatever he said next was lost to me as the wind picked up once more and another wave hit us. The faithful continued to use the grace against us, so I had no choice but to use up the last of my own. We shot forward again, punching through the waves. I felt that familiar hollowness inside me again.

"Draw grace from the sketch so that we may escape," Morgana cried as if she had read my mind.

"I have other plans for the sketch," I said.

Then I saw Borromeo striding down the pier, waves surging up around him. Those same waves swept over the rocks and carried the faithful into the water. A sudden wall of rain fell around us, obscuring the island from sight. And obscuring us from the eyes of the faithful.

I rowed as hard as I could as more waves slammed into us, spinning us around. Lightning struck the water on the port side, then on the starboard, dozens of feet away each time. But it did not strike us again, to Puck's obvious disappointment. For a moment the waves tossed us in one direction and then another, until I wasn't sure which way we had been rowing. I stuck with it, though, and then the worst of the storm was behind us. We were in choppy water still, and the wind continued to howl, but the rain let up and I could see the lagoon around us once more, the mast sticking up out of the water in the distance.

"Did we escape the island?" Morgana asked, peering back the way we had come.

"I think so," I said, although I wasn't entirely certain.

"Do you think they will follow us?" Puck asked wistfully.

"Probably," I said. "With any luck they'll run into the angels and keep each other busy."

"Perhaps we could go back and steal the rest of their wine while they're occupied," he said. He reached behind his back and pulled a bottle out of his pants, then took a long drink from it.

I paused in my rowing and lifted Puck's shirt to inspect his wound. The hole in his chest was large and ragged, and I could see through to muscle and bone.

"Why, Cross, I didn't know you were interested in me in that way." Puck grinned.

"I'm interested in figuring out how you're still alive," I said. The plan we'd worked out back in our room had involved the faithful taking out Puck so he could sneak away and steal the sketch while they chased us. But I had thought they'd most likely knock him out and maybe give him a few flesh wounds in the process. Instead, they had given him a fatal blow. Only he was somehow still alive.

"I don't know either," Puck said. "Maybe one of your gods persists after all. Perhaps that crucifix used on me came with some sort of blessing."

"You're going to need more than a blessing to remain alive," I said. He'd lost a lot of blood, and the wound was of a sort that practically guaranteed infection.

"We'll find him a new body," Morgana said. "Preferably one that has no mouth."

I let Puck's shirt fall and resumed rowing. "Or we could find a hospital and fix the body he has."

"So where do we go now?" Morgana asked, not deigning to respond to my suggestion.

"Rome," I said.

"Did you go mad back on the island?" she asked. "Those lunatics told us Raphael is hidden away in the heart of the angels' power."

"That's what I'm counting on."

"And how exactly is a dead angel supposed to help us, even if we can find it?"

"All those times over the ages where something tore you away from me, or me from you, how often did each of us go looking for the other?" I asked.

Morgana made a face. "That's different. We're not lowly mundanes or mindless angels. Well, I'm not anyway."

"I'm betting it's the same thing with da Vinci." I gazed toward the distant shore, shimmering on the horizon like a mirage. "Wherever that dead angel is, da Vinci is nearby."

THE DIFFERENCE BETWEEN BEING AWAKE AND DREAMING

It was dawn when we reached the island of Murano, which was famous with tourists mainly for its glassmaking shops but also for the Church of Santa Maria e San Donato. The church was rumoured to contain the relics of Saint Donatus of Euroea, as well as the bones of a dragon he killed, but the rumours left out the parts about Donatus's troubled spirit continuing to hunt the dragon in death. That's an entirely different story, though. There were no tourists this early, or dragons. The only locals awake were a pair of weathered old fishermen heading out to the open water. They didn't look our way as they passed. Maybe they knew of the secret island and wanted nothing to do with any who came from its direction.

I took us down one of the canals and left the boat tied to a dock in case the faithful had some way of tracking it. I didn't know if they'd leave the island to pursue us, but there was no point making it easy for them if they did.

We stole another boat from a different dock and rowed it out into the lagoon, far enough that we could start the engine without alerting the owner, then took it to Venice. All of us were quiet and exhausted, but at least the wind had mostly dried our clothes.

I tied the boat to a pier and turned to find Amelia slumped over and asleep in the back seat. I shook her shoulder gently, but she did not rouse. I shook her again, to the same effect. She didn't seem to be drawing breath.

I kneeled before her, and Morgana stepped to my side.

"Amelia," we said at the same time. I held one of her hands and Morgana the other. She felt colder than ever, if that was possible.

Amelia took a breath then, and another several seconds later.

"I'm here," she said, slowly opening her eyes. She stared at us, but her eyes were unfocused and glassy, as if she didn't see us. "I'm still here."

"What's wrong with her?" Puck asked. "Did the zealots work some magic upon her soul?"

"No," I said. "I don't think it was the faithful."

Morgana lifted Amelia in her arms and carried her out of the boat and to shore. She propped Amelia up against a stone wall, then turned to me. "No more," she said. "I am done with this mad quest. And my court is done with me."

"We haven't found da Vinci yet," I said with a weary sigh.

"No, but we have lost Mustardseed. We have lost Cobweb. We have lost all my fey. I still don't understand how Puck is alive after that damned island, and we nearly lost Amelia there as well. She could have drowned and been dead for real."

"I am dead for real," Amelia said.

"You know what I mean," Morgana said without looking at her. "No more."

"I understand," I said, and I did. "I'll carry on alone then. Because I'm not giving up."

"You won't be alone." Amelia pushed herself to her feet. "I am going with you."

"No, you're not." Morgana turned to her. "Did you not hear what I just said? I am your queen. Your mother."

"I heard," Amelia said. "But Alice needs us. We cannot abandon her after all she has done for the living and the dead. If we split up, the angels will hunt us down one by one. If we stay together, we may have a chance to see this through and rescue her. And the court may yet survive."

Morgana was very still for a moment. "Well, she's certainly your daughter," she said and walked away.

We left the dock behind and wandered the streets of Venice until we found an open café, where we consumed several shots of espresso and a matching number of pain au chocolat. That was enough to get us to the train station, and soon we were on a train moving through the rolling hills and olive groves of Tuscany and on our way to Rome. Morgana sat beside me in the window seat, and Amelia and Puck were across from us.

"I once held court in that villa for a decade of your years," Morgana said, nodding at some ruins atop one of the hills we passed. "Faerie came from all over to pay tribute and gave me fey of their own."

"I remember that," Puck said. "I played a card game with Cobweb and Peaseblossom that lasted a week. And that one with the antlers – what was her name?"

"Nyx," Morgana said. "She was slain during the last Wild Hunt. Many years ago."

Puck laughed. "Nyx. Why couldn't I remember that?"

"We are slipping into the mists at the end of time," Morgana said. "Just like the Chaos Court."

The sunlight fell upon her then, as if on cue, and I could see the lines on her face. Her hair was all grey now.

"Maybe there's a way to save your court," I said, even though I suspected the world may be better off without the faerie. But we had a history, and I was reluctant to see the last of Morgana. Chalk it up to the remains of the enchantment she had once cast upon me. "After we save Alice, then I'll help you."

"I suppose we must come up with a plan to find the dead angel in that case," Morgana said and tore her gaze away from the window. She looked at Amelia sitting beside Puck and I knew what she was thinking, but I shook my head.

"Not Amelia," I said.

"She is the only one of us who can," Morgana said. "None of us have that kind of power with the dead."

"And every time she uses that power she slips more out of this world and back into the realm of the dead." I turned to Amelia. "Isn't that right? I noticed it first at the cemetery in Paris, when you found the secret tunnel so we could escape. You were exhausted then, but I passed it off to the battle and our flight from the angels. But every time you use your powers, you become more tired. You had to be roused at the Tuileries when we escaped the angel there. And we could barely bring you back to this world after everything that happened on that island."

Amelia nodded slowly. "I suppose it's like your grace. Every time I use my ability, I am drained a bit more of my remaining life. Only there is no way for me to replenish it. And when all that life is gone . . ."

"You don't need to find Raphael's body," I said. "Besides, if what Borromeo said is true, we likely wouldn't be able to get to it if you did."

"But how do we find da Vinci without the angel?" Morgana asked.

"I think I may have a new plan," I said.

"Why do I not feel reassured to hear that?" she asked.

Amelia looked out the window at the ruins fading away in the distance. "This world and that of the dead aren't really different. It's like the difference between being awake or dreaming."

"Do you see Cobweb there in that other state?" Puck asked. "Or Peaseblossom?"

"Everyone is there eventually," Amelia said.

THE HEART OF ROME

I had lied to Morgana when I told her I had a plan. I was out of ideas except for one, which was really more of a suicidal gesture. I didn't want to share that with Morgana, though, because I was afraid she really would abandon me if she knew the truth, no matter what Amelia said. And no matter what I said, I didn't know what I would do without her.

We arrived in Rome around lunch hour, which is actually several hours in Italy. We left the train station and I led our small group to a pizzeria in a hidden square that had been there for several generations. It was one of those places the locals all knew about but didn't breathe a word of to tourists, for fear of it being ruined. We ate inside the pizzeria despite the day being warm and the sky clear. I didn't want anyone spotting us quite yet. There'd be time for that later.

The walls of the pizzeria were lined with faded photos of other people that had eaten there, mostly black-and-white images from the postwar years. One of the previous owners had been an amateur photographer and had taken the photos. I was in one or two of them, but I didn't bother looking for myself. I don't like to be reminded of who I once was.

We each finished a pizza of our own and then crossed the square to a café that had a similar history to the pizzeria. We drank shots of espresso standing at the counter, then went back out into the streets of Rome.

"Is your plan to gorge ourselves until one of the angels stumbles across us?" Morgana asked. "Because while I don't mind indulging myself, I don't see how this is getting us any closer to what we seek."

"We needed to fortify ourselves for what comes next," I said and headed deeper into Rome.

We made our way to the Colosseum on foot and then split into two groups and walked a few dozen yards apart so as to draw less attention to ourselves. I walked with Amelia at the front while Morgana and Puck brought up the rear. I couldn't help but look over my shoulder every now and then to make sure they were still there.

We didn't stop at the Colosseum but instead wound our way through the crowds surrounding it, and then turned and headed to the northwest. I used the cover of the crowd to stop and check behind us a few times, as well as to the sides. I wanted to know if we were being tailed before we moved on to our real destination.

"Do you see anyone?" Amelia asked me as we stopped at a gelato shop and bought cups for ourselves. The day was hot and I was already sweating. Not all of it was from the heat, though. Being this close to the Colosseum always brought back unpleasant memories.

"I don't see any signs of the angels or the faithful," I said. We both knew that didn't mean much, though. "What about you?"

Amelia turned away from the Colosseum looming above us. "This place is too overpowering. I see the dead without even trying. So many that I have trouble seeing anything else." She closed her eyes. "You were among their number, long ago."

"Let's keep moving before they find us." I tossed my cup in a garbage can and walked away from the Colosseum. I didn't want Amelia to see the first time I had died, when Judas, disguised as the Roman emperor Commodus, killed me in gladiatorial combat on the sands in front of a cheering crowd. Hell, I didn't want to think about that time again myself, or all the blood I had spilled after I had resurrected in a grave outside Rome.

We walked past the Trevi Fountain, where I lifted some coins from the pockets of tourists and threw them into the fountain for good luck. I figured we needed all the luck we could get. Then we took the Ponte Umberto bridge across the Tiber and walked alongside the river until we reached Via della Conciliazione. Amelia and I stopped and studied the dome of St. Peter's Basilica in the distance as we waited for Morgana and Puck to catch up.

"Have you lost what little is left of your sanity?" Morgana asked as she joined us. "Do you actually mean to take us into the heart of your religious cult?"

"It's not my cult," I said. "But yes. Borromeo said that's where Raphael's body lies."

"I thought perhaps we would wander the surrounding streets until we found da Vinci," Morgana said, nodding at the alleys that led away to different parts of the city.

"That could take time we don't have," I said and went down the street to St. Peter's Square. "We find Raphael's body and I suspect we will also find da Vinci."

The square was crowded with more throngs of tourists, which I hoped would make it harder for anyone to notice us. They filled the open plaza and milled about the colonnades that swept to either side, forming a semicircle around us. I stopped near the ancient stone obelisk that stood at the centre of the square. It was pink granite, maybe twenty-five metres tall – which was impressive, considering it had been carved from a single block of stone. There were inscriptions on the base on all four sides, but I didn't pay any attention to them – I was too busy considering the bronze cross affixed to the top of the obelisk. I could feel the grace in it from here.

"What is it?" Morgana asked, alternating between eyeing the cross and the statues decorating the top of the colonnades and the basilica's facade. "Is it some sort of ward or surveillance device?"

"It's a relic," I said. "Actually, both are relics. The Romans brought the obelisk from Egypt, the prize from some pharaoh or another they defeated. They stuck an orb on top containing the ashes of Julius Caesar. I suppose that was their way of claiming the obelisk as their own. Then the Christians came along and pulled off the orb and stuck that cross up there. Legend is it contains a piece of the true cross. Which is why I can feel grace within it."

"The cross you were crucified upon?" Puck asked. He looked up at the cross with a rapturous expression that made me feel uncomfortable.

"Not me," I said. "Christ. I was only born into the body he left behind after all that crucifixion business."

"What do you think would happen if we crucified you?" Puck mused.

"Ask the legionnaires who did it to Christ." I tore my gaze away from the cross atop the obelisk. I craved the grace within it, like an addict needing his next fix. It was a feeling I knew far too well. But there was no way for me to climb the obelisk without drawing a lot of attention. And I wasn't quite ready for that yet.

"It's not just grace that is contained within this," Amelia said, laying her hand on the obelisk. "There are many dead trapped as well."

"Don't waste your power like that," I said.

"I can't help it. They are calling to me."

"It's probably the spirits of the workers who died moving the obelisk," I said. "It was originally erected in Nero's circus, which was some distance from here. They pulled it down and moved it when they built the new basilica to replace the old temple that had been in this spot. Many people lost their lives in the effort."

Amelia shook her head. "No, it's not the spirits of the dead who died near the obelisk in the past. I mean there are dozens of the dead trapped within the obelisk right now. They are held in undeath, like unwilling ghosts."

We all stared at the obelisk for a moment, while tourists around us took photos of it and each other.

"Well, this just keeps getting better and better," Morgana said. "Can we hurry things along? If I'm going to die today, I'd like to get it over with."

I gave all the statues on the roofs another glance, but none of them had moved as far as I could tell. We crossed the square to St. Peter's Basilica.

"Give me the sketch of Raphael," I said to Amelia, and she pulled it out of her shirt and handed it to me.

"What are you going to do with it?" she asked.

"I'm going to make a statement."

THE HOLY DOOR

We made our way to the front of the basilica, where there were five large doors spaced at intervals with nine windows above them. The centre window had a balcony, and it was where the pope made appearances from time to time, to remind people he was still alive. I was really hoping we wouldn't see any popes today, though.

I took us to the large bronze door farthest to the right. It measured a little under four metres in height and was cast with typical biblical scenes: an angel at the gates of paradise, Christ's appearance to his disciples, the crucifixion and so on. None of them were historically accurate, but that's never bothered the faithful.

"This is the Holy Door," I told the others. "You can actually only use it on holy years, whatever those are. The rest of the time it's locked up and bricked on the other side."

"Is this one of those years?" Morgana asked.

"I don't keep track of that sort of thing." I turned to Puck. "I hope you have another knife or something sharp hidden away."

Puck grinned at me and pulled a long, rusty spike out of his pants pocket.

"Close enough," I said and took the spike from him.

I unrolled the sketch of Raphael and placed it against the door. Then I rammed the spike through the top of it and into the door, lodging the point in a gap between the panels. I stepped away. The sketch hung there, the edges curling and uncurling slightly. It probably wouldn't hold for long, but I was hoping not to linger at the basilica.

"I take it this is your statement," Morgana said. "But I have no idea what you are trying to say."

"I'm saying look at me," I said. "Just like when Martin Luther nailed his ninety-five theses to the door of Wittenberg's Castle Church."

"Well, I suppose it's worked then," Morgana said, glancing about. Already several tourists were staring at us and a few were taking videos on their phones.

"It's not them I want to notice," I said. "It's whoever is guarding this place."

"I have more nails," Puck said. "If you want to do a crucifixion."

"I want you to stay here with the sketch," I told him. "At the first sign of an angel or anyone that looks like they serve the angels, I want you to take this sketch back to the obelisk and wait for us there."

"That doesn't sound like much of a plan," Puck said with a frown.

"He's right," Morgana said. "They'll just follow him."

I nodded. "I hope so. I want to draw them out of the basilica."

"Ah," she said. "A diversion while we go inside. To do what exactly?"

"I have no idea," I said. "But Borromeo said Raphael was hidden away in the heart of the church's power, and this is it. However we find da Vinci, the answer lies inside."

And with that I approached the nearby Door of Sacraments, which bore images depicting the ways in which Christ was supposed to redeem us all. As if any of us are worthy of redemption. I took a deep breath and then stepped through the door, into the basilica.

Even I had to admit it was one of the most stunning churches in the world, and I'm usually not a fan of such places. The nave stretched hundreds of feet before me with great pilasters supporting a barrel-vaulted ceiling high overhead. The pilasters were adorned with statues of important figures in the church's history. I even recognized a few of them from my past lives. At the far end of the nave, underneath the great dome that rose up, was an altar with a large bronze canopy supported by four sculpted pillars.

"They created a glamour all of their own here," Morgana murmured, stepping into the nave. She stopped on a circle of red stone set into the tiled floor, as if drawn to it.

"That glamour is called history," I said. "Every piece of wood and stone in this place has a story. For instance, that red porphyry you're standing on comes from the old basilica. There's a whole line of emperors who were crowned on it by popes, starting with Charlemagne."

"Perhaps we should get one of those popes to crown me then," Morgana said.

"I don't think you quite qualify. You have to be human." More or less anyway. I headed for the altar at the end of the nave. I could sense grace emanating from there all the way across the room – perhaps from Raphael's secret tomb, perhaps from some relic I could drain. Whatever happened in here, I would no doubt need more grace to deal with it.

There were men and women that were clearly undercover security guards stationed around the basilica. You could tell by the way they weren't staring in awe at their surroundings. Instead, they were just scanning the crowd. I was somewhat heartened by the fact that none of them paid me any attention, although a few let their gaze linger on Morgana. We were halfway across the nave before a handful of them turned and began to quickly walk toward the door we had come through.

"It looks like our distraction is working," I said to Morgana.

"If you want someone to cause trouble, then Puck is your man," she said. "And sometimes your woman or wild beast."

We reached the Confessio, a sort of sunken but open chapel in the shape of a semicircle in the floor before the great altar. It was surrounded by a white marble balustrade that was lined with dozens of oil lamps. A gate of two golden doors was at the near end, with a short double staircase leading down into the Confessio. There was another set of doors in the wall below the altar, flanked by statues of St. Peter and St. Paul. More doors were to the left and right – they led to the grottoes under the basilica, where the popes and others were buried. The grace was coming through each of these doors.

"Whatever it is we're going to do next, we should set about it," Morgana said at my side. I was dimly aware of shouting somewhere in the distance. "There's no telling what Puck will do when left unsupervised."

I nodded and jumped over the gates to the Confessio, then motioned for them to follow me.

"There are many restless dead down there," Amelia said, which made Morgana pause.

"They'll be more at peace when I take their grace from them," I said. "Then maybe we can locate Raphael's body."

Morgana uttered a few curses that should never be uttered in a place like this but opened the gate to join me, and Amelia reluctantly followed her. That was when the bell began to sound. It wasn't a typical blaring klaxon like a fire alarm but was instead an actual bell. It rang slow and deep, each peal echoing through the basilica like it was announcing something of import.

"They definitely know we're here now," I said.

"Let's find whatever is hidden in this necropolis quickly then," Morgana said. She opened the set of doors in the middle of the Confessio, but they only revealed a niche holding a small bronze coffer. Staring back at me on the rear wall was a mosaic of myself from other times. Sadly, no grace came from it.

"The necropolis is a few levels deeper," I said. "This is just the Niche of the Pallia, where they keep some accessories."

Morgana reached into the niche and opened the coffer, then took out one of the bands of white wool decorated with black crosses inside. "Is it a mystical relic?"

"A relic of no power maybe," I said. "The popes wear them as some sort of symbol of authority. Or maybe it's the archbishops. I can never keep track of whatever rituals they invent for themselves."

I looked back and forth between the doors to either side, trying to decide which one to take. I wasn't sure why they both emanated grace, as I had never been in the burial grottoes underneath the basilica before. Perhaps the place was rich with heavenly corpses. Or perhaps it was some kind of trap.

"What kind of faerie queen would I be if I didn't adorn myself in the relics of other gods?" Morgana said and slipped the band of wool over her head and around her neck, like a curious necklace.

The bell continued to toll and I was relatively certain that it tolled for me. Also, I heard the sounds of running feet approaching.

I chose the door on the left and opened it. A hall with a low vaulted ceiling was on the other side. The ceiling and walls were lined with frescoes of people as familiar to me as the statues in the nave of the basilica. The stone tile floor had been worn down by countless feet. I waved Morgana and Amelia through, then quickly closed the door behind us. There was no way to lock it, so I moved down the hall to where it branched off to either side. The sounds of the bell faded behind me but not entirely.

"Why is it that, when I travel with you, we always wind up surrounded by the dead?" Morgana said.

"I was going to ask you the same thing." I looked down both branches of the hall. The grace was stronger in the one that led to the north, if I had my directions right, so I went that way.

We came to a small chapel lit by candles, the hallway beyond continuing into darkness. Inside the chapel was a row of wooden pews that led to an altar. A painting of the Madonna with an infant in her arms hung on the wall behind the altar, with large broken tablets depicting stone angels suspended on either side. The remaining walls were covered in painted panels of various biblical scenes, but I paid them little attention – the grace I sensed was coming from behind the wall that held the Madonna and the angels. I drew close to the painting and considered it for a moment.

"This is no time for prayer," Morgana said.

"I don't think prayer is the point of this chapel," I said. "There's something behind this wall."

"The dead angel?"

I placed my hand on the painting. If there was a secret room behind the wall, there had to be a secret door somewhere. That meant there was some mechanism in the chapel to open it. Nothing happened when I laid my hand on the Madonna in the painting, so I tried the angel on the left instead. When I touched my hand to his, I felt a small trickle of grace in my fingers, draining from me and into the statue. Nothing else happened, though, so I reached out with my right hand and did the same thing with the angel on the other side of the painting. I felt the grace there, too, and then one of the panels on the back wall slid aside with a rumble, revealing a passageway.

"That doesn't seem very well hidden," Morgana said.

"It's hidden enough," I said. "You need grace to operate the mechanism. Which tells me we're in the right place."

I grabbed a candle from the altar and slipped through the opening in the wall and into the secret passageway beyond. Grace pulled at me from somewhere in the shadows ahead.

The others followed me in, and I turned to inspect the panel from this side. There was a simple metal handle attached to the back of it, which I used to slide the panel shut, so no one else would stumble in after us. Then I led us down the passageway.

The walls were ancient, crumbling stone in a state of serious disrepair. Cracks ran along the floor and walls, and the ceiling sagged in places.

"This doesn't look particularly safe," Morgana said.

"Of course it's not safe," I said. "It's a church."

A gust of wind came from somewhere before us, as if a great door had been opened. It snuffed out my candle, but Amelia was able to shelter hers with her body and keep it alight. I relit my candle using her flame and turned back in the direction we had been heading. I stopped, though, when I noticed the hall had changed. The walls, ceiling and floor were now made of human bones mortared together, many of them broken into pieces. As if someone or something had ripped apart hundreds of skeletons to line the hall. The air was suddenly chill and had the musty scent of catacombs. All in all, it wasn't a good sign.

"I don't suppose this is of your doing," I said to Morgana.

She fingered the cloth around her neck. "This is not part of my glamour."

I thought about asking Amelia if she knew what lay before us but decided against it. We would find out soon enough.

I let the grace pull me forward. I could hear the whispering of dozens of voices. I couldn't quite make out what they were saying, perhaps because they were speaking in different tongues.

"It's too bad Puck isn't here," Morgana said. "He would adore this."

We went around a bend and down a flight of stairs. I tried not to dwell on the fact that I was walking on the dead. The bones in the walls and ceiling became full skeletons the farther we descended, the stairs ending in an arch made of skulls that all faced us. We stopped at the threshold and stared into the chamber beyond.

The skeletal walls were maybe ten metres away on either side and lined with alcoves that contained sculpted stone caskets. In between each alcove a stone cross the size of a man hung suspended in the bones. The arched ceiling climbed high enough overhead that it faded out of sight, as did the other end of the room.

A throne made of skulls was in the centre of the room, and a skeleton in mouldy, disintegrating robes sat upon it. The skeleton's hands rested upon a white tome in its lap, which glowed with a light that lit up the room. I recognized it immediately despite all the years that had passed since I'd last seen it. Gabriel's bible that I had sold to Borromeo, although it hadn't been glowing back then. The light flickered as if the tome were burning with invisible flames. The whispering voices grew into a loud chorus, like a worsening wind. I could feel the grace emanating from that skeleton, pulling at the emptiness inside me.

But the strangest thing was the skeleton spoke, even though it had no tongue with which to form words, or even a lower jawbone for that matter.

"The prodigal son finally returns," the skeleton said. "And just when I was beginning to lose hope I would ever see you again."

THE POPE

I considered the skeleton for a moment, then the caskets in the walls. But there were no answers anywhere for all the questions I had.

"Do I know you?" I asked.

The skeleton stared at me with empty eye sockets. "I'm the pope!"

"Of course," I said. "I should have known. But remind me which pope exactly?"

"I know which one," Amelia murmured.

I held up a hand to her. "We don't need to waste your ability on some random pope."

"I am no random pope!" the pope said – if it was indeed a pope. It wouldn't have been the first time I'd encountered a deceitful skeleton. "I am the pope who made you what you are. Without me, you would still be a lost soul wandering the wilderness."

"Actually, you are describing pretty much who he has always been," Morgana said.

I snapped my fingers and pointed at him. "I remember now. You're that pope that tortured me. Back when I was only a few centuries old."

"Sounds delightful," Morgana said. "And you didn't invite me?"

"This was before you and I met. I didn't really know who I was back then. I was a little careless around an angel and the next thing I knew I woke up in a dungeon with the angel and this pope. It worked out all right in the end, though, because it's how I met Victory. They were holding her in a neighbouring cell while they tried to figure out what each of us were."

That had certainly been a wasted effort.

"You're neglecting to mention the act of blasphemy you committed," the pope said.

"You'll have to be more specific," I said. "I've committed a lot of acts of blasphemy."

"The murder and violation of an angel."

"I've killed many an angel but I've never violated one." Not that I could remember anyway.

"Why not?" Morgana asked.

"You stole its grace!" the pope cried. "And used it to become the abomination you are now!"

"Oh, that." I shook my head. "I'm sorry to break it to you, but I was already an abomination before I woke up in your little cell. But I understand how you wouldn't have known that. We didn't have a chance to talk much because of the torture and all. But enough reminiscing. What is this place and what are you doing here?"

The pope waved a hand at the caskets. "It is the true tomb of the popes. And I have been waiting to make it your tomb as well."

"That's overly dramatic. Besides, I've had a lot of tombs, but none have ever held me." I moved to my right, to put some distance between myself and the others. There was no sense in being bunched together when he tried whatever it was he was going to try.

"So it's a trap then?" Morgana sighed.

"Yes," the pope and I said at the same time.

"You certainly got their attention," Morgana said. She went to the left, maybe to flank him, maybe to get as far away from me as possible.

"Hang on, this doesn't add up," I told the pope. "The last time we crossed paths was centuries ago and far from here. You expect me to believe that you've carried this grudge all this time? And been hiding in this place on the off chance that I might show up?"

The pope turned his head to follow me but made no move to spring whatever trap he had planned. I couldn't decide if that was a good thing or not.

"I have not been hiding here waiting for you," the pope said. "I have been imprisoned here to keep watch over the dead popes and their secrets. But I have hoped over the ages that you would manifest one day and free me."

"After all that torture business?" I snorted. "You'll have to find someone else to bust you out of here."

Now that I was closer to the caskets lining the walls, I felt the pull of grace from them as well. The whispering came from inside the caskets. I thought of all the other popes I'd crossed over the ages and wondered if any of them were entombed here.

"All right, I'll ask the obvious question," Morgana said from the other side of the chamber. "Who imprisoned you in this place?"

"The angel Gabriel," the pope said.

"Excellent," Morgana said. "He also has some kind of grudge with Cross. We can work together to finish him."

The pope kept his gaze fixed on me. "Gabriel imprisoned me because I let Cross escape into the world once. I will not make that mistake again." He waved a hand in the direction we had come and muttered a word that seemed to cross the distance between us like a sudden wave, swelling in my ears and then just as quickly fading away. *"Ruina."*

The hallway we had come down collapsed then, the skeletons that made up its roof and walls falling in a jumbled mess. We could likely pull them apart to find our way back out, but it would take time – time that I suspected we did not have.

There was nothing special about the word itself, which was Latin for *collapse*, or maybe *fall*. But I had sensed the grace flow across the room – too far away to intercept, unfortunately. The glow of Gabriel's bible faded a little and the flickering nearly died away, before it flared up again. The pope had used the book to work his magic. Given he was wielding an angel's bible and trying to keep us here rather than get rid of us, we were likely in trouble.

"Now you are trapped here along with us," the pope said. "And we will have what we seek."

"And what exactly is that?" I asked, then charged him. I figured we may as well get on with it. And I wanted to drain his grace before he used it on me.

Unfortunately, my plan worked about as well as they normally did. The distance between us didn't seem to change, even though I was sprinting all out. In fact, he drew farther away, as if the room were lengthening to match my strides.

"We have long wanted to know the answer to your true nature," the pope continued, as if he hadn't noticed me running at him. "Are you as human as you are divine, like some Nestorian aberration? Or, as the Tome of Leo suggests, does even your tainted fallen flesh contain the divine?"

"Oh, he's quite mad, isn't he?" Morgana said from across the room. She was also trying to close with the pope, with similar results.

"You would be too if you'd had to deal with centuries of theological schisms," I said. I tried leaping at the pope, to no more effect than running at him. "How are you managing that trick anyway?"

The pope chuckled and shook a finger at me. "As you say, we have interpreted the mysteries of the world for centuries. Perhaps we are indeed mad because of it. But we have discovered secret knowledge within those mysteries. With our madness has come dominion over the world itself. You have no more chance of reaching us to corrupt our nature than we have of reaching Heaven."

I tried running to the side instead but still got nowhere. So I stopped and caught my breath. "All right, I'll answer your questions if you answer one of mine first. Where have you hidden Raphael away? Is he in one of these crypts?"

"Let me first set the tone for our conversation," the pope said. *"Carpe eos!"*

Bony arms snapped up from the floor and caught on to both Morgana and me, grabbing our legs and trapping us in place. I noticed the light from Gabriel's bible dim again. At the same time, the shadows around the crypts grew darker.

"You may have power in your glamour, but the afterlife is our eternal glamour even if it is not the afterlife we were promised," the pope said to Morgana as he rose from his throne. "We have the power here. And the grace."

I suspected he wasn't exactly being honest about everything, though. I mean, I'd felt the grace when he commanded the skeletal arms to rise up and seize us. It had flowed from him into the skeletal remains that made up the floor of this place. But the grace seemed to be connected with Gabriel's bible and perhaps the crypts.

"Why haven't you used the grace to escape?" I asked. "Like I did, remember?"

The pope walked toward me. "The angel Gabriel has seen to it that I need more than grace to leave here. We must all earn our salvation. Even the popes, it seems."

More bones climbed up my body, twisting impossibly around my legs and torso like rope. They reached my shoulders and wound around my arms, down to my wrists. I fought to throw them off but they clung to me tightly. Then I was wrenched up into the air and my arms pulled to either side, my feet pinned. I hung a body's length above the ground, crucified on a cross made of bone.

"You have always belonged on the cross, not off it," the pope said.

"Don't even think about doing that to me!" Morgana said, glaring at the pope.

"We are not interested in you," the pope said. "We are interested in unravelling another mystery. Perhaps the greatest mystery ever known to mankind."

I struggled against my bonds as he walked toward me, but the bones may as well have been unbreakable chains. I didn't have enough grace to break free, and he had all the grace in the world.

"Don't you even want to ask me about God's bible?" I said, trying to buy some time. "Everyone else seems obsessed with it."

The pope stopped at my feet. "Don't tell me you've done something to it."

"You mean they haven't told you?" I forced a laugh. "Typical angels. Even the popes don't know what they're up to. Let me down from here and I'll explain everything."

"I don't think so," the pope said. "I will make inquiries when I'm done with you. Now it's time to determine your true nature. Does any of the divine in fact remain within you? If so, perhaps you can finally deliver us to Heaven and free us from our mortal bindings."

"I promise that you're going to find out just how divine I am." I spat at him.

The pope laid a hand on my leg, almost caressing it. "If, however, you truly are a mix of the human and divine, and the human element of you is an accident as so much of this world seems to be, then perhaps that human element could be replaced with another."

The bones grew spikes then, which dug into my flesh. And kept going. They punctured my skin like a thousand knives and then began twisting inside me, like tendrils seeking who knew what.

I screamed and cursed him with everything I could think of. I really hated being crucified.

"We will hollow your soul out of that body," the pope murmured. "And make room for a new soul. Imagine the power of the popes in the body of Christ. Imagine what we would do in your stead."

I was really in need of a deus ex machina, but I was in the wrong place for that. Luckily, I had something just as good.

Amelia stepped out from behind the throne of skulls then and came at the pope from behind. I'd forgotten she was even in the chamber with us. I didn't know how she'd crossed the room without him noticing, but I suspected it was another of her tricks. He didn't seem to notice her, so I kept my gaze fixed on him.

"I think history has already shown us what you would do," I said. "Thankfully that will never happen."

Amelia snatched the bible away from the pope, and smashed it into his skull in the same motion. The blow knocked the skull from the rest of the skeleton and sent it tumbling across the bones to the foot of the crucifix I'd become. The body staggered around in a wild circle.

"You cannot end the popes so easily!" the pope cried.

"Amelia, the bible!" I said.

She ran to me and threw the book up to my right hand. I was able to grab it with my fingers and barely hold on. But it was enough. I felt the grace inside, like electricity buzzing against my fingers. It wanted out of the bible so I obliged.

I drew it forth and let it flow through me and into the crucifix, crumbling the bones to dust. I fell to the ground, nearly crushing the pope's skull underfoot. I picked it up with my other hand. I felt no more than a tickle of grace in the skull. Barely enough to have bound the skeleton together and animated it. Certainly not enough to have been working the tricks the pope had done.

"*Ruina!*" the pope said, but this time nothing happened.

"Perhaps you could destroy him and then get around to freeing me,"

Morgana called from across the room, still struggling with the bones holding her.

I lifted the skull so I could look it in the eyes. Well, eye sockets. It was like some twisted production of *Hamlet*.

"He can't do anything now," I said. "The bible was his power."

The pope didn't say anything. The body stopped its aimless wandering and stood still, as if confused.

"Always the damned bibles," Morgana said as Amelia went to free her. "This world would be better off without all of them."

"They do have some uses," I said, drawing the grace from the bible until there was nothing left. I used a significant amount of it to heal my wounds. Then I gave the pope my full attention. "Raphael. Where is he?"

"Such information seems to be the only thing keeping me alive at the moment," the pope pointed out.

I squeezed the skull with my fingers. "I think we have very different definitions of life. But here's the thing. I don't care what you were doing down here before I set foot in this room and I won't care what you do down here when I leave. The only question is what state you want to be in when I walk out of here."

The pope hesitated, but then the skeleton sagged a little as if the pope had accepted defeat. "The angels have hidden him away in a prison where none can find him. Even the popes."

"So this has been another exercise in futility?" Morgana said as she came to my side, brushing finger bones from her legs. "At least you're consistent."

"Someone must know how to find him," I said to the pope. "Who built his prison?"

"Da Vinci," the pope said. "But he disappeared centuries ago."

Morgana grabbed the skull from me and glared at it. "Let me get this straight. We need to find Raphael because he's the only one who can lead us to da Vinci. But the only one who knows how to find Raphael is da Vinci?"

"What do you want with da Vinci?" the pope asked. "I thought you were here for –"

But I never found out why the pope thought we had come because Morgana threw his skull to the ground then, shattering it into pieces. She stomped on each of the shards, grinding them to powder under her feet. The pope's body started wandering in circles again.

"That wasn't very helpful," I pointed out.

"And yet I feel better."

I inspected Gabriel's bible. The glow was gone from it now, and it was just another old, crumbling tome. I opened it and flipped through the pages, but they were all still ash.

"I thought you said that tome was the source of his power," Morgana said. "It certainly doesn't look like much."

I dropped the bible on the throne and carried on to the nearest crypt. I shoved the lid aside to reveal another skeleton in decayed robes inside. This one at least stayed dead. This close, though, I felt more grace in the bones before me. I laid my hand on the skeleton and pulled the grace from it.

"I think the bible was just some sort of tool to steal the grace from these dead popes," I said. "A conduit crafted for such a purpose perhaps."

"Why do they have grace?" Morgana asked. "Were they trading favours with the angels?"

"Probably," I said. "But not the kind of favours you're thinking of. The angels have given them grace over the ages to help the popes further their own agendas."

"Let's get rid of all the other dead ones before they come to life as well." Morgana turned to Amelia. "Will they come to life?"

"Don't waste your power," I told Amelia. "If they were going to come to life like the other one, they would have by now."

I moved to the next casket and opened it. The rags the skeleton wore were a little different but everything else was pretty much the same.

"So we've learned nothing by our little misadventure here," Morgana said. "Will you both let this mad quest go now?"

I drew the grace from this dead pope and eyed the other caskets. "Maybe Raphael was imprisoned here along with these popes. It would be a secure place to keep him."

"Hardly," Morgana said. "We defeated their champion easily. And without most of my court even."

"Amelia defeated the pope," I said. "I was getting crucified. And I suspect a similar fate was in store for you. Now let's search the dead to see what we can find."

But the dead had different ideas. The lids of the crypts were all shoved open at once, and dozens of skeletons in mouldy robes climbed out.

"What was that you said about them not coming to life?" Morgana asked.

As if the situation weren't bad enough, the bones blocking the entrance to the chamber tumbled aside and a new figure stepped into the room.

It was Gabriel, of course.

CHAOS

I went to step in front of Amelia, to get between her and Gabriel, but Morgana had already beaten me to it – so I stepped in front of both of them. Not that it would do much good with the popes surrounding us now. Although I couldn't help but note the popes all turned to Gabriel when he entered the chamber. It was clear who was in charge.

"If you killed Mona Lisa to find me, there's really going to be Hell to pay," I told Gabriel. I wasn't certain any of the angels were capable of killing Mona Lisa, as she was more ancient and powerful than them even. But if one of them stood a chance, it was Gabriel.

He chuckled and waved a hand dismissively at me. "I suspect Mona Lisa would not tell me what I wanted to know even if faced with death. Too much has passed between us. But she is not the only one who knows what you are up to, is she?"

"Judas," I said. Who else could have betrayed me so?

"He told me what Mona Lisa said to you. It was all I needed to know that you would be coming to find Raphael's body next." Gabriel began to walk toward us, and the popes moved aside to let him pass. "I don't think you'll be going anywhere else now, though. So this is your last chance to work with me to find God's bible. Or I'll kill these two slowly before your eyes and condemn them to a worse fate than the pope I placed here."

"If I ever come across that damned bible, I'm going to rip out all the pages and use them to wipe my bloody arse," Morgana said with a snarl.

"You would end your world as well as ours then," Gabriel said. "The bibles of the gods and the holy stories are all that fix the world into being and hold the chaos at bay. Without them, we would be no more than one of your faerie courts – a fleeting moment of madness in an endless sea of even deeper chaos."

As he drew near, I could see cracks in his body that I hadn't noticed before, and chunks of stone missing from his frame. I wasn't sure if they were from our past encounters or from some other battle. Hell, I wasn't even sure why Gabriel was still masquerading as a statue and hadn't taken some other form. But I was determined to open up a few more cracks in him before this day was done. And Gabriel's words had given me an idea.

"We cannot defeat them all," Morgana said softly. "Especially if they have more of those books."

"Let's give them a different book then," I said and nodded at Amelia.

She pulled *Through the Looking-Glass* from her pocket without hesitation and tossed it to me. Gabriel froze, as did the popes.

I slammed some grace down through my fingers and into the book, then tossed it at Gabriel's feet. At the same time, I uttered a single word.

"Chaos."

The floor exploded suddenly in a shower of bone shards, and large, thick tentacles snapped up from the book and started lashing about. They were so black as to be no colour at all, voids in the shapes of tentacles. There were maybe half a dozen of them, each one twice as long as myself and as thick as one of my legs. They radiated that mad grace I had felt with the White Knight, and I felt dizzy in their presence, the world tilting one way and then another. The scent of chrysanthemums filled the air, and then the smell of burned rubber.

"You would release chaos itself into this holy place?" Gabriel cried. "You are more corrupted than I thought!" He waved a hand at the tentacles and the popes surged forward as one.

"What exactly did you summon with that book?" Morgana murmured to me.

"I don't really know," I admitted. "I was just trying to give it a little guidance."

"What kind of guidance?" Morgana asked as one of the tentacles swept to the side, sending popes flying into the depths of the chamber. "Something from your nightmares?"

I backed away from the book before a tentacle could come for us, and I pulled the others after me. "I thought maybe if the power of the bible is somehow interacting with the Wonderland books, then the book could be influenced by other things as well. I was hoping to cause some diversion that we could use to escape." Although a mass of nightmare tentacles wasn't exactly what I'd had in mind.

Gabriel strode forward instead of retreating. He'd never been one to back away from a fight.

"You forget the angels were born to bring order to the chaos." He grabbed one of the tentacles with both hands and began wrestling with it, as if trying to tear it in two. He was grinning, as if this madness made him happy. Maybe it did.

More tentacles lashed out then and wrapped around him, and Gabriel roared in rage. Or maybe glee. But the popes swarmed the other writhing tentacles, grabbing on to them and slowing them with the weight of their numbers.

"I don't think we want to face whoever wins this fight," Morgana said.

"Probably not," I agreed.

We couldn't escape the way we had come, though. There were too many popes in the way, to say nothing of the fact we'd have to get too close to Gabriel and those tentacles if we made our way back across the chamber. But I'd learned over the ages that when someone created a chamber like this, they almost always included a secret exit in case someone like me came along and started wrecking things.

"Amelia, is there another way out?" I asked. I didn't want her to weaken herself more by using her ability, but we had no choice.

She turned and pointed at a stone cross on the wall behind us. "You need to bow down before it and say the words *salvum me*," she said.

"Save me," I said through gritted teeth. "Of course."

There was no way around it, though, so I went over to the cross and kneeled on the bones before it and spoke the words. The bones holding the cross rearranged themselves then, moving to the sides to reveal a dark passageway beyond. I quickly got up and ushered the others into it.

I looked back to Gabriel, who had produced a long sword that burned with white flames from the air. He was using it to cut apart a tentacle now, even as more strange limbs wreaked havoc among the popes, although he paused long enough to raise the sword in salute. He knew we'd won this round. But, like me, he also knew it wasn't over yet.

"It's a shame we couldn't work together," he said. "Imagine the Heaven we could have made of this world."

"That's exactly what I'm afraid of," I said.

I saw several of the popes turn away from the battle, toward me, so I quickly threw myself into the secret passage. I propelled the last of my grace down through my feet and into the bones underfoot, using it to draw those bones up into a wall between us. I don't know what the popes tried to do, but I heard the bones snap and crack behind me, then hiss and bubble as something melted them.

Then I was in the tunnel and moving up in a sharp incline as we left the chamber behind. We quickly ascended, following a number of twists and turns, until the tunnel dead-ended. A stone slab was suspended in the ceiling there, held in place by skeletal hands. There was space to push it to the side, so I slid it through the hands until we could see the inside of a sarcophagus above us. Another stone lid covered the top of the sarcophagus, but I was able to shove it open. We stepped out of the sarcophagus and back into one of the grottoes underneath the basilica. And if you think I'll tell you which sarcophagus it was, you're madder than Puck.

"We're lucky to have escaped that without losing anyone else," Morgana said as we hurried back to the basilica. "What now?"

"We keep looking for Raphael," I said.

She grabbed me by the arm and turned me to look at her. "The whole thing was a trap," she said. "The pope was waiting for us. Gabriel knew exactly where to find us. Again."

"Gabriel knew we would come in search of Raphael," I said. "Which means the dead angel must be nearby or he wouldn't have come looking for us here." I threw off her hand and continued up into the Confessio and back into the nave of the basilica.

"I concede your point," Morgana said, her voice echoing through the basilica, which was empty now. "But we can't possibly find Raphael with Gabriel and an army of dead popes pursuing us."

"Maybe not," I said as I headed for the door. "Or maybe that's exactly the sort of thing to make da Vinci take notice of us."

"Let's collect Puck and get out of here then," Morgana said. "I hope he hasn't gotten into any trouble in our absence."

That was when the screaming started outside the basilica.

THE DEAD MAKE THEIR ESCAPE

We hurried outside to find the square largely emptied out, with only pockets of people remaining, huddled in the colonnades. The ground was broken in places, having been heaved up from some force underneath or torn open in rifts. A black tentacle rose from one such rift and probed the area around it, then was pulled back down.

"What exactly did you summon?" Morgana asked, raising an eyebrow. "And why that of all things?"

"I'm not entirely certain," I said, although I had an idea. The tentacles reminded me of some of the abominations Noah had imprisoned in his ark before his armada had been destroyed in the battle at the Sunken City. My grace and call for chaos must have caused the power leaking out of the bible and into the Wonderland books to transform itself into a monstrosity reminiscent of that battle.

Another tentacle waved from a different rift and smashed into pillars of a nearby colonnade, sending them tumbling to the ground and causing the roof to collapse. The back wall of the colonnade cracked open, and I glimpsed a wall lined with paintings. Then this tentacle snapped back into the rift, too.

"Just once, it would be lovely if you didn't think with your grace first," Morgana said.

"Let's just hope Gabriel and the popes can handle it," I said, trying not to let the doubt I felt carry to my voice.

I turned to the obelisk and saw a half-dozen men and women sprawled unmoving on the ground around the structure – the security guards from inside the basilica. I couldn't tell from this distance if they were dead or just unconscious. They were the least of my concerns, though, as I saw Puck standing atop the obelisk. He had broken off the cross and was swinging it wildly at a statue clinging to the obelisk a few feet below the top. The statue parried Puck's blows with a stone violin – it was one of the angels that had been pursuing us. Like Gabriel, it was deteriorating, with large cracks running the length of its body.

I checked the Holy Door and saw the sketch of Raphael still there, hanging from the spike. Yes, we had definitely made a statement here today. I was worried it was too much of a statement, though, as the people hiding in the colonnades were all recording Puck's battle with the angel on their phones. I pulled the sketch off the spike and handed it to Amelia, who rolled it up and tucked it inside her shirt. I left the spike in the Holy Door. Maybe it would become a relic for someone.

Puck took a two-handed swing at the angel's head, which the angel blocked again. The blow was strong enough to knock stone chips from the violin, though, and bend the cross a little. I felt more than saw the grace coming from it, like tendrils pulling at me, and then I was running across the square toward them. I leapt over the rifts and heard distant shouts drifting up from them.

"Throw me the cross!" I cried to Puck. I figured there was no point trying to be stealthy or blend into what was left of the crowd. If the angel didn't care about being seen by all the tourists then it already had a plan to make sure none of what was happening here got outside of the square. Hopefully that just meant wiping everyone's phones and cameras and a bit of their memories. If it was more than that, well, it wouldn't be the first time an angel had turned on the faithful.

"I think I need it more than you," Puck said, leaping up in the air as the angel swung the violin at his feet.

"I have –" I began, but Morgana cut me off.

"Don't you dare say you have a plan! Not after how the others have worked out."

"Who do you think has a better chance of beating that angel?" I said. "Puck or me?"

Morgana glared at me, then muttered a curse. "Give him the cross. We may as well get this over with."

"But what if I have a plan?" Puck asked.

That drew a laugh from Morgana. "When have you ever had a plan?"

Puck dodged another blow from the violin by somersaulting backward onto the other side of the obelisk. "How am I supposed to defend myself?"

"You could have gone anywhere in this square, but you chose that stage!" Morgana snapped. "Now stop putting on your show and get down here."

Puck grinned and disappeared around the back of the obelisk as the angel scuttled sideways to get at him like a spider, digging its feet and free hand into the obelisk and gouging out great chunks of it. Puck threw himself off the obelisk, flipping through the air and landing atop one of the fallen security guards, who let out a sharp exhalation of air at the impact. So he was still alive.

Puck gave a bow like a stage actor at the end of a performance and then tossed me the cross. I caught it in my left hand and put my right upon the obelisk. I felt the grace in the cross, and the dead in the obelisk. The angel threw itself down at us. I drained all the grace from the cross and shoved it into the obelisk in less time than it took to draw a breath.

A number of things happened then.

I felt the heavenly power of the grace surge through me like a current that filled me with joy and wonder and then left me feeling hollow and brittle in its wake.

The grace ripped through the obelisk, undoing whatever bonds had trapped the spirits within it.

And the dead came rushing out.

They were so ancient and faded that each was little more than a wisp. You probably wouldn't even notice one if you happened upon it. But there were enough of them that they formed a white cloud, like the smoke that rose from the Vatican when a new pope was announced.

I glimpsed faces here and there, crying out in a chorus of howls and wails, and limbs flailing in sudden freedom. Then the cloud ripped apart as the spirits flew in every direction. They streaked across the square in the blink of an eye. Some went up and over the colonnades and disappeared from sight. Others sank into the people huddled there, who fell to the ground and began to shake. Still more slid into the bodies of the security guards, who began to twitch and stir. And a handful threw themselves into the stone body of the angel as it fell toward us, slipping into the cracks in its form and vanishing from sight.

The angel crashed heavily to the ground. It landed close enough that it could have swung the violin at us from its prone position. But instead it began to spasm like the security guards. It stared at me and babbled in a tongue I didn't understand.

"I don't know what's happening," Puck murmured, looking about. "But I approve of your plan nevertheless."

"I freed the spirits trapped in the obelisk," I said. "Some just wanted to escape, but some want to feel what it is to live again, so they're trying to possess the others in the square."

Puck reached for the cross. "Let's finish off the angel while it's occupied then."

I pushed him away. "It'll take us forever to put a dent in that statue without more grace. And it'll cast out those spirits any second now. We need to get out of here while we still can."

As if on cue, the angel fixed me with its gaze. "Blasphemy," it said.

"You're a fine one to talk." I threw the cross at its face. "Have you even been inside that basilica?"

The ground collapsed in pockets around the square then, filling in the rifts. I grabbed Amelia and headed for the edge of the square. It was time to leave. But I saw soldiers gathered there, forcing fleeing tourists into the back of armoured cars. I paused and searched for another way out. My gaze settled on the part of the colonnade the tentacle had wrecked. Now that the dust had settled, I could see that there was indeed some sort of gallery of paintings on the other side of the colonnade wall. I was looking into the Vatican. I remembered the da Vinci sketch of the Sistine Chapel from the scriptorium on Isola Malcontenta then, and the grace I had drawn from it. I changed direction and headed toward the opening.

"Now where are you going?" Morgana asked. "There's no escape that way."

"Maybe not," I said. "But we may yet find da Vinci."

CHAOS CHRISTS

We climbed through the crack in the wall and found ourselves in an artistic madhouse. There was a small gallery on the other side with three paintings I recognized right away: van Gogh's *Pietà*, in which a woman holds the dying Christ in a stark landscape; Chagall's *Le Christ et le peintre*, which depicted the crucifixion as only Chagall could; and Dalí's *L'Annuncio*, which featured a naked Christ caught in mid-ascension, face hidden behind his outstretched hand, while Mary and the angel Gabriel look on.

Only the gallery wasn't exactly *holding* the paintings, because the Christ in each of them was pulling itself from the canvas and out into the room, growing in size and shape to a full-grown man as they did so.

"Cross, please tell me this is your doing," Morgana said, but the tone of her voice told me she already didn't believe that.

"I generally leave the Christs alone," I said. "I think this is more of the chaos at work."

The Dalí Christ came at us then, holding both hands before his head so I couldn't see his face. Which was probably just as well. I stepped aside from the opening in the wall and pulled Morgana and Amelia after me. Puck stood there, grinning at the Christ, until Morgana yanked him out of the way as well.

The Dalí Christ ignored us and went through the crack and out into the square. It left a trail of wet paint footprints behind. Once outside, it spread its arms wide, and the fallen bodies across the square begin to drift toward the sky.

"Why can't you be more like these Christs?" Puck said, shaking his head.

"We should probably get out of here," I said as the Chagall Christ started toward us. I cast about and saw a tall wooden door at the other end of the room, and I pushed Morgana and Amelia toward it.

Just then a shadow fell across the room, as someone blocked the light from the square outside. Gabriel stepped through the crack and into the gallery. His body was scored with fissures and was smoking, but he still had that flaming sword.

"Now what madness have you wrought?" he asked.

"Why does everyone always think I'm to blame?" I muttered.

"I believe you are exactly the one to blame in this case," Morgana said.

The van Gogh Christ lunged at Gabriel with surprising speed, moving so fast that paint spun off it and splattered across the room. A few drops fell upon my arms, and I felt the grace in them, but it was mad grace just like the copy of *Through the Looking-Glass*. The Christ grabbed hold of Gabriel before he could react, spun and slammed him *into* the painting it had just climbed out of. His body sank into the canvas, until his wings hit the cross. He dropped the sword and managed to grab on to the edges of the frame, to stop himself from being shoved in all the way.

"It's trying to crucify him!" Puck cackled. "Should we help?"

"We should run," I said. The Chagall Christ was coming at us now, and I didn't want to be the next one forced into a painting. I'd had enough of that for a lifetime. For all my lifetimes.

Luckily Morgana and Amelia had already gone through the door. Puck and I followed them, slamming the door shut behind us. I wasn't sure if the painted Christ would know how to open a door or not, but I broke into a run just in case.

We were in a hallway adorned with more biblical murals, but thankfully these ones remained on the walls. We made our way to the end, where another wooden door awaited us. I glanced over my shoulder and saw paint pouring through the lock of the door behind us and forming into the shape of the Chagall Christ once more.

"I believe that Christ is chasing us," I said.

"They can be annoying that way," Morgana said.

We passed through a room full of Matisse sculptures, and then another hall lined with paintings by artists that must have been contemporary because I didn't know them. Then we were in another gallery, this one lined with a Francis Bacon study of a pope in a red smock on the left wall and a Graham Sutherland painting of an emaciated Christ hanging on a cross on the right. There was a doorway beyond each of the paintings, shrouded in shadows. And the Chagall Christ stood before the doorways, blocking our exit from the room.

"How did it manage that?" Morgana asked.

"Chaos," Puck breathed.

I didn't know how the painted Christ had managed to get in front of us, but it was blocking our path deeper into the Vatican.

"Do you have any more spikes?" I asked Puck.

"I always have spikes," he said with a grin and produced a handful of long rusty nails.

"Whatever you're thinking of doing, you should probably not do it," Morgana said, backing away. "Let's go back the way we came and hope there is still a path out of this madhouse."

"I'm not leaving here until I find something that points me toward da Vinci," I said.

"Did you not see what that other Christ did to Gabriel?" Morgana asked as the Christ came at us.

"That's what gave me the idea for this," I said and sprang at the Chagall Christ. I hit it with my shoulder and knocked it back toward the Sutherland Crucifixion scene. It was like hitting a wave – paint splashed all over my head and upper body. But the Christ stumbled back, until it collided with the painting behind it. The Christ threw its arms out as it tried to regain its balance, and I rammed one of Puck's spikes into its left hand. It went through the hand and into the painting beyond, driving into the cross. The Christ tried to reach across its body to pull the spike out with its other hand, but I caught its wrist with both my hands. For a moment we strained against each other, and then Puck was at my side, grabbing on to the Christ's arm and helping force it back against the painting. I rammed another spike into its right hand, and now it was pinned to the cross atop the emaciated Christ.

"Look at me!" Puck cried, doing a little dance. "I'm a crucifier! I'm a Judas!"

I wanted to pin him to the painting next for saying that, but I was too tired. Instead, I stepped back out of range of the Chagall Christ's kicking feet and looked at Morgana and Amelia to make sure they were all right.

They hadn't been harmed in the struggle, but Morgana came toward me with an expression I couldn't read.

"We could have all been lost," she said. "Again."

"But we're not," I said. "Now let's continue on and find da Vinci."

She raised a hand to my cheek and held it there for a moment. When she pulled her hand back, it was covered with paint.

"What have you become?" she said.

THE SISTINE CHAPEL'S SECRET

We ventured deeper into the Vatican, winding our way to the Sistine Chapel without encountering another living soul. The entire place must have been shut down. That wouldn't be surprising given what was happening next door, to say nothing of a few rooms behind us. But even though we didn't see anyone else, we were likely being watched. That we were able to just walk into the empty Sistine Chapel told me that whoever was watching wanted to see what we were going to do next.

I had no idea what to do next.

I walked over to the *Last Judgment* fresco at the end of the chapel while the others took in the paintings on all the walls and the ceiling overhead.

"Imagine what I could do with a little spray paint in here," Puck said while gazing up at God and Adam reaching out to each other. "Or a blowtorch."

I considered the angels and saints floating in the sky over the risen dead and the sinners being dragged to Hell by demons. At least the Christ that hung in the centre of the scene didn't resemble me, unlike da Vinci's sketch back in the scriptorium on Isola Malcontenta.

"What is it you see here?" Morgana asked, coming to my side and frowning at the wall. "It looks no different than any of the other ridiculous drawings."

"I don't know," I murmured. "But I think da Vinci tried to leave me a message about this place."

"What message?" she asked. "What are you talking about?"

"There was a sketch of this painting back on the island," I told her. "Only it was me up there instead of Christ. And there was grace in the sketch. Why would da Vinci create a sketch like that if he wasn't trying to send a message?"

A low chuckle echoed through the chapel then, and I knew from the sound of it that it didn't belong to any of us.

"I was wondering if I would ever see you again," a man's voice said. It took me a few seconds to realize it was coming from the painting in front of me.

Then I saw him: A bald man with a wild beard in a filthy, paint-stained robe making his way through the demons and the damned in the lower right corner of the fresco. Walking out of the mouth of Hell itself. And he was actually walking, moving around the other figures that were painted on the wall, until he stepped to the forefront of the fresco and gazed out at us.

"I left that sketch on the island in case you ever needed to find me again," he said, studying me. "Took you long enough."

"Da Vinci," I breathed.

"Oh, thank all the gods," Morgana said. "Even yours. Grab him from the painting and let's get out of here."

"I'm not sure I know how to do that," I said.

"It's probably best you come with me instead," da Vinci said. "They're looking for you and there's no way out now."

"Of course not." Morgana sighed. "Curse you and all your gods."

"And how exactly do we accompany you?" I asked him.

Da Vinci smiled and extended his hand out of the fresco, into the air between the painting and me.

"Take my hand and join the damned," he said.

DA VINCI'S SANCTUARY

I took da Vinci's hand. It was cool to the touch, as if I were holding the hand of a mannequin. He pulled me closer, and just like that I was among the crowd of sinners. It was familiar company.

I hadn't known what to expect, but I was still surprised. I felt heat on my face and arms from the glowing passageway, which was now before me. The light flickered, and the air was filled with the cries of the damned, who struggled with the demons that dragged them toward distant flames. They reached out as if I could do anything to save them. The demons rolled their eyes and laughed. Maybe they knew me.

To my left was the river I had seen in the painting, with the same boat disgorging the same crowd of the damned. Above me, more of them were falling through the air toward us. Beyond them was Christ floating in the sky, Mary at his side. He felt as distant to me as the real Christ. I felt pulled toward him nevertheless, as though he could offer me some salvation I couldn't find for myself.

"I was hoping never to see you again," da Vinci grunted. He squinted in the distance. "Who are your friends? Or are they your enemies? It's always hard to say with you."

I turned to look behind me, but I couldn't see anything but more damned and demons milling about.

"Friends," I said. "And they need sanctuary as well, for all the angels of Heaven are after us."

"That's nothing new," da Vinci said. He reached out his hand again, into the writhing crowd, and then pulled Morgana forth. "You didn't tell me they were faerie." He wiped his hand on his filthy tunic.

"A faerie *queen*," Morgana said. She looked around and muttered a curse. "All the centuries I've managed to avoid your ridiculous little mythos. And now here I am, trapped in the midst of it."

"If it's any consolation, I know how you feel," I said.

"I could put you both back in the chapel," da Vinci said, yanking Puck through next. He continued to grip Puck's hand and frowned, and it was the faerie who pulled away. "Curious," da Vinci muttered.

"You haven't seen anything yet," I said.

Da Vinci took Amelia from the crowd of the damned and stared at her. "Just when I thought I knew everything there was. What an intriguing mystery you lot are."

I took a moment to look around. The scene we found ourselves in was alive yet strangely unchanging. The demons wrestled with the damned but didn't seem to pull them any deeper into the cave. The poor souls in the boat hung on to the sides and screamed, not wanting to go any farther – and they didn't. Even those falling from above didn't seem to descend any as they frantically twisted and flailed to avoid their fate. Christ remained as far away as ever. It was much like the time the angels trapped me in a different painting, although *Hadleigh Castle* had been a little more relaxing.

Then da Vinci pushed past me and headed back toward the cave. "I wouldn't tarry if I were you," he said, twisting to slide between a pair of demons on one side and some sort of snake-creature half coiled around a man on the right. "The angels are nearly here and they will notice you don't belong."

"And I thought that ghost play was the worst place you had ever brought me," Morgana said.

"I rather like this place," Puck said. He patted one of the demons on its rump. "This corner of it anyway. The other parts look rather dull."

We followed da Vinci through the crowd of the damned and the demons. I felt hot breath upon me, and the lost souls being dragged away to whatever fate awaited them cried out in tongues I hadn't heard in centuries. I didn't tell them I couldn't help because I didn't want to leave them completely without hope. So I said nothing as I went into Hell.

The tunnel sloped down before me, with more monstrous demons silhouetted against the distant flames. But da Vinci moved to the side instead, to a door in a rock wall that was hidden behind the bodies of the damned. He produced a key and used it to unlock the door, then made the key disappear again without me seeing where it went.

"The damned cannot escape their fate, but sometimes the demons act in peculiar fashions and attempt to enter my sanctuary," he said. "I must take precautions."

He opened the door to reveal a study that belonged in some palace or villa, not a cave connected to Hell. It was around twenty metres wide and the same across, with white walls and a high ceiling painted with a blue sky and a scattering of clouds. The ceiling gave off a natural light as if we were standing outside, although there were deep shadows along the right wall where a bed rested.

The centre of the room was crowded with tables covered in sketches and journals, with quills and pots of ink here and there. The wall to the left was blocked by a dozen easels with half-finished paintings set upon them. Some of the paintings were portraits of people vaguely familiar to me – perhaps they were acquaintances that we had both known. But there was also a painting of what I was pretty sure was a Valkyrie, and another of Victory striding knee-deep through a lake of blood.

I didn't give the room much more than a quick glance before I saw what was on the opposite wall. A painting of a crypt, with walls made of the bones of the dead, much like the chamber of the popes. A platform made of full skeletons intertwined with each other was in the centre of the crypt. Upon the skeletal platform rested the body of an angel, its limbs broken and bent at unnatural angles and its wings torn off and cast onto the floor. I recognized the angel right away as Raphael, the same angel in the sketch we had taken from Borromeo's island.

"I don't suppose you have any wine?" Puck asked.

Da Vinci pointed at an amphora on one of the tables. "Drink all you like. It replenishes itself."

"This place is Heaven then, not Hell," Puck said. He busied himself testing the limits of the amphora while Morgana wandered over to the paintings along the left wall to inspect them. Amelia studied the painting of the angel, and da Vinci studied her.

"I have never seen such a creature before," he said. "Although I have theorized it was possible. Where did she come from?"

"From me, I suppose," I said. "And her mother, who is dead and ash now. And also the faerie queen over there." I nodded at Morgana.

"Hmm. I imagine there is an interesting tale to be told, but that is not why you are here," da Vinci said.

"No," I said. "We need your help."

"Many have sought me before. But none have found me."

"That's why we brought Raphael's soul to you. You didn't pull us into this painting because you missed my company, did you?"

Amelia placed the sketch down on the table, still rolled up. Da Vinci gazed upon it for a moment, then smiled.

"I sensed it the moment you nailed it to the Holy Door in the basilica," he said. "And I suspected you would come this way. You have always been one to add more troubles to the considerable troubles you already own."

"He is very predictable that way," Morgana said.

Da Vinci stepped over to the sketch and unrolled it. He stared at it for a long moment.

"And what is it you would have of me?" he asked.

"I need to find my way into a book. You seemed like the person to talk to about such things." I waved my hand at his study.

"What book?" he asked, not looking away from the sketch.

I told him everything because I didn't see any point in keeping things from him. He listened in silence until I was done, then remained silent for a time longer. I looked at Amelia considering the dead angel. Morgana was leaning close to the painting of Victory and whispering in her ear. Puck had staggered to da Vinci's bed with the amphora. I imagine we made quite the tableaux. If any art critics could have seen us, they would have been talking for ages.

"Books are a different sort of magic than a painting," da Vinci finally said. "But I think I may know of a way. First, I need your help with one thing."

"It's always one more thing," Puck called from the bed. "When do we get to the last thing?"

"Hush," Morgana said. Puck promptly fell asleep.

"I must reunite Raphael's soul with his body," da Vinci said.

I felt like I needed an amphora of never-ending wine myself. "And how exactly do we do that?" I asked.

Da Vinci tapped the sketch with his hand. "We need to take this into there." He pointed at the painting of the angel's crypt. "Once we are in the crypt, I believe I know what to do next to restore Raphael's soul."

"You believe?" Morgana asked.

Da Vinci shrugged. "I have never had the opportunity to test my hypothesis. But I have spent centuries working it out." He waved at the sketches and journals on the tables.

"So you want us to just walk into a painting within a painting, which we can't get out of on our own," Morgana said. "A painting of a crypt no less."

"The crypt is a real place if that's what you're worried about," da Vinci said. "It is deep in the necropolis under St. Peter's Basilica. This painting is simply my own personal window into that crypt, which I constructed over time. But you don't have to use it to enter or exit the crypt. You can try the basilica."

"The same absurd temple to your dead god that we just narrowly escaped from," Morgana said. She stepped to me. "How do you know you can even trust this man? This mural we have sought sanctuary in looks like it could be home to the very angels that pursue us. Perhaps he is in league with them."

"I didn't paint *The Last Judgment*," da Vinci said. "That was Michelangelo. Although I understand your point. He was allied with the angels, after all."

"I had heard rumours that there was more to his paintings than talent," I said.

"They favoured him with their grace," da Vinci said.

"But not you. For you were rivals."

"No." Da Vinci looked at the dead angel. "They did not favour me. Except for Raphael. But therein lies the problem, for he also favoured Michelangelo."

"Are you hidden away in here out of jealousy then?" Morgana asked. "You seek to spoil your romantic rival's accomplishment by corrupting it from within?"

"I did not see him as a rival," da Vinci said. "When Raphael was with me that was enough. What he did with others did not concern me."

"I've heard that before," Morgana muttered.

"But the same could not be said for Michelangelo. When Raphael finally tired of him, Michelangelo would not let him go. It was Michelangelo who betrayed Raphael. We tried to escape but . . ." He trailed off. "If you have the sketch from Borromeo, then you know the rest of the story."

"I do, but Morgana makes a good point," I said. "Why are you hiding in this painting of all places?"

"The angels have never sought me here. Perhaps they never thought I would enter one of the greatest works of my rival. But I have used his own painting against him to plan how to undo his betrayal of Raphael."

I thought things over, but what da Vinci said was enough for me. Besides, it wasn't like we had any other options.

"All right, if you have a plan then let's get on with it," I said.

"There's just one problem," da Vinci said.

"Of course there is." I sighed. "Let me guess, you don't actually know how to enter that painting yet."

"Oh no, that's the easy part. The hard part will be defeating the dead Raphael long enough that I can carry out the procedure."

I stared at the crypt, rubbed my eyes, then stared some more. "Explain it to me like I don't understand, because he looks dead to me."

"You should know better than any that an angel does not stay dead if you don't drain it of its heavenly grace," da Vinci said. "Raphael has slowly been healing all this time. But that body has no soul. It has returned to life empty of the Raphael that I knew and loved. It is no more than a mindless revenant now, bound by the decree of the other angels to destroy any who enter its tomb."

We all considered the painting for a time. I liked it considerably less now.

"That's no problem for Cross," Morgana said. "He kills angels all the time. And lots of other things, too. Why, he's gotten most of my court killed."

I shook my head. "I can take an angel when I have grace, but right now I'm as empty of that as Raphael's body is a soul."

"Perhaps there is a way to find what you need," da Vinci said with a small smile.

ASCENSION

We left the study and returned to *The Last Judgment.* We stayed deep in the crowd to avoid being seen by anyone outside the painting. The demons whispered greetings to me in some infernal tongue, or perhaps it was invitations. It was hard to tell from the leers. The damned moaned at the sight of me, because they knew by now that I would be of no use to them.

I tried peering around one of the demons and out of the painting, into the Sistine Chapel. I couldn't see anything but more damned stretching toward a vanishing point. It was a painter's trick. I'm as good a painter as I am a poet, which meant I'd never figure it out.

"There's no one out there at the moment," da Vinci said. "But I suspect that will soon change. We don't have much time."

"Time for what, exactly?" Morgana asked.

"Something I'd really rather not do," I said.

I made my way along a sliver of shoreline at the bottom of the painting and climbed up on some rocks overlooking the river. A group of angels hung over me, some of them blowing on long horns. I recalled there being a bit about that in the Book of Revelation, but it had been a long time since I'd read it. Their horns made sounds like trumpets, only very far away. The angels looked disappointed but only mildly so, as if they were used to disappointment. Some of the others were holding books open and one of them was facing my way. Given the nature of the painting, I figured the books listed the names of the damned and the saved. My name was written in the book – I could see it over and over. I didn't know which book it was, though.

I reached up and caught hold of one of those horns and used it to pull myself onto the angels' little cloud. They gave me disapproving looks, but I was as used to that as they were to disappointment. I lingered there for a moment, hoping to sense some grace in them. That would have been the easier option. But there was nothing, so I carried on.

Another cloud hovered over me, with a man dangling his own flayed skin from one hand. A neat trick that, and presumably an impossible one for any regular mortal. I had once seen an angel flay itself in an underground bar in Berlin, but this man didn't strike me as an angel. I figured him for a saint or some other forgotten character. All that mattered was his skin hung low enough I could climb up it like I had the horn.

Then I was standing on the cloud just below Christ, who wore only a wisp of cloth that ran around his genitals. It wouldn't do to show his real body. People might get ideas, and we all know what the religious texts have to say about that. He gazed down at me with what I could only call disdainful curiosity.

"Don't give me that look," I said. "You don't know the kind of world you left me."

Mary was at his side, curled away so she didn't have to set her eyes on me. I couldn't blame her. I was no doubt the sort of son that made you regret your life choices.

But I wasn't here for their approval. I was here for the grace I felt within my namesake. It leaked out of the holes in his hands and feet.

"Raphael gifted Michelangelo's brushes with some of his grace," da Vinci called from the damned below. "The ones that he used to paint Christ. It was the only way he could make his dull works so compelling."

"I've never known the angels to share their grace unless there was something in it for them," I said. "Was it because they were lovers?"

"Because he foresaw this day and knew you would need grace," Amelia said. "It was the reason he agreed to be Michelangelo's lover."

Da Vinci stared at her, then up at Christ. "Fool," he breathed. He must not have known.

"Save your energy," I said to Amelia. "I've got it from here." I reached up and laid my hands on Christ's feet, and I felt the grace flow from him into me. His eyes widened, then grew still.

"Sorry about that," I said. "If I find more, I'll come back and give it to you."

I think both of us knew that was a lie.

The flow of grace ended too quickly. There had been enough in him that I could do some minor miracle, but I wouldn't be raising anyone from the dead with it. Still, it was better than the emptiness that had been inside of me.

I felt a different feeling then, a sense of being watched. Mary was still turned away from me, though, and when I glanced around the painting everyone else was looking elsewhere as well. It was as if they were all embarrassed to see what I had just done. Or maybe at what I had become.

No, it wasn't any of them.

Someone was watching me from the Sistine Chapel.

"We are discovered," da Vinci said. "We must abandon this place quickly."

I hurried back down the way I had come and retreated back toward Hell. I hated to show the angels where da Vinci was hiding, but there was nothing to be done now.

We re-entered the studio and da Vinci lit a candle, even though the light hadn't changed any. He touched it to the sketches and journals, and they caught fire immediately. The flames quickly raced along the table and jumped to the neighbouring ones. The fire and smoke were enough to rouse Puck, who cheered at the sight.

"Can we not take them with us or hide them away?" I asked. I couldn't even imagine what sort of secret knowledge was burning up before my eyes.

"I remember everything I've worked out here," da Vinci said. "Perhaps I'll record them again someday."

"I'll burn the paintings," Puck said, leaping off the bed and hurrying over to the tables.

Da Vinci held up a hand to block him. "Leave them, for I have hidden a few surprises among their number, for intruders. We burn only the one." He took a scrap of flaming parchment and touched it to the painting of the dead angel. The canvas caught fire as quickly as the papers and began to burn. "We must hurry through now, while we still can."

Morgana arched her brows at the burning painting. "After you."

Da Vinci smiled and stepped into the painting, and just like that he was in the crypt. He didn't turn and help us into it this time. Instead, he just stood there with the sketch of Raphael in his hands, looking at the dead angel laid out before him.

I stepped in after him. It was like stepping into another tunnel, only this one was made of bones. They stretched out past me, to another vanishing point in the distance. Da Vinci and the dead angel shrunk away to nothing there, then snapped back. Only they were all out of shape, with limbs sticking out at weird angles like some sort of cubist painting. Gradually they flowed into their proper shapes, as if they were actually made of paint, and then I was in the crypt with them.

I turned to give a word of warning, so Morgana and the others would know what to expect. But they were already stepping out of the burning wall behind me, blinking as if they were trying to make sense of what they now saw.

I looked for da Vinci's studio, but there was no sign of it. There was just a rectangle of ash on the bones that made up the wall, the same dimensions as the painting. I suspected no one would be able to follow us through that.

I turned back to da Vinci, just in time for the dead angel to leap off the platform it lay upon and run me through with a sword made of fused bones.

MICHELANGELO'S SECRET

Perhaps I could have dodged Raphael's blade with the grace I had taken from the Christ in *The Last Judgment*. But Amelia was standing directly behind me, and if I'd stepped aside then the angel would have skewered her. So instead I lunged at it to try and close the distance before its arm reached full extension.

The blade went in my right side. It hurt as bad as all the other times I'd been stabbed – it never gets any easier. I managed not to scream or swear or make too many other noises this time, though, as I didn't know if there were any other angels nearby to hear. I reflexively twisted to the right to get away from the blade and snapped my left hand up at the same time. I caught hold of Raphael's throat, pushing the angel off balance. Between that and me stepping in, it wasn't able to strike with full force, so the sword only sank a few inches into me. I hammered down on Raphael's sword arm with my right hand then, using grace to add extra force to the blow.

It probably wouldn't have done much to an angel that hadn't been dead for hundreds of years, but Raphael's limbs were still bent and twisted at odd angles from whatever torture its fellow angels had inflicted upon him and hadn't fully healed yet. The arm snapped under my blow, and Raphael's fingers let go.

I tried to grab the hilt of the bone sword, which was still stuck in me, but Raphael gripped my left arm and twisted to the side, trying to break it like I had broken its arm. I had no choice but to go with the motion. I was flipped through the air and landed hard on my back on the platform.

The hard landing left me too dazed to do anything for a couple of seconds.

With an angel, a couple of seconds can be the difference between life and death. I knew even as I lay there, trying to collect my senses, that I wouldn't be able to stop Raphael.

But Raphael didn't come for me. Instead, it spun and lunged for Amelia, who stood looking at it with the same curious expression as when she'd regarded the painting of the crypt.

Morgana threw herself between Amelia and the angel with a snarl, but it was Puck that actually stopped the angel, at least for a few more seconds. He leapt at it and smashed the amphora down on its head, shattering the clay jug. Wine splashed everywhere, and the angel stumbled a few steps, enough that Morgana was able to pull Amelia away from its reaching hands.

I rolled off the platform, took a deep breath and pulled the sword from my body. It hurt in the way such things hurt and I nearly fell back to the ground. Then I saw Raphael straighten and turn to Amelia once more. I ran at the dead angel, sword in hand.

Morgana and Amelia darted behind me, and Raphael went to follow them. It opened itself up to me as it did so, and I buried the blade in its heart.

Grace spilled out of the wound and I breathed it in, replenishing myself. The angel tried the same thing I had, grabbing my neck with one hand and striking my sword arm with the other. I quickly used its own grace to harden my skin to the strength of stone so it couldn't crush my throat or break my arm. I felt so heavy I didn't think I could run anymore, so I hung on to Raphael. And I took in more of the grace that bled from its wound.

We strained against each other for a moment, like Michelangelo's *Two Wrestlers*. And then da Vinci came out of the shadows with the sketch holding Raphael's soul. He embraced the angel's dead body, pressing the sketch into its back. The angel spasmed, as if having a seizure. The paper melted into the dead angel's skin, and the charcoal flowed from it like ink, into the angel.

The angel relaxed his grip on my throat and arm, and I pulled the sword free for another strike. I hesitated, though, because da Vinci still clung to Raphael's body.

The angel fell to his knees, sliding from da Vinci's embrace. Da Vinci stared down at him for a moment, then nodded and stepped around him. He came over to me.

"Give me the sword," he said.

I looked back and forth between them, then flipped the sword around and offered it to him hilt first.

Da Vinci took it from me and then turned and slid the blade into the angel's heart. He struck a mere inch from where I had, but the effect of his blow was far different. Raphael opened his eyes wide as he stared up at da Vinci. He let out a long breath, filled with more grace. And then he slid off the blade to the floor. He was still now, not drawing any more breath. The grace flowed out of him like blood.

"Angels don't usually go down that easily," I said, for I wasn't certain that he was dead.

"Angels don't usually want to die," da Vinci said. He squatted down beside Raphael and laid a hand on the angel's breast.

I cast a glance at the others. Puck was staring down sadly at the remains of the amphora. Morgana stood with Amelia on the other side of the platform, watching warily.

"The angel was trying to kill you," I said to Amelia. I didn't think it had even meant to stab me. It had been going for Amelia and I had simply been in the way.

"The revenant had little consciousness without its soul," Amelia said. "It sensed I was an abomination like itself. The angel wanted to die, so in its state of mind it tried to do to me what it could not do to itself because of its bindings."

"Perhaps you don't belong in this world any more than the angels," Morgana said. "But you are not an abomination like they are. You are one of the faerie court." She brushed the hair from Amelia's face.

I should have said something, but I just turned away to see da Vinci pull the sword out of Raphael and toss it to the floor. He produced a small crystal vial the size of an inkpot from his robes and held it against Raphael's chest. The dying angel's blood flowed into it. When the vial was full, da Vinci stood and put a stopper in it and then held it out to me.

"It will serve well enough as ink," he said. "Combined with the faerie magic of the journal where your Alice seems to have taken refuge and the grace you have taken from Raphael, you should be able to find a way in."

"And if I can't?" I asked.

"If the blood of an angel isn't good enough ink to work your magic, then there is nothing that will help you."

I nodded and took the vial from him. It felt heavier than it should have, but perhaps that was just exhaustion setting in. Or maybe my own blood loss from the wound in my side. I slipped the vial into a pocket and inspected the crypt. It was bone all the way around. I didn't see a door anywhere.

"So how exactly do we get out of here?" I asked.

"The angels meant this to be an unescapable prison," da Vinci said. "It is buried deep in the Earth, beneath the necropolis even, with no entrance or exit. At least, that's what the angels think."

"You have another painting that can get us out of here?" Morgana asked.

"Or another jug of wine?" Puck asked.

"I have neither," da Vinci said. "But Michelangelo created this place, and he could not let Raphael go so easily. He built a secret passage that the angels did not know about. We just have to find it."

"How do you know there's a secret passage if you don't know where it is?" I asked.

"It's what I would have done." He lifted up Raphael and laid him on the platform. The sketch melted into Raphael's back was now a blurry mess of charcoal. The angel appeared less substantial, as if he were withering away.

"Let's hurry up and discover the passage before the angels find their way in here," I said and moved around the crypt, searching for a way out. The bones that made up the walls weren't even mortared together. I could see there were more bones behind the first layer of bones. Who knew how far the layers of the dead carried on?

Puck tried pushing the platform, but it didn't move.

"Too obvious," da Vinci said, shaking his head. "Even for Michelangelo."

"If we're trapped in here forever, I'm eating you first," Puck told him.

"I don't think you'd find me to your taste," da Vinci said.

"My tastes might surprise you," Puck said with a grin.

I walked the walls, looking for gaps in the bones that would reveal the secret passage, or perhaps hidden switches or levers. I didn't see anything until I came across a skull in one of the corners. It looked out into the room, and I could see its left side appeared smoother, polished even. It was like the statues that people kissed and the part they kissed got worn smooth.

I took hold of the skull, wrapping my fingers around the place where it was smoother, and shifted it so it was facing away from the room. The back of it was worn as well.

"What did you find?" Morgana asked.

"I'm not sure." I turned to study the room again. Then I saw it: The skulls in each of the other corners stared into the room like the first one had. I went over to the next one. It was worn smooth on the sides as well. I turned its face away from the room just like the first one.

Morgana did the same with the third, and then da Vinci nodded and stepped to the fourth.

"So simple it's easy to overlook," he said and turned the last skull.

The bones of the north wall receded then and pulled away to either side to form a hallway. That trick of perspective again. The hallway ended in a white rectangle of light in the distance. A figure was silhouetted there, sitting on a chair with a book in one hand. For a moment I thought maybe the angels had found us after all. But he had his back to me and was looking to the side.

I motioned for the others to be quiet and slipped down the hall toward him, moving as quietly as I could on a floor made of bones. Drawing near, I saw he was a giant of a man, for he was taller than me even sitting down. And more muscular as well. The horns atop his head did little to reassure me.

He hadn't moved the entire time, though, and when I was within arm's reach I saw why. He was a statue. Only he wasn't cracked and worn by the elements like the angels. He was as polished as if he'd been carved only yesterday.

Da Vinci came up behind me then, making no effort to be quiet. "I should have known," he sighed.

The statue made no sign it had heard him, so it must have really been a statue. "Who is it?" I asked.

"Moses," da Vinci said. He went up to the statue and turned sideways to slide past it. "Hurry now, for I do not know how long the passage will last."

I passed the statue the same way he had and found myself in another church, but smaller this time. I stood on a stone ledge raised slightly above a marble floor. An altar with a golden canopy supported by four pillars was a few dozen metres before me. The far wall housed a golden balcony with an organ for the church. The dome above the altar was decorated with more painted frescoes, while two rows of wooden pews stretched across the nave to a pair of double wooden doors. The church was empty and dark except for recessed lights in the ceiling that cast more shadows than light.

I turned around to look the way I had come. The statue of Moses was part of a larger sculpture that stretched two storeys high. He was flanked by statues of people in robes that I imagined were notables in their day, but I didn't recognize any of them.

"The Tomb of Pope Julius the Second," da Vinci said. "We are still in Rome, in the Basilica of San Pietro in Vincoli."

"There's another pope in here?" Morgana asked as she came out from behind Moses with Amelia. "They are like roaches."

"It was originally meant to be a monumental tomb for Pope Julius the Second at Saint Peter's Basilica," da Vinci said. "But Michelangelo had a falling out with the pope and it was moved here and finished on a smaller scale, with no actual chamber for a body. It always seemed like there was more to the story. I suspect Michelangelo created whatever dispute he had with the pope so he could hide his secret passage to Raphael's crypt here. He would have had enough influence that he could have asked to worship at this basilica in solitude and travelled back and forth with none the wiser."

"You artists are a devious bunch," Puck said, following the others out and juggling three bones. "I should have spent more time consorting with your like."

"Let's close the passage then and get out of here before someone notices us," I said. "Any idea how we do that?"

Da Vinci stroked his tangled beard. "I believe the way to close the passage is to turn the skulls back to face the room once more. To leave them facing the other way would be risky, after all. If the angels have their own way of entering the crypt, they might notice the skulls had been moved. There is probably some mechanism that delays the passage from closing that would have given Michelangelo time to exit back here."

"If you're wrong, whoever goes back there to try it risks being trapped," I said.

"That is why I will go," he said. "That and I wish to spend some time alone with Raphael before he fades away entirely to whatever Heaven awaits him."

"I hoped you would journey with us," I said.

"I have spent these past centuries watching over Raphael," da Vinci said. "I no longer wish to be involved with the matters of angels or mortals. I will take some time to mourn Raphael, and then I will travel the world for a time to see what has changed."

I nodded. "You're in for some surprises."

"I certainly hope so," he said.

"Safe travels then." I offered him my hand. He clasped it with both of his, which were still smeared with Raphael's blood.

"And safe travels to you," he said. "I hope you are able to free this Alice from her prison."

With that he returned to the hall of bones behind Moses. A moment later the bones faded away and there was nothing but stone behind the statue. I looked Moses up and down and realized I should have asked da Vinci why he had horns on his head. But then maybe some things in this world are just meant to be mysteries.

We went through the wooden doors of the basilica and out into the streets of Rome. It was night now, and the sounds of sirens were in the distance.

"Back to England then?" Morgana asked.

I nodded. "Let's go find Alice."

TO THOSE WE HAVE LEFT BEHIND

We made our way back across the continent by means of trains, stolen cars, cabs and at one point a school bus. The less said about that the better, although the school bus did have a first aid kit I used to clean and bandage the wound in my side. It was an ugly hole, but the fact that I wasn't dead yet meant it probably wouldn't kill me. Thankfully, my body has a hell of an immune system, so I rarely have to worry about infection.

At a café somewhere along the way we saw a news segment on the television about a gas leak and explosion at St. Peter's Basilica that had caused severe damage to the area and hallucinations in scores of tourists. There was no footage from the scene, however – the angels had been at work suppressing the incident. It was probably just as well. Sometimes the truth is best not known.

We returned to the beach where Coal had left us. It was evening again, and a cool wind swept off the water and chilled us. I was hoping the inflatable Coal had given us was still there, tucked in the bushes, so we could use it to cross the Channel. I'd done crazier things. Although, granted, I hadn't survived them all.

I was surprised, however, to see Coal's boat anchored a hundred metres or so off the shore. I didn't see Coal, though, and no lights were visible in the cabin.

"I've got a bad feeling about this," I said.

"How could things possibly get worse?" Morgana asked.

We pulled the inflatable from the bushes and rowed it out to Coal's boat. There was no sound from the boat beyond the lap of water against its hull. I pulled myself aboard and found it empty. There was no sign of Coal in the cabin or anywhere else. There was only a half-full bottle of whisky on the table in the cabin, with an empty glass beside it.

"Maybe he ventured ashore to look for us," Morgana said. "Or to fetch provisions."

"I hope he brings back more spirits," Puck said, picking up the bottle and taking a long drink from it.

I nodded at Amelia, and she looked out at the ocean.

"He's in a current several leagues away," she said. "Deep down, where light cannot reach."

"So no more spirits then." Puck sighed.

I grabbed the whisky from Puck and stepped to the side of the boat. I took a long drink and then another.

"Maybe he fell overboard," Morgana said.

"Maybe," I said, although neither of us believed that.

I gave Coal a moment of silence, then started the engine and hauled up the anchor. I took us away from that beach and headed back to England. I kept the bottle with me. Coal wasn't the first person I'd gotten killed simply because he knew me, and he likely wouldn't be the last, but it still stung. I needed something to dull the pain. But the whisky ran out and the pain didn't.

I searched the boat while we crossed. I was looking for clues as to what had happened to Coal, but of course I didn't find any. I was also looking for a weapon or anything else I could use, but I didn't find that either. I did find a set of car keys, though, which I pocketed.

We reached the marina where Coal's boat had been docked the next morning. I eased the boat into his slip and killed the engine, and Morgana tied us off. We stepped onto the dock and I turned and gave the boat one last look.

"We should set it free to drift on the tides," Puck said.

"Coal wouldn't like that," I said. "It's still a good boat. Someone else will make use of it."

We left it there and went to the nearby car park. I hit the unlock button on the key fob as we wandered, until we found Coal's car – a Volvo as weathered as Coal had been.

"Is there nothing better?" Morgana asked, surveying the parking lot. But it was a marina for working sailors, so the vehicles were all in similar states of disrepair.

"We don't want to attract attention," I said, getting behind the wheel and starting the engine.

"I think the ship has sailed on that point," Morgana said, settling into the passenger's seat.

Puck and Amelia got in the back, where Puck found another half-full bottle of whisky underneath some rags that looked as if they had been used for cleaning engine parts. "To those we have left behind," he said and passed the bottle around so each of us could drink from it.

And then we drove back to Christ Church to save Alice.

THE DOOR TO THE WONDER LANDS

We entered Christ Church the same way as before, by joining a tour group walking into the building. This day was grey and chill, so the people in the group mostly huddled in their coats and paid little attention to us.

We made our way straight to the library and up to the second floor, where there were only a couple of students and a sole librarian. They were gathered around a table looking at a book the librarian was handling with white gloves. They didn't notice us come up the stairs or take the letter from the display case once more.

I returned to the shelf with the copy of Homer and found it still covered in a thick layer of dust. There were no signs it had been handled by me or anyone else recently. I pulled it from the shelf and slid the letter inside its pages.

The book changed in my hand again, transforming into the green volume with the icy cursive writing on the cover: *The Elements of Fancy*. The doorway was back in the middle of the shelves, too, and we quickly stepped through it and closed the door behind us.

The small study was the same as we had left it, with the wooden desk and chair carved with curious characters in the middle of the room, facing the opposite wall. The scattered papers remained atop the desk alongside the quill and inkpot. Everything was still damp and the smell of salt water lingered.

I pulled the journal from the bottom drawer, then set it down on the desk. I felt that same bit of grace in it that I had before. I was tempted once again to use the grace I had to heal the wound in my side, which continued to ache. But I knew I would need it for more important things.

I sat in the chair and the others gathered around the desk. I flipped through the stained pages with their strange waves of ink that hinted at the shapes of creatures I couldn't quite comprehend. Then I paused, for there was something else . . .

"What is it?" Morgana asked, looking back and forth between the book and me.

"The journal seems lighter," I said. "As if it's missing pages."

"So what if it is? It's a magic journal. Is the page we need still there?"

I turned to the end of the journal and there she was: Alice amid the ruins, fallen stone blocks all around her. Characters from Wonderland were in the background now, fighting with one another. The White Rabbit ripped the throat from the Hatter with fierce fangs, while the Cheshire Cat mauled a figure that was half playing card, half man. Alice continued to fight the angel erupting from the bible at her feet, trying to force it back into the book's pages. She did not turn her head to look at me this time, though.

"It's rather different," I said.

"It was created by the Chaos Court," Morgana said, as if that explained everything.

I put the missing pages from my mind and took out the vial that da Vinci had given me. I pulled out the stopper, and the air smelled of cinnamon, although I didn't know if it was from the angel's blood or some effect of the room. I poured some of the blood into the inkpot and then picked up the raven's quill. I hesitated as I considered the mad scene on the page.

"Let us enter the journal and snatch Alice while we still can," Morgana said. "Hurry and draw us on the page."

Puck let out a cheer and smashed the empty whisky bottle on the desk, then brandished the jagged remnants at the journal. I hadn't even known he was still carrying the bottle.

I dipped the quill in the angel's blood and then drew us on the page in a semicircle around Alice, protecting her from the other characters in the mad scene. My rendering was unusually accurate, which I attributed to the blood – I've never been much of an artist. Or maybe it was the quill, or perhaps the room itself. Who knew? Sometimes it's best not to dwell too much on the creative process.

Satisfied with the drawing, I sat back and waited. What I was waiting for, I didn't know. Maybe for the ink to start swirling and suck us down into the page, maybe for a tunnel to open up into the page like it had into da Vinci's painting of Raphael's crypt.

"How long does this sort of thing usually take?" Puck asked. He poked the journal a bit, as if to hurry it along.

I stared at Alice. "She's lost."

"Maybe," Morgana said. "But perhaps we can find her yet."

Something in her voice drew my gaze toward her, and then I saw what she was looking at. A new door had appeared in the far wall. The door was painted white, but the paint was peeling to reveal, well, nothing underneath. It was as if the spots where the paint had fallen away simply didn't exist. There was no wood, no wall, nothing at all.

"I don't understand," Puck said. "I thought we were going into the book."

I set the quill on the desk and put the vial of blood away. Then I stood and went around to the door. "I was wrong all along. Alice isn't in the journal. The journal is just the key that unlocks the door to where she is really hiding."

"And where is that?" Puck asked.

"The Wonder Lands," I said and opened the door.

THE WONDER LANDS

There was another room on the other side – or rather, the remains of a room. It had been a small library with wooden bookshelves lining the walls. The wood was a deep purple in colour and uneven in width and depth. Many of the shelves were broken, and all were empty of books. A small table made of the same wood and two stuffed chairs had been overturned in the middle of the room. Dried bloodstains marked the floor.

The opposite wall had been knocked down, and chunks of stone littered the ground. There was no other door that I could see. On the other side of the fallen wall was a wasteland. A grey rocky plain stretched to a forest in the distance, with large pools of water here and there. The sky overhead was made of churning orange clouds, and I heard the sound of distant thunder. The air smelled of the sea one moment, rotting garbage the next, then . . . was that rosemary?

"This is the place, isn't it?" I asked Morgana. "The Wonder Lands."

She crossed the room and stood at the ruined wall, gazing out at the strange landscape. "It is the home of the Chaos Court. Or rather, it used to be."

I joined Morgana and then turned to look back at the library. Through the broken wall I could see it was the end of a wing of a great mansion. The building was several hundred feet long and made of different materials at different places. The library's walls were stone but they gave way to white wood, then glass, then melted black stone, then sheets of emerald. There were stained glass windows with abstract patterns and shutters made of what appeared to be leather. Sections of the mansion were charred from some fire or maybe fires, and smoke still drifted from the wreckage in places.

"What happened to it?" I asked. "Did the angels do this?"

"It was the chaos," Puck breathed.

Morgana nodded. "The chaos is leaking back into the glamour the Chaos Court created. Soon it will be no more."

"How much time before this place is lost?" I asked.

"There's no way of knowing," Morgana said. "That's what makes it chaos. Years, perhaps. Or maybe mere minutes."

"So we're racing against the clock, but the clock is broken," I said.

"A broken clock is right twice a day," Puck said. "I heard that from one of the fey the angels killed."

Morgana pointed past the far end of the mansion, to where the plain abruptly ended at a sea. Only it was no normal body of water. It was a churning mass of . . . well, I didn't know how to describe it other than nothingness. Yet in that nothingness shapes and colours appeared and then melted away, lightning flashed in every shade of the rainbow and waves of it fell upon the land and carried pieces of rock and soil away to disappear.

"That is the chaos," Morgana said.

"I thought it might be," I said.

"It was much more distant the last time I was here. This place is not safe. I have helped to bring you here, but we can go no farther. I will not risk what remains of my court."

"I can't do this on my own," I said, and I knew that to be true.

Morgana turned to me. "You have proven time and time again that your own life means nothing to you. And I know you may be willing to risk me to save Alice. But what of Amelia? You would risk her as well?"

"It's not safe for us to split up," I said. "Not with the angels chasing us."

"I suspect even you don't believe that anymore," Morgana said. "This place may very well be more dangerous than Gabriel and his minions."

Mountains shimmered in the distance to the left. One of them was spewing lava into the sky, but it was blue lava. To the right, the plain eventually gave way to a wall of whirlwinds, twisting and turning through each other.

She was right. But it didn't matter.

"I am going to save Alice," I said, "because it's the right thing to do."

"The right thing to do is to cut our losses while we can," Morgana said.

"If I don't try, then all those times that Alice saved me were for nothing," I replied. "If I don't try, then I'll be no different from the man I used to be."

"Sometimes I like that man better anyway," Morgana said softly. "But it doesn't matter. I have made my decision."

"And I have made mine," Amelia said. She stepped over the ruined wall, into the Wonder Lands. "We go in search of Alice. Together."

Morgana grabbed hold of the wall in front of her so tightly she ground one of the blocks into powder. "You are of my court. You are *my* daughter."

"And he is my father," Amelia said. "I'll no more leave him than I would you."

"Well, that's settled then," Puck said with a grin and somersaulted over the broken wall.

"And what if this doorway is not here when we return?" Morgana asked.

I held up the journal. "Then I'll draw another way out. I still have enough of Raphael's blood."

Morgana said nothing more for a long moment, then joined the others. "We will discuss how my court came to be such an unseemly democracy later. But we should not linger, as this place could become undone around us."

I stepped over the threshold. The ground was wet underfoot, and water oozed out from beneath my shoes. I didn't have time to dwell on it, though, for at that moment something snatched the journal from my hand and fled with it. I say "something" because I couldn't get a clear look at it. The air rippled in front of me, as if from the heat, and then there was a flash of sharp teeth. I lurched back, but the teeth weren't coming for me. Instead, they latched on to the journal and took it from my hand.

I tried to grab it back, but the creature that took it was already out on the plain. I could make out its shape from the way the air blurred as it moved. Some sort of long cat, maybe the length of a panther, holding the journal in its fangs. It bounded across the land, making its way around the pools of water and heading for the forest.

"Was that the Cheshire Cat?" I asked. "Is it one of the Chaos Court?"

"Perhaps it is one of their creations," Morgana said. "Or perhaps it is some creature of the chaos itself."

"Whatever it is, we need to stop it before it gets away with the journal," I said and gave chase.

We followed its path, detouring around the pools of water as it had. In one of them I saw a dead siren floating in the depths. Its body had been hacked savagely by blades, and I knew who was to blame.

"Friend of yours?" Morgana asked as I slowed to gaze down at the siren.

I shook my head. "Neither friend nor foe. She was killed during the battle to stop Noah at the Sunken City. The whirlpool that took Alice away must have brought them both here."

"I'll fetch her," Puck said, readying himself to dive into the pool. "Perhaps she has some weapon hidden on her that we can use."

"The sirens are weapons all on their own," I said.

Morgana put her arm out to stop Puck. "Not all of these pools are merely water. Some of them are chaos pools, filled with the same madness that is devouring these lands. Enter into one of them and you will be changed in ways no one can predict." She picked up a fallen stick and shoved the siren deeper into the pool until it disappeared into the darkness. When Morgana pulled the stick back out, the end that had been submerged writhed like a serpent.

"This is all very interesting but we're losing the cat," I said.

Morgana tossed the stick aside and we continued on, although Puck gave the pool a yearning look.

I couldn't even see the cat now because it blended into the land too well at this distance. I headed toward the forest, for it was the closest place the creature could likely lose itself and shake us off.

As we drew near the forest I saw all the trees were dead, their branches bare and twisting. Yet they swayed back and forth. "This is what inspired the Wonderland books?" I said. "It looks more like some sort of apocalyptic wasteland."

"It was a different place in the time of the Chaos Court," Morgana said. "But nothing ever remains the same. Whatever you do, don't fall asleep in the woods."

"I'm really hoping not to stay that long."

We slowed as we made our way through the forest, trying to find the cat again. White-and-black mushrooms began to spot the ground, then carpet it. The mushrooms grew larger and larger the deeper we went, until they were knee-high and as wide around as my legs. We had to force our way through them and were slowed even more.

They gave way and we stumbled into a clearing with another pool of water at its centre, along with the remains of some great creature. It had a body made of massive serpents all twined together, some of which ended in heads of various creatures – a crocodile, a turtle and so on. The creature's body was torn all over, and its blood stained the ground – blood and ink. It was the hydra we had fought in the British Library, but it was clearly dead now.

The angel archivist lay nearby, just as dead judging by the gaping wounds covering its broken body. Yet it shook and twitched as if still alive. I nudged it with a foot. I sensed grace within, but somehow distant and beyond my reach.

"Does it yet persist?" Morgana asked as she stepped around the hydra and angel, keeping her distance from both. "Perhaps you should replenish your grace if so."

"I'm not entirely certain," I said and looked at Amelia. It seemed one of those times where we should probably know.

She studied the angel. "It is dead. Yet there is some life hidden within it that I do not understand."

That wasn't at all helpful, but I knew it wasn't her fault. It was this odd place. "Could the chaos be causing this?"

"The chaos can cause anything," Morgana said. "Have you not been paying attention? That is why it is not safe here."

"Then we'd best hurry and find Alice," I said and headed for the other side of the clearing.

Before I could reach it, though, there was a sudden chiming somewhere in the distance, like a grandfather clock, followed by the sounds of trees falling. The sounds came our way, rapidly.

Morgana muttered a curse as she caught up to me. "Perhaps we don't want to get caught in the open by whatever that is," she said.

We quickly left the clearing behind and moved into the forest. A tree grew sideways out of a boulder before us, and we crouched down behind it, scanning the woods. The sounds were coming closer, but I couldn't see what was causing them yet.

Then I spotted the cat again. It came dashing through the woods with the journal still in its mouth, obviously fleeing whatever was making the noise. It leapt over the tree we hid behind – and I jumped up and slammed my shoulder into its stomach. The cat flashed a sudden rainbow of colours and somersaulted backward. I tried to grab the journal from its jaws but couldn't pull it free, and the cat wrenched itself away.

A tree fell behind us, and a creature stepped out of the woods with a giant axe in its hands. It was humanoid but covered with dirty white fur streaked with blood. More fur covered its face, along with a set of whiskers hard as wire. It had long pointed ears and sharp teeth that jutted out of its mouth.

"Is that some sort of *rabbit*?" Morgana asked, peering over the tree.

"I suppose that would be fitting," I said.

The cat stopped and spun with a snarl. The creature with the axe strode forward, pointing the weapon at the cat. "Give me the book!" it cried in a shrill voice. "It's almost too late to escape this place! Too late!"

Then the chiming of the clock suddenly sounded all around us, and other creatures slid out from behind the trees.

ALICE IN THE WONDER LANDS

There were a half-dozen of them. A giant mechanical beetle with a rusting body that should have been too large to hide behind the trees yet somehow had. A diamond man in silver chain mail, who bore a long pike. A wooden man whose body was compartmented and covered in hatches. A half-man, half-otter creature bearing a long and dented metal shield. A humanoid being made of clocks of all different shapes and sizes bound together by bent springs.

And then there was Alice. She looked much like I had seen her last, only her clothes were reduced to rags and her skin was as pale as a corpse. Her hair was wet and matted, and there were scrapes and cuts and burns all over her body. She rode a black horse that appeared to be made of marble and had the distinct appearance of a chess piece. She hunched over its neck as if she were exhausted.

"I have a book that you'll like better," Alice said, and I realized she was talking to the creature with the axe. "Or maybe I'll like better. I can't remember which it is, but someone will like it, and that's all a book ever wants."

She reached out her hand and the wooden man pulled a white book from one of the compartments in his body and handed it to her. Grace filled the air.

The rabbit man threw himself at the cat, and I stepped up to meet him. I didn't know what was going on here, but he was at odds with Alice and that was enough for me. I wasn't sure how I was going to deal with his axe, but as it turned out I didn't have to do anything.

Alice threw the white book and it opened as it hurtled toward the rabbit. The pages fluttered and then expanded to several feet in length. The book fell upon the strange creature, and the pages wrapped around it like a net. The rabbit man shrieked once and then disappeared as the paper stretched like a blanket covering someone. I saw arms thrusting up and trying to break free. Words swirled in that paper, although they were the same white as the pages themselves. In fact, now that I looked closer, the pages seemed to be made of those words. Then the book shrank down to its previous size and fell to the ground, where it lay still. There was no sign of the creature with the axe.

Alice dismounted the black horse and walked over to pick up the book. She was still partially hunched over and moved slowly. She turned the book in her hands for a moment, inspecting it, then tossed it to the wooden man. He caught it with one hand and opened a door in his chest with another. There was a chamber inside him that held another dozen or so books just like that one. He added the new book to them and then closed the door, and I heard the sound of a lock sliding into place.

Alice turned to look at me, and I ran to her and gathered her in my arms. Her body was cold and damp, but I didn't mind.

"I've been looking all over for you," I said.

"I know," she said. "Because I've been everywhere you haven't been. Which is here. And now that you're here and you've brought me the journal, you have to leave and go back to the places I'm not."

I stepped back. "Alice, what is going on?"

The cat came over and sat beside her. She laid her hand on its head and then took the journal from its mouth. She didn't give it to me but instead slipped it into a pocket. One of the clocks in the clock man let out a single chime that sounded longer than it should have.

"We're fighting a war in the Wonder Lands," Alice said. "The bible is damaged and words keep escaping from it. They turn into creatures like the poor white rabbit."

"We've encountered a few of them back in our world," I said, nodding.

"They found the books left behind by the Chaos Court," Alice said. "The ones Lewis Carroll wrote just for the faerie. Or maybe the ones the faerie made him write. They've been using them as portals to the Wonderland books in your world to escape."

"And how exactly does that work?" I asked.

Alice gave me a sad smile. "Haven't you realized yet that books are magic?"

"I knew there was a reason I didn't like them," Puck muttered.

"We've been destroying the books left here," Alice continued. "Which I hate to do because the books didn't do anything. They're just being books. I think we found them all. But the journal was still a possible doorway, so I needed you to bring it to me. Which you have, because you always find me."

"The illustrations of you fighting the angel, that was you sending me a message, wasn't it?" I said.

"I think it was me. Or maybe it was the journal. Things are confusing here. More confusing than normal I mean."

"Well, we're here now. And we'll bring you back through that door, and the bible with us. We'll find a way to repair it and put an end to all the madness."

"I can't find any way to repair it. And every time a word gets out it makes things worse. If we go back through that door with the bible, it may turn your world into a place like the Wonder Lands, and I don't think anyone wants that. Do you?"

"Well," Puck said, but Morgana gave him a look and he fell silent.

"The bible should stay here, where it can't harm anywhere else," Alice said. "Because there's no other place for it."

"You know the chaos will soon undo this place," Morgana said.

"Chaos always finds a way," Alice said, nodding.

"And what will happen if the bible is lost to the chaos?" I asked. "Doesn't our world need it to hold itself together?" That was what the popes had led me to believe anyway.

Alice hugged herself. "I don't know what the world needs. If I did, maybe I would be a book instead of an Alice."

"Perhaps the holy texts of the other gods are enough to keep the world the world," Morgana said, although she didn't sound certain. "They all keep the chaos at bay in their own manner."

"Maybe," I said. "But I've got a feeling the world would be changed if the bible was lost."

"Would that be a bad thing?" Morgana asked.

"That probably depends on who you ask," I said. "But that's for the angels to worry about, not us. Let's just get out of here. Leave the bible, though. If what you said about the books is true, then it can't harm our world anymore if it's stuck here."

"I can't leave," Alice said and patted the strange cat.

"Bring your friends if you want," I said. "We'll find a place to hide them away."

"They are servants of the Chaos Court," Morgana said. "They may not survive outside of this glamour."

"Hess is no servant," Alice said, nodding at the cat. Even though I stood beside the creature I still could only see it when it moved and the ground and trees rippled in its shape. "It was the last thing left alive in the Wonder Lands when I arrived. It was so lonely that it was happy to help me by scouring the lands for the last of the books. Or maybe it was not lonely but sad. It's hard to tell with invisible cats. Or other cats, for that matter."

"I don't think it's the last living thing in this place," I said. "There's an angel in a clearing behind us that has some sort of life left in it."

Alice looked back the way we had come. "Oh no, that can't be right," she said. "Because if it is, that's very wrong."

Morgana put a hand to her head and closed her eyes. "Please do tell us why that can't be right."

Alice pulled herself back up onto the black horse. "Because that angel was dead the last time we saw it."

SOMETHING WICKED THIS WAY COMES

We made our way back to the clearing in the woods accompanied by Alice and her strange group.

"Do you have the bible with you?" I asked. I was curious to see it again.

Alice laughed like I had made a joke. "Of course not. What if some words from the bible escaped into us? Then we'd be like the angels."

"So what has become of it?" I tried not to think too much about the meaning of her words.

"It's in the graveyard where the Chaos Court are buried," she said. "At least the ones that didn't go back into the chaos. And we buried the servants that fell in battle with the bible's creations in the graveyard, too. There are a lot of them. It's been a long war. It feels like forever, but most hard things do. Or maybe they're hard because they feel like forever."

"Is the bible safe in such a place?" I asked.

"It's not safe anywhere," Alice said. "I thought you knew that. But the graveyard will be the last place that the chaos claims of the Wonder Lands."

"How do you know that?"

"Because the Chaos Court still exert an influence on the Wonder Lands even in death," Amelia said.

"It's true," Morgana said, nodding. "They are the ones that created the Wonder Lands out of the chaos, after all."

"Are you going to take those white books there?" I asked, glancing at the wooden man. "Have you found a way to put the escaped words back in the bible?"

"I think only God can do that," Alice said. "And he's not here, if he ever was at all. So the other books are like a new set of bibles. A new New Testament maybe. Or maybe a different translation of the old one. I don't know. I don't like to think about it too much because that's the sort of thing that starts wars and I've already got a war and don't need another."

"Maybe I could drain the grace from the books," I mused. "That would make them less dangerous. And I could use the grace."

Alice's wet hair curled like tentacles. "What if one of those books infected you and the bible got into you? And then what if you got loose back in the world? It'd be the Second Coming but in a way nobody would want, not even the angels. And not me."

Luckily, I didn't have to think about that too much because we came to the clearing then and there was much to distract me.

The hydra still lay where it had fallen, but the dead angel was on its feet now. It staggered around the clearing, ripping at its body with its hands. The fingers had sharpened into talons, and it tore great strips of its flesh away. I could feel the grace emanating from it, stronger now.

"Oh, this is most curious," Alice said. "And not in any of the good ways."

"We could try and kill it," Puck suggested.

"It's already dead," I pointed out.

"So are you," Puck said. "And yet here you are, annoying me."

"We don't need to become involved with whatever madness is happening here," Morgana said. "We've found Alice. Let's escape this place while we still can."

"But what if it's a word we missed?" Alice said.

As if that were some cue, the creatures of her entourage spread out in a circle around the clearing and surrounded the dead angel.

"And what if it's worse than a mere word?" Morgana asked sharply.

The angel dugs its hands into its chest then and pulled in different directions. There was the sound of bones snapping and flesh tearing. A stream of blood spilled forth, staining the ground the angel stood upon. The angel continued to rip itself apart, and then it ripped what was left of its flesh downward, as if it were tearing off clothing.

"Something wicked this way comes," Puck said and giggled.

A man suddenly lunged out of the dead angel, covered in gore.
No, not a man.
Gabriel.

THE LAST STAND OF THE FAERIE COURT

Gabriel was still in the same statue form as before but larger chunks of him were missing now, and deep fissures crossed his body. The chaos creature I had summoned into the popes' chamber had taken its toll on him. But it hadn't slowed him any.

He slammed into Puck before any of us had time to react, knocking the faerie back and into the pool at the centre of the clearing. Morgana lunged for Puck, trying to catch him, but she was too late. Puck disappeared into the water without a splash or even a ripple. It was a chaos pool.

Alice and her servants swarmed Gabriel. The soldier rammed his pike into Gabriel's chest, but the point caught in one of the cracks and lodged there, so that the pike broke when Gabriel twisted to the side. The otter man leapt at him, teeth going for his throat, but Gabriel grabbed him by his neck and squeezed until we heard the sound of bones snapping. The otter man went limp, and Gabriel tossed him into the clock man, who began to chime with multiple bells. Teeth flashed in the air around Gabriel, but his stone flesh was too hard for the cat's fangs.

"I just want the bible, not you lot," Gabriel said. "Give it to me, and I'll let you be on your way." He stared at the wooden man as if he could sense the books hidden inside him. Perhaps he could.

"Who says we will let you be on your way?" Morgana asked, striding toward him with murder and much more in her eyes.

I stepped forward, so Gabriel had to face me next. I figured I had the best chance of taking him, although I had to admit it wasn't a good chance.

He pulled the point of the pike from the crack in his chest and considered it, as if determining its worth as a weapon.

"How did you get here?" Alice asked, circling him on her black horse. "You don't belong in the Wonder Lands. And the things that don't belong shouldn't be."

Gabriel pointed the pike at me and smiled. "You can thank Cross for that. I've been following him for some time, making him think that I was about to catch him and undo all his plans. I applied just enough pressure that he would eventually make a mistake. Which he always does. He's remarkably predictable that way."

I cursed then, realizing Gabriel had played me all along. "It was you who took me from Prague and dumped me underneath that bridge in Paris, wasn't it?"

"You would have found your drunken way to Paris again eventually. I just helped move things along a little when I planted you there and did the same with the book in the Mazarine."

The battle at the cemetery in Paris, at Mona Lisa's hidden ruins, at St. Peter's Basilica even – they were all just tricks to keep me on the run, so I would try desperately to find Alice before Gabriel caught me. And I had led him straight here, even if I didn't understand how he had come to be here.

"Eventually you led me to that secret room in the library," Gabriel said. "And that's when I –"

"How am I supposed to know which library you mean?" Alice said. "They all have secret rooms."

"The one the Chaos Court created for Lewis Carroll of course," Gabriel said. He leaned on the pike. "After you visited the first time, I found the journal and knew you would return. I took some pages from the journal just in case. When you unlocked the door to the Wonder Lands I tried to follow you through but the door wouldn't open for me."

"The journal was the only thing holding back the chaos," Alice said. "Because it was born of this glamour, it exerted enough of a presence into the Wonder Lands that it kept the chaos at bay. Once Hess brought the journal to me, there was nothing to hold off the chaos and it consumed the mansion. There is no door now."

Gabriel shrugged. "Luckily, I had already learned of the archivist following the hydra back to wherever it came from in that battle at the British Library. When I realized it was likely the same place the doorway had led to, I used the pages from the journal to find my own way here." He gazed around the clearing, his eyes lingering on the chaos pool. "A strange journey to an even stranger place."

So that explained the missing pages I had noticed earlier. I scanned the clearing, searching for some weapon I could use, but there was nothing beyond a few fallen branches. I was going to have to do this the hard way. Amelia had climbed up on top of the mechanical beetle's back, as if preparing for us to escape. I didn't see Morgana any more, and I didn't know what to make of that. Had she simply faded away now that the last member of her court was gone?

"All right, if you won't give me the bible then I'll just have to take it," Gabriel said and came at us.

The soldier threw himself forward to meet Gabriel before I could, and the two grappled. The soldier wrapped his hands around Gabriel's neck, and the stone there cracked a bit more. But then Gabriel grabbed hold of the soldier's skull and squeezed, and I heard the grinding of his fingers on the diamond of the soldier's skull.

I moved forward, looking for an angle where I could tie up Gabriel's arms or grab him in some sort of lock from behind. Maybe I could hold him long enough that someone else could do some damage to him.

"Can you catch him with one of those books?" I asked Alice.

She laughed. "He's no word escaped from the bible. He's just an angel."

Just an angel. Right.

Gabriel saw me coming, and spun the soldier around to keep him between us. He kept squeezing, turning the soldier's skull into powder that drifted to the ground. The clock man began to chime with more alarm. The cat prowled around the outskirts of the battle, but there was little it could do.

Then Morgana stepped out of the shadows behind Gabriel as if she had just appeared from thin air. I didn't know if she had moved so stealthily I hadn't seen her, or if she had used the glamour to get behind Gabriel. She threw herself into him, striking him square in his back and sending him stumbling forward. She kicked the broken shaft of the pike up into her hand with one foot and then rammed it into him in one motion while he was off balance, sending him into the pool.

Gabriel tried to hang on to the soldier to pull himself out, but the soldier understood what was happening and threw himself into the pool, disappearing into the chaos. Gabriel teetered on the edge, and then fell in.

And then Puck rose from the pool and sent Gabriel flying.

THE BANDERSNATCH

For a moment I thought I must have been struck on the head and it was affecting my vision, for Puck looked all wrong. His limbs were bent like they were broken and out of place – his right arm was lower down on his side while his left arm sprouted from his back, and each of his legs was split in two so he seemed like some sort of massive, grotesque insect.

There was also the fact that he had knocked Gabriel high into the air – something that I hadn't even been able to do. The angel crashed into the upper branches of a dead tree and hung there for a moment, as if he were surprised by what had just happened.

But when I glanced at the others to check my vision, they appeared normal and seemed just as confused as I was by the turn of events. Alice stared wide-eyed at Puck while Morgana frowned at him. Amelia squinted at him as if trying to see him more clearly.

Puck stepped from the pool with a grin and tried to speak, but his words came out as musical notes.

"Morgana?" I said, stepping back from Puck. "Is this some faerie thing?"

"It's not my doing," she said, also retreating. "And I doubt Puck possessed the power for such a transformation on his own. The chaos must have gotten into him."

"I think he has become a bandersnatch," Alice said. "And that is not good. In fact, it is the very opposite of not good, which is even worse."

"It's time someone explained to me exactly what a bandersnatch is," I said.

"It's any creature that enters the chaos and then returns from it," Alice said. "They are the most dangerous of all for they bring the chaos with them and can unleash it in this land. But such a transformation should not happen so quickly."

"Oh, the chaos has been within me for some time," Puck said. This time I was able to understand his words, although his voice was a gurgle now. "Ever since I took that book from Cross back at the library. It crept into me then, but it was most welcome."

I remembered Puck going through the book after he had stolen it from me, and I cursed. The chaos must have been the reason the grace I had drained from the White Knight had affected me so strangely. The knight had had the chaos within him when he sprang from the book and attacked me. I had used up the grace quickly, so the chaos had passed from me with it. But it had been within Puck this whole time, infecting him.

Morgana shook her head. "That's what you've been hiding from us. You used the power of chaos for your little tricks, didn't you?"

"Don't think of it as chaos," Puck said. "Think of it as the way things are supposed to be."

I picked up the remains of the pike, although I suspected the broken weapon wouldn't be much use. I cast a wary glance at Gabriel – I didn't want him sneaking up on me from behind – as he was pulling himself down from the tree. That's when I realized he was floating and not falling, as if gravity no longer applied to him. He didn't look entirely comfortable with the fact, so I assumed he wasn't behind it.

"Do you finally see why I need the bible?" Gabriel asked, grabbing on to the tree trunk and somersaulting down to the ground. "When the world is full of abominations like this?"

For a moment I thought he was talking about me because the angels usually were when they started using words like *abomination* and *heresy*. But he was looking at Puck.

"I would also like the bible," Puck said, "but for different reasons."

Puck reached down and touched an exposed tree root on the ground, and it caught fire. More flames erupted from the roots of the trees all around the clearing and quickly raced up their trunks and along their branches. Smoke billowed from the burning trees, only it was smoke made of tiny black bats.

"This is so much fun," Puck said, winking at me. "I see why you are always killing those angels and stealing their grace."

"Puck, you will stop all this nonsense and return to your rightful place at my heel," Morgana said, stepping to my side.

Puck grinned, showing crooked but sharp fangs. "I'm not a member of your court anymore. I belong to the chaos now. I'm going to start a new Chaos Court."

He threw himself at me and was suddenly a rolling ball of limbs and teeth surrounding a body that morphed and twisted. I thrust the pike at him, but it met only air and then he was rising up and smashing it aside with a snarl.

Gabriel leapt over Morgana and me and descended upon Puck with a broken and burning tree branch like it was a flaming sword. He rammed the jagged end of the branch into Puck's neck, where his jugular should have been. He drove it into the faerie so hard it came out Puck's side, still burning.

A cloud of those tiny black bats erupted from Puck and flew around us, obscuring him from sight. Gabriel wrenched the branch free, but it had become a burning serpent made of wood, and it sank its fangs into a crack in Gabriel's skin. By the time the bats had flown away and disappeared into the woods, Puck was gone.

"Where is he?" I asked, pivoting in a quick circle. I eyed the chaos pool, but it was unchanged.

"He's somewhere not here," Alice said. "And that's probably even worse than being here."

"Does she always talk like that?" Gabriel asked as he pulled the snake from his body and then broke it in two like it was still a branch.

"I can't tell you how much I've missed hearing her talk like that," I said.

"We must make sure the bandersnatch doesn't find the bible," Alice said. "I don't know what a bandersnatch would do with it. For that matter, I don't know what a bible might do with a bandersnatch."

I locked my gaze with Gabriel's. "We need to work together right now to stop Puck. I can wait to kill you until after that."

"This is what I've been saying to you all along," he said. "Your lives would be so much easier if you listened to the angels."

“I doubt that,” I said.

“Why not leave the damned bible to him?” Morgana asked. “We should be trying to find a way out of here, not getting ourselves into more trouble.”

“If Alice says we need to protect the bible from the bandersnatch, then that is what we’ll do,” I said.

“Is that what I said?” Alice asked. “Sometimes even I don’t know what the words that come out of me mean.” She stuck a couple of fingers in her mouth and probed inside, as if searching for more words.

Gabriel offered his hand and I shook it, for I’ve always been one for meaningless symbolic gestures. Morgana spat on the ground in a gesture of her own.

“Let’s go find God’s bible then,” I said. “Before it brings more ruin to the world.”

THE CHAOS CEMETERY

We climbed atop the mechanical beetle along with the surviving automatons and the cat. They pulled the remains of the otter man along with them, which earned a frown from Gabriel.

"Why bother with that?" he asked. "Dead weight will just slow us down."

"We need to bury him in the graveyard," Alice said. "The dead belong in graveyards, not among the living. What if someone left us in a graveyard for the rest of time?"

"Don't get him started on that," I said. I turned to Gabriel. "Make yourself useful and have a fly about to make sure Puck isn't lingering somewhere nearby."

"Perhaps later," Gabriel said, eyeing the burning trees. "Let's leave this place before some branch falls and incapacitates one of your frail number."

"What's wrong with flying around now?" I asked, and then I knew the answer. "You can't fly anymore?"

Gabriel didn't say anything. It may have been the very first time I'd seen an angel embarrassed.

"Did Puck do something to you?" I asked. The idea of that made me a little envious, for I'd never been able to really harm Gabriel over the ages.

"It's the bible," he said. "The more grace that escapes from it, the more the angels fall. And the more it changes the world. And us."

"So that's why you haven't changed form since the cemetery in Paris? You're stuck as a statue."

"The angels have been finding it difficult to transform," Gabriel muttered.

I couldn't help but laugh. "That almost makes me want to let more words out of the bible."

Gabriel glared at me. "Imagine a world with no angels."

"I do that all the time."

"Now imagine it with bandersnatches running amok," he said. "Who will ensure the survival of our world if not the angels? You?"

"I've saved the world a time or two," I pointed out.

"And how many times have your misadventures nearly led to its end?"

That was a fair point. The two of us settled into an uncomfortable silence as we left the clearing atop the mechanical beetle. Alice took us through the flaming trees and into the woods beyond. A few of the bats fluttered overhead but then scattered in different directions. The scent of ripe mangoes filled the air and then faded as quickly as it came. A face formed in the churning violet clouds overhead for a few brief seconds, a young boy with elfin features and pointed ears, and then it was gone.

"Was that Puck again?" I asked, watching the sky.

Morgana snorted. "That was Pan, the ruler of the Chaos Court. If you could say anyone ruled it. But he was one of the first to disappear."

"What happened to him?" I asked.

"He fell under the thrall of a vampire," Morgana said. "He fed on children in their dreams until he was lost in one of those dreams."

I forced my gaze from the sky and moved closer to Amelia. "You were puzzled in a way I haven't seen before when Puck came out of that chaos pool," I said to her.

She took a moment to answer. "He is neither dead nor alive now, nor even in between. It is like he exists outside of such things."

"That's chaos," Morgana said. "I wouldn't think upon it too deeply for that way lies madness."

"Can we even kill him then?" I asked.

"I don't know," Amelia said. "How do you kill something that shouldn't even exist?"

"We'll find a way," Gabriel said, looking sideways at me.

Alice took us to a jumble of fallen trees that blocked our path. The way forward looked impassable but there was a wooden door set into one of the trees, with a worn bronze handle and a knocker in the shape of an owl's head. Alice slid off her black horse, skipped to the door and hit the knocker twice against the wood.

"There's no need to be so rough," the owl said. "I saw you coming from the moment you left the clearing with that bandersnatch."

"Did the bandersnatch see you?" Alice asked. "For I think it might be rougher than me."

The owl swivelled its head to the left and then the right. "I don't see it anywhere. So perhaps it has found a door of its own."

"I certainly hope not," Alice said. "Doors always lead somewhere, and a creature like the bandersnatch should be nowhere."

"Well, we shall all be nowhere soon enough," the owl said. With that, the door opened and Alice led the horse through.

We slid off the beetle for it was too large to fit through the door, and followed Alice. We were in a tunnel now, which seemed to have been chewed out of the wood. There was a soft green light at the end of the tunnel, which was only a few dozen metres away. Yet we had to linger and wait for Gabriel, who moved at the pace of an elderly man.

"Don't tell me you're turning into an actual statue," I said.

"Poison from that snake," he said through gritted teeth. "It's slowing me down."

"Maybe I should just take your grace and put you out of your suffering. I can probably use it better than you in your state."

"I suspect you have never put grace to good use," Gabriel said.

We went toward that green light and then through it to a graveyard beyond. The graveyard was as much a mad, disorderly mess as everything else in the Wonder Lands. There were a half-dozen stone crypts in various states of crumbling, with doors hanging off their hinges and pink-and-yellow moss growing on them. A tower made of some blue wood I had never seen before loomed over the scene, with cages full of skeletons hanging from the top. A Viking ship floated in a long pool of black water on the far side, listing to port. A couple of raised platforms were surrounded by loose bones, as if something had been eating up there and cast the bones over the edge. And there were dozens of graves, both filled and open, with worn grave markers jutting out of the ground. A long wooden table also sat amid the graves, surrounded by fallen chairs and covered in wine bottles and pastries. A crimson stain covered the middle of the table, and I wasn't certain if it was wine or blood.

There was a scraping sound from behind me and I turned to see the mechanical beetle pushing itself out of the tunnel, even though it was too large for it. And now I saw the tunnel emerged not from more fallen trees on this side but from the entrance to a large stone tomb carved with the scene of the forest we had left behind. I wasn't sure what to make of that so I passed it off to the curious nature of this place. The beetle squeezed out of the tunnel, expanding to nearly twice its size, and lumbered into the graveyard.

Alice stepped forward and closed the door, and it simply faded away into the stone. "The bandersnatch won't be able to follow us this way," she said. "Unless of course it can, I suppose."

Gabriel stared at her, then turned to me. "This is who you've been risking your life for?"

"Alice helped save the world," I reminded him. "And your god's bible. So maybe give her a little more respect."

"It's all right," Alice said. "The angels don't know any better because no one taught them."

Gabriel opened his mouth but didn't say anything. Maybe he thought better of it. Or maybe he just didn't know what to say.

Alice left the black horse and whispered in the ear of the wooden man. He nodded and strode toward a distant crypt. At the same time, the clockwork man dragged the otter man off the beetle to an open grave. I saw a shine of teeth as the cat slunk off somewhere to do whatever it was invisible cats do.

"Is this where the Chaos Court are buried?" I asked.

"Most of them," Alice said, pirouetting back to us. "Others are fallen elsewhere or lost to the chaos. And the chaos has taken over some of those tombs, so don't open any doors that we don't open. I don't want you to become the Chaos Court."

I glanced at Morgana and saw her studying the graves. She looked more worn and tired than I had ever seen before.

The wooden man wrenched open the door of the crypt. I saw bookshelves lining the walls inside. Each was stacked with more of those white books. Hundreds of them. The wooden man opened the compartment in his chest and took out the books he was carrying and added them to one of the shelves.

The clock man began to chime in alarm.

Then Puck climbed out of an open grave next to the crypt.

PUCK'S GLAMOUR

Puck was transformed again, his skin crawling with those black bats. He had grown more arms, and they were scattered around his body as if at random. He had six legs and scuttled now. His head swivelled around like an owl's and fixed on the wooden man. He grabbed the wooden man before anyone could move and pulled him from the crypt, then smashed him into the ground.

I threw the pike shaft at Puck like a spear. It had been some time since I'd thrown a spear, but my aim was still true. It struck Puck in the chest and knocked him down. I ran at him, and I heard Gabriel lumbering along beside me. For once I didn't mind having an angel at my side.

Puck leapt back up and pulled the shaft from his body like he didn't even feel it. He threw it at us, and for a second I thought he was going to turn it into another serpent. But instead it hit the ground a few metres before me and turned into a fallen tree that bounced across the ground in our direction.

I cursed and threw myself down, and the tree passed close enough over my head that I felt the wind of its passage. Gabriel was not as quick, and I heard him grunt as it slammed into him and carried him backward.

I leapt to my feet again as Puck stepped to the wooden man, who kicked at him to no effect. Puck ripped one leg off and then the other, casting them aside. Then he did the same with the wooden man's arms even as I ran at him again.

"I thought I was finally done with you," I said.

"Chaos always finds a way." Puck laughed.

I wasn't sure what I was going to do, as I no longer had a weapon. But I had to do something. Perhaps I could use one of the wooden man's limbs to beat Puck.

Puck ripped open the wooden man's chest and peered inside, but it was empty. He kicked the remains of the wooden man into the grave he had climbed out of, and suddenly the ground opened up beneath me and I fell into another grave. I landed on the wooden man, who had grown still, and I realized I had somehow been transported to the grave behind Puck.

"He's using the chaos like his own glamour!" Morgana cried from across the cemetery. She had pulled herself atop the black horse and was trying to ride it at Puck, but it didn't move at all. It had grown as still as a statue. Maybe because it only responded to Alice, maybe because it had run out of life in this place.

"Can you cast a glamour of your own?" I asked, pulling myself out of the grave.

"I have little power in this place for it is not of my court," she said. "And my own court is mostly gone thanks to you." She threw herself off the horse and rushed to put herself between Amelia and Puck.

A few feet away, Gabriel lay underneath the tree, with fallen gravestones all around him. Gabriel pushed the tree off and picked himself up, but he was moving even slower than before. Beyond him, the clockwork man continued to sound the alarm while Alice stood and just watched the scene unfold, chewing on the end of a lock of hair.

Puck turned toward the crypt with all the books, and I knew he meant to use them to unleash some chaos. He hesitated, then spun his head around to look at Alice.

And that was when I realized she'd had the bible all along.

GOD'S BIBLE

Puck scrambled across the broken ground of the graveyard toward Alice, moving as fast as the insect he resembled.

I lunged at him, but he had already passed me. Maybe if I had used the bit of grace I had left, I could have caught him. But I had a feeling I would still need that.

"Alice, the bible!" I called.

Alice watched Puck come at her, then pulled aside the rags covering her stomach. I saw a gaping wound in her side. I wasn't sure if it was from the battle at the Sunken City or some creature here in the Wonder Lands. It didn't matter. What mattered was that God's bible was jammed into it. That explained all the grace I'd sensed when she had shown up in the forest.

Alice pulled out the bible and held it up. She cried out when she did so and sagged against Amelia, who leapt to her side to keep her standing.

Then Gabriel was at her side as well, and he ripped the bible from her grasp. He stared at it as if he had forgotten about everyone else. But Puck was almost upon him, his many twisted hands reaching for that bible.

I did the only thing I could think of. I grabbed a fallen tombstone from the ground and threw it across the graveyard. It hit the top edge of the bible, catching the front cover enough to lift it away from the pages a fraction of an inch.

And a word slipped out.

I didn't get a good look at it, for Puck had moved between the others and me. I saw long black arms like those of a mantis grab on to Puck and snap him forward. Something like the tail of a giant scorpion rammed through him, spraying white blood across the graveyard.

"Oh well done!" Puck cried. "Let's free all the words and see what happens!"

"Alice!" I cried as I ran toward them. "Bind it now!"

But Alice was already in motion. She pulled another of those white books from her rags and threw it at Puck and the other creature. The book flipped open and expanded as it came down on them. Puck understood what was happening too late.

"No, not a book!" he cried. Then he was lost underneath it as it carried him down to the ground. For a moment the pages writhed as they had with the other book, thrusting up as Puck and the creature that had escaped the bible struggled to free themselves. But the struggling eventually subsided and then the book lay still on the ground. Alice picked it up and handed it to Morgana.

"You should be the one to shelve it," she said. "The bandersnatch was from your court, after all. Although you don't really have a court now, so maybe it wasn't. Anyway, someone should probably shelve it and soon."

Morgana took the book and stared down at it, then nodded once.

"Where did you even get those books?" I asked as I reached Alice. I expected to see bones and muscles and organs in her wound. Instead, I saw a jumble of letters of different fonts and sizes and even colours jammed together to form a mess of words that made up her insides.

"From the bible, of course," Alice said. "What else would be able to make a book that can bind words from God's bible?"

The words within her made me feel dizzy, so I looked away from them and tried to focus on her face. "How exactly did you manage to get books from the bible? Everything else that has escaped it has been considerably less helpful."

"They were with me when the whirlpool cast me out here," she said. "I didn't know what they were at first, but I figured it out. Books always create other books, after all."

"Perhaps the bible is attempting to repair itself," Gabriel said, turning the tome over in his hands. "Perhaps God foresaw such a day."

"And maybe it's just random like me," I said. I nodded at the white book Morgana held. "The question is how long that one will contain Puck. Or the bandersnatch or whatever the hell he's become."

"It won't need to hold him for long," Morgana said. She stepped over to the clockwork man and whispered in his ear, then gave him the book.

He strode across the graveyard to a nearby tomb, clocks still chiming. He opened the door to the tomb, but there was no chamber inside. Instead, there were swirling purple clouds with little forks of lightning flashing through them. The clockwork man stepped through the door with the book and disappeared into the clouds. Morgana closed the door behind him. She stood there for a moment and spoke without turning around. "Puck was enamoured of the chaos, so I have set him free and returned him to it. I think we will not see him again." She turned to Amelia. "And now my court is down to one."

I put my hand on Alice's wound without looking at it again and eased grace through my fingertips and into her. The wound shrunk as my grace healed her, more words spreading out to twist together to form flesh, until there was only a scar. Now it was my turn to sag and feel exhausted as that familiar emptiness returned.

"You shouldn't have done that," Alice said, straightening up.

"I'm not going to let you die," I said. "Especially not after I just found you."

"But you're going to need that grace to fight Gabriel."

A DEAL WITH THE DEVIL

"We don't need to fight," Gabriel said. "As long as you hand over that journal. I suspect it's now my only way out of here."

"Can't you just go out the way you came in?" I asked. I eyed the bible, wondering if I could wrest it away from him. He was obviously in a weakened and damaged state. But he was still Gabriel, the toughest angel I had ever known.

"I'm afraid that was a one-way trip," he said. "I have no more journal pages left. So I really must insist."

I glanced at Alice, and she nodded. "We've destroyed all the other books," she said. "The journal is the last thing left of the Chaos Court that can be used as a doorway to your world."

I considered Gabriel. I already knew how this would go. "You said the journal is *your* only way out of here. It doesn't sound like you plan on taking us with you."

"You can find another way," Gabriel said.

"You heard Alice. There isn't another way."

"That hasn't stopped you in the past. And I will not risk losing the bible to you now."

"Well, then we have a problem," I said. "Because I'm not giving you the journal."

"I think you will," Gabriel said. "And not just because you're out of grace."

He leapt forward, moving faster than he had before. But he wasn't coming for me. Instead, he grabbed Amelia and pulled her toward him, putting her between us. "Your daughter for the journal. Hardly a fair trade, I know, but your kind always have been overly sentimental."

I stalked toward him, but stopped when he put his stone hand around Amelia's neck.

"Damn you, Cross," Morgana said. "You have ended us all."

I ignored her and kept my attention on Gabriel. "Let me guess. There was no poison slowing you down."

"Oh, there was," Gabriel said with a chuckle. "Its effects faded rather quickly, but I decided not to let you know that. I thought that perhaps –"

"You will not have my daughter!" Morgana screamed.

At the same time, hands erupted from the ground all around the three of them and reached up. They were varied in nature – some made of rusted metal, others made of wood and one that seemed made of ice. For a moment, I thought they were reaching for Gabriel. But then they caught on to Morgana and Amelia. They pulled them down in the blink of an eye – down and *into* the ground. The two of them sank into the dirt and faded away. Morgana had escaped with Amelia into the glamour. She must have been holding a trick or two back, just like I'd held my last bit of grace in reserve.

Gabriel started to reach down, as if he was going to dig through the dirt after them, and then the cat crashed into him and sent him tumbling through the graveyard. He knocked more tombstones flying and then slammed into and through the tower's supports. The tower collapsed upon him with the sound of falling trees and he disappeared under the wreckage, hunched over to protect the bible.

I ran toward the fallen tower, but Gabriel shoved a couple of beams aside and stood before I could reach it. He still had the bible, but now a chunk of wood was lodged in its cover. Gabriel pulled the wood out and threw it at me like a knife.

If I'd still had some grace, maybe I could have dodged it. The number of times I'd said that to myself over the years. I threw up my left hand and the wood shard slammed into my palm and came out the other side, the point stopping centimetres before my eye. It wasn't a particularly serious wound in the general scheme of things, but it was enough to distract me from the broken timber that he kicked into my path. I tripped over it and tumbled to the ground.

I looked up to see Gabriel lay his hand on the bible and whisper something I couldn't hear. I felt grace in the air, and when he pulled his hand away the hole in the cover was gone, as were the other marks upon the bible. He had healed the damage to it, or at least some of the damage. It had cost him, though – he leaned against a pile of fallen beams as if he were poisoned again.

Morgana rose up from the rubble behind him then and tried to grab the bible. Maybe she didn't have enough power left to use the glamour to escape back to our world. Or maybe she just didn't want to abandon us here with Gabriel. But Gabriel must have heard or sensed her for he turned and knocked her aside.

The attack had been a diversion, though. Amelia stepped out of a different part of the rubble and tried to snatch the bible from his hand while he was occupied with Morgana. Gabriel spun to the side to evade her, lashing out with a kick that threw her back.

The ground shook, and then a crack opened up between the fallen tower and myself. It was full of water that churned and frothed, as if there were a creature moving about in there. But I knew it was just the chaos. I glanced around and saw another crack running through the sky overhead, with bits of lava dripping from its edges. Somewhere in the distance, a bell began to chime, but each peal sounded like a different bell. We were running out of time. The Wonder Lands were coming apart.

"We can keep wearing him down," Morgana said, rising again. "He'll run out of grace eventually."

"And then what?" Gabriel said. "You've seen what happens when the bible cannot be contained. Do you really think any of you can repair it before it gets worse and the chaos spreads to other realms?"

"We'll find a way," Morgana spat at him. "I am the faerie queen and as long as I have a court of even one –"

"He's right," I said.

Everyone stopped and looked at me. I got wearily to my feet and stood at the edge of the rift between us.

"Gabriel is right," I said. "I can't fix the bible and I don't think any of you can either. But maybe he can. Or maybe some other angel can if he takes it back to them."

"Need I remind you of everyone he has killed?" Morgana said. "Of what he has done?"

"The same things we've all done over the ages," I said. "Just for different causes. Maybe he'll try to repair the bible to save the world. Maybe he'll try to build a new Heaven with it. I don't know anymore. But he's right. The angels are the only ones who stand a chance of stopping the bible from tearing itself apart and making things even worse."

Morgana glared at me, then at Gabriel. "The other gods and their bibles. Surely, they can do something."

"The other gods seem as gone as his god. And who even knows about the state of their holy texts. I think we're the only ones that can help ourselves now."

"Cross may be right," Alice said, coming to stand beside me. "Or may be wrong. I'm not sure. Only time will tell, but it never tells me."

"So we just give him the journal and let him go with the bible?" Morgana said.

"We use the journal to bring us *all* out," I said. "And then we go our separate ways. He can keep the bible in return for our safe passage."

"That's a real deal with the devil," Morgana said. The ground shook again and she sighed as she turned back to Gabriel. "Touch my daughter again, though, and I'll end you, even if I have to burn the whole world to do so."

He looked at me instead of answering her. "How do I know I can trust you?"

"Because I care more about saving the world than killing you," I said.

THE END OF THE WORLD

We gathered in the middle of the graveyard, well away from the rift. I found a shard of bone that would serve as a quill and then took out the vial of Raphael's blood. Thankfully it had survived all I had been through. Alice took the journal from her pocket and gave it to me. I dipped the bone into the blood, then opened the journal and drew the tomb that had contained all of the white books, with the door open. Instead of the back wall, though, I drew the cemetery in Paris, with a crypt in the background – the one we had used to escape Gabriel and the other angels. I couldn't remember it that well, so Amelia helped me. She gave me the dimensions of the crypt and described the surrounding graves. Soon I had a passable rendering of it, although it took most of the blood to draw.

When I was done, we went over to the tomb. The books were still there, but the back wall was gone. The Paris cemetery was on the other side, just like in the drawing.

"How do I know that's even real?" Gabriel asked.

Amelia stepped into the tomb and walked through it, into the other cemetery. She turned back to us. "It's real," she said.

Morgana followed her and stood among the graves, looking around and breathing deeply. "I never thought I'd be so happy to see Paris again," she said.

Gabriel hesitated, then stepped into the tomb. He stopped and began to pull books from the shelves and toss them to Morgana and Amelia.

"Hide them in there," he said, nodding to the crypt we had used to flee into the catacombs. "I'll come back for them later."

Morgana caught one of the books and considered it for a moment, as if wondering what mischief she could get up to with it. I shook my head at her. She sighed and caught more of the books, then took them over to the crypt in the other cemetery. I handed the journal to Alice and then began to help Gabriel. I didn't know how long we had and I wanted to be done with this place.

When we had finally transferred all the books over, Gabriel stepped through with the bible and turned back to me. "Come through so we can seal off the Wonder Lands," he said.

I turned back to Alice. "You heard the angel. Let's get out of here before this whole place descends into chaos."

"I'm not going anywhere," Alice said. "Other than here, that is. And I'm already here."

"What are you talking about? You can't stay here because here isn't going to exist soon."

"I know," she said. "And that's why I have to stay here. Someone has to use the journal to close this doorway again. And then destroy the journal on this side so nothing from the Wonder Lands can ever get through to the other side again."

I opened my mouth to argue with her, but she was right. "I didn't search the entire world to lose you now," I said. "We'll find another way."

"There is no other way. It's been the only way all along, since the whirlpool cast me out here. I've tried to reach the journal so I could destroy it, but I couldn't manage to find a way out of this place. So instead I found a way to send messages into the journal itself."

"The drawings of you fighting the angel."

"I knew you would find the journal one day and use it to come into the Wonder Lands. You would find me because you always do. That's why I had Hess wait for you at the mansion of the Chaos Court. To steal the journal as soon as you had entered so the doorway you had created would be destroyed by the chaos and there would be no way out. Now there is only this doorway and I'm going to get rid of it once you go through."

"Fine, you stay on this side," I said. "We'll leave you some books. You can do your little trick of walking between libraries to find your way back to our world."

"Cross, you're not listening to me," Alice said. "Or maybe I'm talking nonsense again. The books would be another doorway. That's why there aren't any more books left here."

I looked to the others, but they had nothing to offer. I knew Gabriel was fine with her sacrifice, because that's just the way angels are. He had the good sense not to say anything, though.

"It's the only way, Cross." Alice stepped into the tomb and hugged me. "Thank you for all the stories."

"No, there is one other way," I said.

I grabbed the journal from her, then pushed her into the cemetery with the others. I saw a rippling in the air as the cat followed her. I crushed the vial in my hand and the rest of Raphael's blood fell onto the page, covering the Paris scene that I had drawn. And just like that, the back wall of the tomb was there again. Paris was gone. The others were gone. I was alone.

I stared at the wall for a long moment. Then I returned to the rift in the ground and dropped the bone and remains of the vial into it.

"It's just you and me now," I said to the mechanical beetle, but it was as still and lifeless as the horse. Whatever animating spirit it'd had was gone.

I went through the other tombs until I found a burning candle in one. I held the journal in the flames until it caught fire. I continued to hold it there until it had burned to ash that sifted between my fingers.

Then I stepped back out into the cemetery and waited for the end of the world.

A GRAVE JOURNEY

Of course, things never end quite the way you thought they would.

"We should get you out of here while we still can," Amelia said from behind me.

I spun to find her before the open door of the tomb. I rushed to her but saw the back wall of the tomb was still there. There was no sign of anyone else.

"I thought you left with the others," I breathed. I must have missed her returning to the tomb. And now I had trapped her here with me.

"I did go with the others," she said. "We waited for you in the Père Lachaise Cemetery, before a sepulchre that looked into the Wonder Lands. Alice came out but you didn't. And then the Wonder Lands faded away and the stone wall of the sepulchre was just a stone wall. So I came back for you."

I stared at her, wondering if this was some trick of the chaos or if I was going mad.

Amelia smiled, and it was the first time I could remember her doing so in a long time.

"I know places of the dead like Alice knows libraries," she said. "I can find my way from one to any other. Here, I'll show you." She offered me her hand, and of course I took it.

She led me back into the tomb, and pushed on a stone in the left wall. A door slid open to reveal a set of wooden stairs spiralling upward in a narrow chamber. We climbed up them for several minutes, long enough that

I knew we had gone beyond the top of the tomb. Yet I had seen nothing rising above that tomb from the outside. Eventually we came to a wooden trapdoor, which Amelia pushed open –

– and we were in catacombs lined with skulls, only they were skulls that weren't quite human. They were longer and flatter, with snouts that contained fangs. We went down the hall, which had a low enough ceiling we couldn't stand straight, until we came to a round metal door to one side. Amelia tapped a complex pattern on it with her fingers, and there was the sound of several bolts sliding open from somewhere on the other side. Amelia pulled the door open and we stepped through –

– into a crematorium with high walls that disappeared into the darkness overhead. The room was hundreds of feet long and filled with bodies on stretchers. Men and women that had been torn apart by some force. The far wall was lined with blazing incinerators and one cold one. Amelia climbed into the cold one and out the other end –

– into an earthen tunnel filled with dead men in uniforms I didn't recognize, who had killed each other in hand-to-hand fighting with knives and shovels. We stepped over them and carried along the tunnel, which descended into a flooded area. The water rose to our ankles, then our knees, then our waists. Amelia took a deep breath and then sank under, so I did the same and followed her –

– into the mess hall of a flooded ship, with dead men and women floating around us. We swam through it, to a hatch on the other side, and passed through –

– and fell into a cold, dark space where we were jammed against one another. Stone walls pressed on us from all sides, and for a moment I panicked, thinking she had brought us to a true dead end –

– and then she pushed the lid off the stone casket we were in and climbed out, and I followed her to find us in a tomb. It was empty except for the casket and a plain wooden door in one wall. She walked to the door and opened it, then looked back at me.

I went through the door and outside. And stopped at what I saw there.

We were back in Père Lachaise Cemetery.

BETWEEN LIFE AND DEATH

It was a cloudy, grey day and the graves were wet with rain, although there was no rain falling now. A scattering of white flower petals lay on the ground along with a couple of loose coins. A clock tower chimed somewhere in the distance but stopped before I could count the number of chimes.

"How did you manage that?" I asked. "Was it some sort of faerie glamour?"

"I have my own kind of glamour," Amelia said.

"Couldn't you have just taken me that way to find Alice at the start of all this? It would have saved a lot of trouble."

"The Wonder Lands is a hidden place that even I did not know until we found the way in."

I cast about but didn't see the others anywhere. For a moment I worried they were trying to find their own way back to me in the Wonder Lands.

"Time is different in the dead places," Amelia said. "Several days have passed since I left them to come for you. Gabriel parted ways to take the bible to a safe location. The others told me they would wait at a library for you. Morgana said you would know which one."

I nodded for I did know.

"Can anything follow us using the same path you took out of the Wonder Lands?" I asked.

"Only I could find that path. And as far as I know, I am one of a kind. Besides, the Wonder Lands will soon be no more."

"Let's get out of here then. I've had my fill of graveyards for a lifetime."

But Amelia didn't move. "I can't leave the cemetery now."

"Are we waiting for someone else?" I eyed a statue of a woman with a sword atop a grave in the distance. "Please tell me it's not more angels."

Amelia didn't blink. "No, I mean that coming for you through the realms of the dead as I did changed my very nature. I had to return to death more fully to be able to make such a journey. I can no longer walk in the world of the living. Graveyards and the other places of the dead are the most I can manage."

I gazed around the cemetery and listened to the wind. But it didn't hold any answers. It never does. It lifted up the flower petals and carried them away behind the graves.

"I'll find a way to bring you back," I finally said. "Morgana will help me. Hell, we'll get the angels on our side if need be. They owe us, after all."

"No," Amelia said. "This cemetery is where I belong. And the places like it. Between life and death."

I sat on a stone casket so worn by time that there were no markings left on it to identify who lay within. I thought things over, but there was nothing I could do.

"Will I be able to find you again?" I asked.

Amelia pointed behind me, and I saw a weathered stone cross in the ground. Her name was carved in it, along with a simple message.

As long as there is someone to remember me, I remain.

I turned back to Amelia but she was gone, and the tomb door was closed. I'd been hoping to give her a final hug, but perhaps it was better this way.

I lingered there in the cemetery for a time, with only my memories for company. Then I went to find the others.

THE FINAL CHAPTER AND A NEW BEGINNING

I returned to the Bibliothèque Mazarine, where everything had begun. The damage from my last visit had been repaired and it was open again. There were dozens of people inside, sitting at the tables or in the stacks. It was like my battle with the White Knight had never happened.

I found Morgana at a table upstairs by a window. She was sitting alone, drinking a glass of wine and gazing out over the city. A half-empty bottle was on the table before her, but no one around us appeared to notice.

I sat down in the chair across from her and she nodded at the wine. I took a drink from the bottle even though I knew better. You should never accept spirits from a faerie. But if there was ever a time I needed a drink, this was it.

"I wasn't sure if you would still be here," I said.

"I was waiting for my court to finally return," she said. "Speaking of which, where is our daughter?"

"She's not coming," I said and told her what had happened. We sat in silence while we finished the wine.

"You'll want to see Alice then," Morgana said when the bottle was finally empty.

"Yes. Where is she?"

"She helped the angel take the bible and the other books to whatever hiding place he had in mind. I haven't seen her since. He's probably imprisoned her like he did Raphael and that pope."

"If he did, we'll find her again."

"Yes, I imagine we will," Morgana said softly.

We left the table with the bottle and wineglass still on it. Let it be a curious mystery for the librarians. I led us to the bookshelf where I'd found the copy of *Through the Looking-Glass* that the White Knight had escaped from. There was only an empty space where it had once been. I scanned the shelves and saw a new edition of the same book misshelved on the top of the next stack. I reached up and pulled it out, and all the books from the shelf came with it and rained down upon me, and then all the books from the entire stack fell to the ground.

I stood there, staring at the hundreds of books on the floor, and then a figure rose up from underneath them and stood before me.

Alice.

She was wearing the simple dress she wore in so many of the illustrations from the Wonderland books, but her eyes were clockfaces and a metal beetle scurried through her hair. One earring was a little wooden man while the other was a black knight chess piece. She had tattoos of a soldier with a pike on her left arm and an owl on her right. An otter stuck its head out of the pocket of her dress and wrinkled its nose at me, then burrowed back down into the fabric with a huff.

"Cross," she said. "You were lost, but I knew that I'd find you here. No one can stay lost in a library."

I hugged her once more, and she was warm to the touch now. I turned to Morgana. "Can Alice join the faerie court?"

Morgana shrugged but couldn't quite hide her smile. "She can't be any worse than Puck."

A librarian appeared at the far end of the aisle and stared at all the books on the floor, then at us standing amid them.

"We should probably leave," I said, because it's never a good idea to be on the bad side of librarians.

I felt something rub against my legs, like a cat, but when I looked down I didn't see anything. I couldn't help but smile, though, for I knew Hess had escaped the chaos as well.

"Where should we go and what should we do?" Alice asked. "I have been in the Wonder Lands so long that I thought it would be my last tale."

I placed *Through the Looking-Glass* back on the empty shelf and then we headed for the exit and the world we had somehow managed to save yet again.

"I think we have many more tales to come," I said.

Peter Darbyshire is the author of six books and more stories than he can remember. He lives near Vancouver, British Columbia, where he spends his time writing, raising children and playing D&D with other writers. It's a good life.